by james leo herlihy

BLUE DENIM (*a play with William Noble*)

CRAZY OCTOBER (*a play*)

THE SLEEP OF BABY FILBERTSON
AND OTHER STORIES

ALL FALL DOWN

MIDNIGHT COWBOY

midnight

NEW YORK

A NOVEL BY

james leo herlihy

cowboy

SIMON AND SCHUSTER

For Dick Duane

"They's no Beatitude for the lonesome. The Book don't say they are blessèd."

—MR. O'DANIEL

part one

part one

1

•

In his new boots, Joe Buck was six-foot-one and life was different. As he walked out of that store in Houston something snapped in the whole bottom half of him: A kind of power he never even knew was there had been released in his pelvis and he was able to feel the world through it. Brand-new muscles came into play in his buttocks and in his legs, and he was aware of a totally new attitude toward the sidewalk. The world was down there, and he was way up here, on top of it, and the space between him and it was now commanded by a beautiful strange animal, himself, Joe Buck. He was strong. He was exultant. He was ready.

"I'm ready," he said to himself, and he wondered what he meant by that.

Joe knew he was no great shakes as a thinker and he knew that what thinking he did was best done looking in a mirror, and so his eyes cast about for something that would show him a reflection of himself. Just ahead was a store window. Ta-click ta-click ta-click ta-click, his boots said to the concrete, meaning power power power power, as he approached the window head on, and there was this new and yet familiar person coming at him, broad-shouldered, swaggering, cool and handsome. Lord, I'm glad I'm you, he said to his image—but not out loud—and then, Hey, what's all this ready crap? What you ready for?

And then he remembered.

When he arrived at the H tel, a hotel that not only had no name but had lost its *O* as well, he felt the absurdity of anyone so rich and hard and juicy as himself ever staying in such a nameless, no-account place. He ran up the stairs two at a time, went to the second floor rear and hurried into the closet, emerging seconds later with a large package. He removed the brown paper and placed on the bed a black-and-white horsehide suitcase.

He folded his arms, stood back and looked at it, shaking his head in awe. The beauty of it never failed to move him. The black was so black and the white so white and the whole thing so lifelike and soft, it was like owning a miracle. He checked his hands for dirt, then brushed at the hide as if it were soiled. But of course it wasn't, he was merely brushing away the possibility of future dirt.

Joe set about removing from their hiding place other treasures purchased in recent months: six brand-new Western-cut shirts, new slacks (black gabardines and black cottons), new underwear, socks (a half dozen pair, still in their cellophanes), two silk handkerchiefs to be worn at his neck, a silver ring from Juarez, an eight-transistor portable radio that brought in Mexico City without a murmur of static, a new electric razor, four packs of Camels and several of Juicy Fruit chewing gum, toilet articles, a stack of old letters, etc.

Then he took a shower and returned to the room to groom himself for the trip. He shaved with his new electric razor, cleaning it carefully before placing it in the suitcase, splashed his face and armpits and crotch with

14

Florida Water, combed a nickel-sized glob of Brylcream into his brown hair, making it appear almost black, sweetened his mouth with a fresh stick of Juicy Fruit and spat it out, applied some special leather lotion to his new boots, put on a fresh, seven-dollar shirt (black, decorated with white piping, a shirt that fit his lean, broad-shouldered frame almost as close and neat as his own skin), tied a blue handkerchief at his throat, arranged the cuffs of his tight-thighed whipcord trousers in such a way that, with a kind of stylish untidiness, they were half in and half out of those richly gleaming black boots so you could still see the yellow sunbursts at the ankles, and finally he put on a cream-colored leather sport coat so soft and supple it seemed to be alive.

Now Joe would appraise the finished product. During the grooming process, he seldom looked at his total image. He would allow himself to focus only upon that patch of face being covered by the razor at a given moment, or at the portion of the head through which the comb was traveling, and so on. For he didn't want to wear out his ability to perceive himself as a whole. He was in some ways like a mother preparing her child to meet some important personage whose judgment will decide the child's fate, and so when all was ready and the time had come to assess the total effect, Joe Buck would actually turn his back on the mirror and walk away from it, roll his shoulders to get the kinks out, take a few deep belly breaths and a couple of quick knee bends, and crack his knuckles. Then he would slouch in a way that he thought attractive and that was his habitual stance anyway—most of his weight on one foot—get hold of a certain image in his mind, probably of some pretty, wide-eyed, adoring girl, smile at it with a kind of crooked, indulgent wisdom, light a Camel and

15

stick it into his mouth, and hook one thumb into his low-riding garrison belt. And now, ready for that fresh look at himself, he would swing his eyes back onto the mirror as if some hidden interloper beyond the glass had suddenly called his name: *Joe Buck!*

On this day of the trip, Joe liked especially what he saw: liked the sweet, dark, dangerous devil he surprised in the dirty mirror of that H tel room. Beyond his own reflection he could see the splendid suitcase lying on the bed, and in his hip pocket he could feel the flat-folded money, two hundred and twenty-four dollars, more than he'd ever at any one time owned before. And he felt most of all the possession of himself, inside his own skin, standing in his own boots, motivator of his own muscles and faculties, possessor of all that beauty and hardness and juice and youngness, box-seat ticket holder to the brilliant big top of his own future, and it was nearly overwhelming to him. Formerly, and not so long ago, there had confronted him always in mirrors a brooding and frightened and lonesome person who was not at all pleased with himself, but he was gone now, put out of the way entirely, while Joe beheld the new. He could not have borne one more scrap of splendor without buckling under the wonder of it, for even as it was he felt that if he savored for one more instant the incredible good fortune of being himself in this time and place and on the move through it, he might easily wreck it all by weeping.

And so he gathered up his possessions and left that H tel for good.

Over the door of the Sunshine Cafeteria was a big yellow sunburst with a clock (twenty to seven) set in it, and on the face of the clock it said TIME TO EAT.

As Joe approached this place he saw enacted in his mind the following scene:

He goes into the Sunshine. His employer, a pink man in a soiled gray suit, is just inside the door holding his pocket watch in his right hand and shaking the forefinger of his left at Joe. "You're due here at four o'clock, four to midnight, understand?" he shouts. Customers stop eating and look up. Joe Buck takes the pink man by the ear and leads him past the astonished diners and into the scullery. A number of cooks and counter girls and dishwashers pause in their work to watch as Joe shoves the pink manager against the dishwashing machine. Joe takes his time lighting a cigarette, lifts a brilliantly booted foot and rests it on a dish crate. Then, exhaling a puff of smoke, he says, "They's something about that dishwashing machine been bothering me. Been bothering me a long long time. Yes it has. What I been wondering is whether or not that dishwashing machine would fit up your ass. Now bend over." "What? What? Bend over? Are you crazy?" the pink man protests. Joe remains dangerously still, looks out from under dark eyebrows: "Did you call me crazy?" "No, no, no, I only meant—" "Bend over," says Joe. The man bends over and Joe sees a billfold sticking out of his hip pocket. "Believe I'll take my pay," he says, removing the money, "plus help m'self to a little bonus." He stuffs a great wad of money into his jockstrap and walks out of the place, all eyes upon him, wide open and profoundly impressed. But no one dares follow or in any way impede his exit. In fact, just to play it safe, the pink man himself remains bent over for several days after Joe has gone.

That was the way Joe imagined it. This is what actually took place:

He clicked across the street, pushed through the revolv-

17

ing door and into the Sunshine Cafeteria, swung his new body past the tables and toward a door that said EMPLOY-EES ONLY on it. This door marked the end of the air conditioning; inside it was hot and steamy. He passed through another doorway that led into the scullery. A colored man of middle age was filling a tray with dirty dishes. Joe watched as the man filled the tray and placed it on a conveyor belt that would carry it through the dish-washing machine. Then he smiled up at Joe and nodded toward a mountain of dish-filled wire baskets stacked on the floor. "Looka that shit, will you?" he said.

Joe stood next to the man. "Listen, uh, it looks like I'm headin' East." He lit a cigarette.

The man looked at Joe's suitcase. "You ain't coming to work?"

"Naw, I don't guess. I just come to say goodbye, tell you I'm headin' East."

"East?"

"Yeah. Oh, hell yeah. Thought I say g'bye, take a look around the place."

A door opened and a fat woman with a splotchy face stood there shouting *"Cups!"* at the top of her voice. Then she closed the door and was gone.

The colored man put his hand forward. "Well. Good-bye." They shook hands and for a moment Joe felt reluctant to release the other man's grip. Inexplicably, he felt like putting on an apron and starting to work, but that was out of the question. "What the hell am I hanging around here for, right?"

"That's right," the man said, looking down at his own hand, still caught in Joe's. "What you going to do back there, East?"

"Women," Joe said. "Eastern women. They got Eastern women back there, and they going to pay for it, too."

"Pay for what?" The man finally got his hand free.

"The men back there," said Joe, "is just faggots mostly, and so the women got to buy what they want. They glad to pay for it 'cause it's just about the only way they can get it."

The colored man shook his head. "That must be some mess back there." He took another empty tray and began filling it with cups.

"Yeah, it's a mess. And I'm going to cash in on some of it. Isn't that right?"

"I don't know. I don't know nothing about it."

"What do you mean? I just told you."

"Yeah, I know, but I don't know."

"Well, they's no use hanging around here. I got places to go. Right?"

Joe Buck, all dressed up like a cowboy, suddenly knew he was not a cowboy at all. He stood there with his mouth slack, his big, slightly bucked teeth showing white, his blue eyes caught on the older man's face. "Papa," his eyes said, "I am going now to seek my fortune and have come to ask your blessing." But of course the poor colored man was not his father. Nor was Joe the son of anyone in particular. And so he walked out of that scullery. The place owed him a day's pay, but he had no stomach for an interview with the pink man who was manager of the Sunshine. Besides, he knew he would never actually tell the man to put the dishwashing machine up his ass.

He walked through the cafeteria and out onto the sidewalk, where it was evening and pleasant and clearly springtime, and pretty soon, with the clicking of his own heels to nourish his heart as he walked toward the bus

19

station, he felt fine and his thoughts were thousands of miles away: walking down Park Avenue in New York City. Rich ladies looking out their windows swooned to see a cowboy there. A butler tapped him on the shoulder, an elevator whirred him up to a penthouse, a golden door opened to admit him to a large apartment carpeted from wall to wall with soft brown fur. Madame was wearing scanties covered by a sheer black negligee. At sight of Joe Buck, breathing became a labor: She was overwhelmed. Quivering with desire, she threw herself at once onto the soft floor. The juices of her womanliness had already risen to meet him. There was no time for undressing. He took her immediately. The butler handed him a check, signed in a florid hand, on which the amount had been left for him to fill in as he chose.

There was a juke box in the depot at Houston. As Joe climbed aboard the bus he heard the voice of some fine, big Western woman singing about a *wheel of fortune turning turning turning,* and it seemed to him that what this woman was getting at, she was sending all the studs East to clean up. Joe smiled his crooked and gleaming white smile all the way down the aisle, knowing and savoring something he had no words for about destiny: that there is a certain way of climbing inside of time that gives a man ownership of the world and everything in it, and when this takes place there is a kind of *click,* and from then on when you hear a juke box, for instance, it plays only what you need to hear, and everything, even Greyhound buses, operates for your convenience—you walk into the station and you say, "What time's a bus to New York City?" and the man says, "Right away," and you just step on the thing and that's all there is to it. The

20

world is music and yours is the rhythm that owns it. You don't even have to snap your fingers, the beat is you, and when you think about those Eastern women, the big broad on the juke box sings the finish of the thought for you, *yearning yearning yearning*, that's what they're doing in the East. (Okay, here it is, lady, it's just climbed on the bus, it's on the way!) And there's a seat for you, two of them in fact, one for your butt and one for your feet, and you don't need a reservation, the whole world is reserved, and the minute you sling your horsehide suitcase onto the overhead rack, the driver shifts into gear and begins to back out on schedule. Maybe not on schedule from the Greyhound's point of view, but from yours. Because you *are* the schedule, and that bus *moves*.

2

now at this time in which Joe Buck was coming out of the West on that Greyhound bus to seek his fortune in the East, he was already twenty-seven years old. But he had behind him as little experience of life as a boy of eighteen, and in some ways even less.

He had been raised by various blondes. The first three, who brought him up to the age of seven, were young and pretty.

There was a great deal of coming and going in the household of the three blondes and he was never certain which of them was which. At various intervals, each of them seemed to be his mother, known as Mama this or Mama that, but he later learned that two of them were merely friends in whose household his real mother shared. But the blondes all were nice to him, allowed him to do as he pleased, brought gifts and fondled him a great deal. And at least one of them sang around the house a lot: *Wonder When My Baby's Comin' Home, The Tumbleweed Song, Accentuate the Positive, The Lady in Red, He Wears a Pair of Silvery Wings,* and others. Thinking back on the matter, Joe Buck always supposed that this singer of the household was his actual mother.

There was in those days a war taking place, and some of the blondes were involved in it. They would go out at all hours wearing slacks and babushkas and carrying lunch pails. Sometimes there were bus trips between Houston and Detroit, and Joe remembered living in those cities some of the time. Wherever he was there would be men in uniform coming into the house, staying awhile and then leaving. Some of these men were known as husbands, but Joe could not remember being told that any of them was his father. (Later he was able to surmise that he had been born out of wedlock.)

At a certain point, which happened to be on the day of an exceptionally still and white sky, he was delivered to a fourth blonde in Albuquerque, New Mexico, and from then on and forever he was never to see the other three again. When he would think of them, he would think also of that special white sky and imagine those yellow-haired women to be hiding somewhere behind it.

Now the fourth blonde was his grandmother, a silly and skinny little thing named Sally Buck. For all her skinniness, she was prettier than all the others put together. She had enormous gray eyes with lashes black as pitch and waxy thick, and knees that made you cry they were so sorry-looking and knobby. If there is some part of every loved one that will make you cry to contemplate it, such for Joe were these poor, sad, bony knees of Sally Buck. Sally ran a beauty shop that kept her away from home ten and twelve hours a day, and so the boy unhappily spent his after-school hours in the company of various cleaning women. These women were never blonde, and they never wore lavender or pale-green or lemon-colored dresses; they never seemed to look at him either, and had they chosen to, it would have been necessary to do so out of very ordinary eyes with lashes that were scarcely visible at all.

Sundays were not much better. Sally usually went on dates. She had a weakness for men, especially outdoor ones, and many of her beaus were ranchers who wore Western hats. These big, broad-shouldered, ruddy-faced Western men went for pretty little Sally in a big way. She was all gossamer and perfume and fingernail polish, and they were all leather and muscle and manure, and each was titillated by the contrast. Sometimes Joe was taken along on these dates and he liked and admired a number of Sally's men, but only one of them paid him any more than a counterfeit token of attention.

This man was named Woodsy Niles. His beard was blue and his eyes were bright, and he showed Joe Buck how to ride a horse and how to make a slingshot, and he taught him how to chew tobacco and how to smoke cigarettes, and a special way of holding his peter so that he could piss an arc higher than his own head. Woodsy Niles was a happy kind of man who had his own pleasurable and snappy way of doing everything, even walking. Yes, he

23

walked as if he believed no moment should pass without pleasure, and he took enjoyment even from such simple acts as moving across a room or opening the corral gates. He sang a lot of songs, too, this Woodsy Niles, sang them in a fine manly voice, accompanying himself on a guitar, and sometimes when they spent the night at his ranch, Joe would awaken as late as three A.M. to the songs that issued from the bedroom where Woodsy and Sally slept. The boy always supposed Woodsy had simply awakened in the night feeling far too strong and handsome and salty to squander himself on mere sleep, and was forced to let off some of the excess in a chorus or two of *The Last Roundup.* He did the "git alongs" in a way that made Sally giggle, and when he got to the part about the place in the sky where the strays are counted and branded, Joe was apt to get the blues, but in a strangely pleasurable way, and he had to restrain himself from joining the beautiful people in the bedroom. This was one of the first things Joe learned about lying with a woman in the night: You sing songs to her. It seemed a splendid way to do, and what's more, the whole house got the good of it.

But inevitably Sally had some falling out or other with this remarkable man—as sooner or later she did with all the others—and Joe was left to pine for him as for a gone-away father. But surely it was in this time of Woodsy Niles that Joe had begun to see himself as some sort of a cowboy.

There was, following this love affair, a flurry of Sundays in which Sally Buck took the boy to church. What she liked best about these mornings was their promenade aspect, the opportunity afforded for daytime dress-up. Spending almost all of her daytimes in the shop, she had, for example, few opportunities to parade around in her lovely hats. And the boy set her off well; everyone said they looked like a mother and son team, an illusion that seemed to chop an entire generation of years from her age.

But for Joe these visits to church were another matter altogether: After the regular services, the adults had coffee and rolls in the church basement while the youngsters attended Sunday school upstairs. It was at these sessions that Jesus replaced Woodsy Niles in Joe's affections. He was taught by a young lady with warm, humorous, kindly eyes that Jesus loved him. There was always a painting on an easel in front of the class; it depicted Jesus walking with a boy child. You could see only the back of the boy's head, but Joe felt that he himself was that child. Songs were sung, songs about how Jesus walked with him and talked with him and told him he was His own. And one day the young lady teacher told about the events of a certain terrible Friday in the life of this gentle, bearded man, and then she passed out small colored pictures that they were allowed to keep. Jesus was looking right at him, and his eyes said: "Let me tell you I have seen an awful lot of misery, and have suffered something fierce in my life, but it sure is a comfort to have a cowboy like you for a friend." Something like that. Something that gave Joe a personal and strong feeling of connection with the suffering that was going on in those eyes, along with a desire to alleviate it in some way. Studying the picture, it occurred to him that, clean-shaven, Jesus might have a blue face like Woodsy's, and he began to wonder if there might be other similarities as well. For several nights he placed on his chest of drawers in front of the Jesus picture a plug of tobacco and a pack of Camels, and each morning he checked to see if anyone had come in the night for a chew or a smoke. No one ever did. And soon he lost completely

25

the belief that there was anyone walking with him or talking with him or telling him he was His own. Jesus joined the people Joe would never see again; He was behind the sky with the three blondes and Woodsy.

That summer flurry of churchgoing ended for good when Sally Buck landed a new beau, a telephone lineman. He walked into her shop one afternoon, his wide leather belt riding low on his hips, heavy with tools, to make an installation. Sally's pupils dilated at the sight of him, and by the time he returned to his truck, the lineman had fallen under her pretty little gray-eyed spell.

There followed a year in which Joe saw hardly anything at all of his grandmother. For that matter he saw very little of anyone at all. A listlessness took possession of him during that fall of his fourteenth year, and by Thanksgiving he had ceased going to school. The effort needed to get there and to remain awake could no longer be summoned in him. Several boys of Joe's temperament, boys unresponsive to talk, drifted away from the school that year. Some few remained for the social life, but this was no lure to Joe, who never had been included in it. No one had disliked him, but then, no one had really noticed him much either. He was simply the one with the big front teeth (sometimes called "Buck" Buck), the one who seldom spoke, never had his lesson, and always managed somehow to angle a seat in the back of the room. Sally was visited at her shop from time to time by truant officers, but this never resulted in any real action on her part or theirs, and Joe was left to do as he pleased. He got up at noon, combed his hair a lot, smoked cigarettes, ate peanut butter and sardines, and watched thousands of miles of film unroll on the television set in Sally Buck's living room. He kept that TV going from noon till long past midnight. Away from it for any length of time he actually

26

became confused and disoriented. He urgently required the images it gave out, and especially the sound it made. His own life made very little noise of its own, and he found that in silence there was something downright perilous: It had enemies in it that only sound could drive out.

Then, too, the TV had lots of blonde women, and every last one of them looked somehow like one of his own. It seemed that every stagecoach and covered wagon, every saloon and every general store, if you watched it long enough, would prove to have a blonde in it: The swinging doors would open, or the curtains would part, and out would come Claire Trevor or Barbara Stanwyck or Constance Bennett, looking for all the world like his own familiar yellow-haired women. And who would that tall man be, riding high in his saddle, face against the sun, jaw squared toward goodness and justice, bursting with his own hardness and strength and purpose, and portrayed by anyone from Tom Mix to Henry Fonda? Why, that was Joe Buck himself. In a sense.

During this time of his television addiction, an astonishing thing was happening to him. He was becoming, day by day and bit by bit and feature by feature, as tall and strong and handsome as a TV cowboy. One day, when summer had come and gone and then had come again and Joe was swimming in the river, there was a moment in which he discovered himself to be inhabiting the body of a man. He climbed out of the water and looked down at himself and there he saw this shimmering new man conveying himself through the mud on a man's strong legs. His arms and body had developed a full muscle structure, and there was on his chest and limbs a perfectly presentable man's growth of dark body hair. He became tremendously excited by these sudden discoveries and hurried home on his bicycle to study the situation in Sally's bedroom mirror. He found that his face too had changed: Its outlines were more squarely defined, and somehow his mouth had grown up to accommodate his big teeth so that they had become a good white shiny asset.

He was so pleased with what he saw that he got dressed up and went strutting about the neighborhood, supposing that others too would see what had taken place in him and find it remarkable. (No one did.) He stopped at Sally's shop. She said, "Good Lord, honey, those clothes look awful on you, they've gotten away too small."

"No," he argued, "they no smaller than they was."

She said, "Oh yes they are," and she gave him money for a new outfit.

Later that afternoon, Joe paraded through the streets of Albuquerque in bright-blue slacks, an orange sport jacket and oxblood shoes with cleats on the heels. Sally said the outfit seemed to clash a little, "but you look real cute, have you got a girl?"

At home, straining his eyes toward the mirror until they were all but inflamed, he wondered what had happened to his delight with himself. The new man was still there with all his beauty intact, but somehow the marvel of him had gone sour, the elation had broken apart and become a misery. And suddenly he knew why. For a dreadful thing had come about in him that day: an awakening to his own lonesomeness.

Never having had a friendship on his own, Joe knew nothing of how to bring such a situation about. His way of proceeding was to pick out a person he liked and then do a lot of hanging around in the hope that a friendship would come into being. He tried this method on: the grocer's widow, two gas station attendants, the girl who issued money orders at the Rio Pharmacy, an old immigrant shoemaker, an usher at the World movie theater. But they never seemed to understand what he hoped to achieve. Gradually it became clear to him that conversation was a necessary part of the development of personal ties, but Joe rarely had anything to say, and on occasions when he did dredge up a few words, his listener as a rule remained unmoved and the effort went for nothing. He was simply no talker. His best conversations were with Sally, but even they were conducted on the run. He'd be sitting, say, on the edge of the bathtub watching her paint herself in the mirror over the sink; the greater part of her attention would be given over to the considerable task of getting some twenty years erased from her face, and very little would be left over for her grandson.

It was during the fall of his seventeenth year, and in this mood of hunger for affectionate connections in the world, that Joe one evening wandered into the World movie theater and began a brief and pleasurable and terrible association with a girl named Anastasia Pratt.

3

the name of Anastasia Pratt, even though the girl herself was only fifteen, was legendary to the young people of Albuquerque. Such legends rarely derive from fact alone: Invention as a rule takes a part in their creation. But the behavior of Anastasia Pratt from the time she was twelve was such that the imagination was stunned; no one by lying could have made it seem to be much more bizarre or improbable than it already was.

She was know as Chalkline Annie, suggesting the order that had to be maintained in order to serve efficiently the large numbers of boys to whom in a single half hour she made her body available.

Behind the silver screen at the World movie theater was a large room in which were stored the letters for the marquee, uniforms for the ushers, towels and soap and various other supplies and equipment. In one corner were stored some ends of carpeting left over from the theater's most recent refurbishing. It was in this corner that the legend of Anastasia Pratt was created in the flesh. She labored as well in various living rooms, bedrooms, parked cars, and garages, in school grounds at night, and even under the sky along certain desert highways in fair weather. But it was on this stack of carpet ends in the storeroom of the World movie theater that Anastasia was most often used and by the greatest numbers.

Neither pretty nor unpretty, she appeared to be an ordinary schoolgirl, so ordinary that in light of her actual behavior the effect seemed almost studied. She wore the usual clothes—skirts, blouses, sweaters, ankle socks, and saddle oxfords. Her hair was chestnut-colored, combed straight back and held with a clip. She wore no makeup to speak of, merely plucked her eyebrows and dabbed on a little lipstick. In the daytime you would see her walking always alone to and from school, carrying her books, and seeming to be as open-eyed and listless and mildly troubled as any virginal and solitary adolescent is apt to be. Unless you knew of her special activities, you would

30

have had no reason to look twice at Anastasia Pratt. But with that knowledge, the contrast between what you imagined and what you saw was astonishing. One young wag referred to her as Virgin Jekyll and Miss Hyde.

Despite the girl's fame there were at least three persons who were totally unaware of her conduct. Two of these, of course, were the girl's parents, the father a strict, hard-working, irritable bank cashier and the mother a thin-lipped, shifty-eyed piano player at the Truth Church. The third ignorant party, until a certain Friday evening in October, was Joe Buck.

They met at the World water fountain. Joe stepped back and held the faucet for her. She drank and then looked at him gratefully and smiled. He smiled back. She said: "Would you like to sit with me?"

They sat on the side, about a third of the way down the aisle. Anastasia immediately placed her knee against Joe's and began to wiggle in an unmistakably provocative way. Suddenly they were holding hands. Just as Joe was beginning to worry about the perspiration emanating from his palm, she took his hand and used it to caress her thigh. Then the girl used her own hand boldly to study the extent of his excitement. Finding it to be considerable she took hold of his face and begged him to kiss her. Joe was not at all disinclined to do so; in all the excitement he simply hadn't thought of it; but there was in her request such urgency, such desperation that when he did kiss her, the girl's lips clung to his mouth as if she were taking from him some life-giving substance. He felt as if he were administering to a person who had been fatally wounded in an accident but who was not yet quite dead.

A pack of boys came down the aisle and sat behind Joe and Anastasia Pratt.

One of them said, "Jesus, it's Anastasia Pratt."

"You're kidding," said another.

A third said, "Who's the guy?"

"He's *kissing* her."

"Hey, somebody's kissing Anastasia Pratt."

"Who is he? Who's the guy kissing Annie?"

"Hey Annie, who you got there?"

Anastasia turned around and in a whining voice said, "Shut up. Please shut up. Give me a chance, will you?"

"Give you a chance? I'll give you a chance."

"Here you are, Annie, here it is."

"Me, too, Annie, how's this? Want me to knock it against the back of your seat a few times for luck?"

Joe did not yet understand what was taking place. He'd seen lots of couples necking in this very theater, and always they had been left unmolested. He was frightened and he was confused. Apparently in his inexperience he was doing something wrong, but he hadn't the faintest notion of what it was, and he knew even less how to handle himself in such a situation.

One of the gang stood up and leaned over the row of seats and recognized Joe Buck from grade-school days. "Hey, it's Buck. It's Joe Buck," he announced, resuming his seat.

Joe didn't know the voices behind him and he was afraid to turn around and look.

"Hey, Joe," one of them whispered to him. "You been kissing Anastasia, you better go swallow a drug store and I ain't kidding. She's copped every joint in Albuquerque." This voice was not hostile, it was in fact friendly and urgent in its tone. Joe then turned and saw a dark Italian boy he remembered from school. His name was Bobby Desmond.

Anastasia Pratt got up from her seat and flounced up the aisle. The gang ran to follow her. Before leaving with the others, Bobby Desmond paused long enough to tap Joe's shoulder and say, "Come on."

Joe got up and followed. In the back of the theater were six boys, all of high-school age, blocking an exit. Anastasia was pleading weakly to be allowed through. A tall, skinny, pimply, loudmouthed blond boy said, "Hey, Annie, Gary Amberger's upstairs and he's dying to see you."

"He is not," said Anastasia, but her eyes said, Is he really?

"Okay, he isn't. I'll go tell him he's not there."

"No, but I mean he is not," Anastasia said.

And then they were all trooping down a side aisle of the World movie theater, this line of boys and Anastasia Pratt, heading toward a red exit sign at the left of the screen. Joe, following behind Bobby Desmond, brought up the rear. As he went through the curtains under the sign he heard the voice of some Hollywood woman on the screen saying: "I tell you, the situation's gotten entirely out of hand. Our only hope is to pretend that nothing's happened."

They all filed up a short flight of steps and into the storeroom. Someone turned on a light. Anastasia said, "Where is he? Where's Gary Amberger?"

The tall blond boy, whose name was Adrian Schmidt, said, "Over on the carpets, Annie, over on the carpets." He went into that corner, saying, "Hi Gare, Anastasia's here."

She said, "You're lying. This is just a trick. To get me

33

here. I know you boys." And then, "Gary? Gary!" she called. "If you're there, say something."

A woman's voice, projected electronically, said, "Blow out your candles now, darling, and make a wish!" "No!" said a little girl's voice. "We haven't sung happy birthday yet!" Then there was much shouting from the screen and a chorus of people sang *Happy Birthday*.

Anastasia said, "I want out of here," and that got the door closed. For everybody in the room except Joe knew she did not want out of there at all.

"I still don't believe he's back there," she said, "but I'm going to take a look just the same."

In the corner Adrian Schmidt was lying on the carpets, exposed, handling himself, and then all the boys were exposing themselves, and then Anastasia Pratt was lying on the carpets, demanding petulantly as she pulled down her panties that "somebody nice has to be first, otherwise nothing doing." Adrian Schmidt was told he had to wait till last as punishment for lying to her about Gary Amberger. But she had known there wasn't any Gary Amberger any more. Gary Amberger had moved to Battle Creek Michigan three years earlier and everybody knew it.

While the young men labored over her, Anastasia lay perfectly still, her head to one side, biting her nails idly and not paying much attention to what was taking place. She was like a doomed cancer patient taking radium treatments that can't possibly help, but taking them nonetheless, just in case.

To one of them she said, "Hurry up, I haven't got all night, what do you think this is?" But nothing the girl said carried much conviction.

At his turn, Joe climbed on, and Anastasia's interest

34

awakened somewhat, perhaps to the novelty of someone new.

When she turned her head to the side again, Joe whispered to her, "What's the matter?"

She said, "Oh, I was just wondering what-all words you could make from those letters." She was looking at the stacks of marquee letters: Put together in a certain way, they would spell out what was to become of her.

Someone said, "I'll bet he's back there *kissing* her," and Bobby Desmond said, "Let him alone." A third young man said, "Somebody give me a cigarette," and Adrian Schmidt said, "Wait'll I get at her, making me be last." Then Bobby Desmond said, "Shut up or she'll cross her legs and go home." And the voice of a very old lady on the screen was heard to say: "No, no! You mustn't tell! If you do, it won't come true!"

Joe whispered to Anastasia Pratt, "Is this all right?"

"Is what all right?"

"Like this."

"Well, why are you asking *me?*"

The voice of Adrian Schmidt was heard again: "What's he doing back there? I mean I'd just like to time him. That's what we ought to do. We ought to all be timed. Otherwise a guy can just, I mean, *crap!* Right, you guys? From now on . . . !"

Anastasia Pratt put her hands on Joe's head and drew him toward her. Then she whispered in his ear, "You're the only one, you're the one, you're the one, the only one since, you're the only one since Gary Amberger, you are, honest, you really, you honestly are. Usually I never feel, I, honest, I mean, you're the best. Kiss me. Please."

Her body had come to life under him and her breathing

began to sound as if she were climbing the steepest hill in the world. This ascent seemed to make more urgent her need for his mouth, as if at these rarefied altitudes her own breathing mechanism were inadequate.

But Joe could think only of what he had been told by Bobby Desmond.

"You've got to," she begged. *"You've got to!"*

The girl's face was wet, and then, too, the thing that was happening to Joe at that moment made everything else unimportant and so in gratitude he clamped his mouth against hers, permitting her to take from that contact something that caused her to shudder and cling to him in a prolonged and violent seizure. Even when the moment had ended, Anastasia Pratt would not release him. She wept quietly and held onto his back for dear life.

"Okay," said Adrian Schmidt, "I've had it. I have had it. I count ten, and then, is that fair or isn't it? I mean I count ten and then— One two three . . ."

The voice of another old lady from Hollywood said: "Now don't forget, children, we're all the family poor Sarah has, and it's our duty as Christians—"

This was followed by a door slam, twenty times louder than life.

Anastasia put on her panties and would not allow Adrian Schmidt to touch her. He came at her as if to beat her up, but the other boys held him away from her. She marched out of the storeroom and down the short flight of stairs and into the passageway, holding her head absurdly high and staggering as if she were slightly drunk.

As she passed under the exit sign, the screen was producing some truly glorious music to accompany her reentry into the dark of the World movie theater.

36

4

•

In adolescence, a person is apt to do a lot of walking past places. He loses his imagination to someone and then, afraid to declare himself openly, he walks past the place of that someone on all sorts of dreamed-up pretexts, hoping for a miracle. Or at least a glimpse.

Joe lost himself to the idea of becoming a part of that pack of boys with whom he had shared Anastasia Pratt in the storeroom at the World. But Adrian Schmidt, the tall, blond, pimpled, impatient loudmouth of the pack, blamed Joe for the rebuff he had suffered that Friday night. And so when Joe took to walking past the magazine store that was their hangout, Adrian glowered at him through the window in a way that would have discouraged almost anyone. And then he turned the others (all except Bobby Desmond) against Joe, so that one day as he passed by they all came out on the sidewalk and made kissing sounds at him.

At the same time, Anastasia Pratt, having lost her imagination to Joe Buck, took to walking past his house. Each afternoon when school was out she could be seen walking slowly down his street. Joe watched from behind the venetian blinds in Sally's living room, noticed how like an infant she cradled the schoolbooks in her arms, was impressed by the coolness with which she kept her face aimed straight ahead while out of the corner of her eye she worked the place over like a burglar casing a jewelry store.

One day she stopped at each house on the street, rang the doorbell and offered for sale tickets to a raffle being held by the Truth Church.

"Oh!" she said, pretending surprise as Joe Buck opened his door to her, "I had no idea you lived here! I was just, I was just, our church is raffling a rotisserie, and I was just, it's electric and all, have you lived here long? I mean would you like to buy one, a ticket?"

Joe looked at her lips as she spoke, and then he looked past her, hearing in his mind the kissing sounds of Adrian Schmidt, and he shook his head, no, he didn't want to buy a raffle ticket.

The girl knew what he was saying no to, and without actually moving, her face strained toward him, her eyes watery and deeply troubled, and she said: "Are you sure?" He nodded. Anastasia quickly turned and walked down the steps and up the path toward the sidewalk. Her rear end moved back and forth, back and forth, in a way that made his stomach jump, and then he noticed how sorry her back was, how sad and lonesome the backs of her knees looked, and then he heard himself saying "Umh" fairly loud. When she turned to him again, Joe said, "I don't know if I got any change," and the tilt of her eyebrows pulled at his heart.

And so Joe's first woman was this fifteen-year-old Chalkline Annie Pratt. They hid like thieves. He was ashamed of her and of himself. He hated paying the price she exacted, those desperate kisses, and yet, because her

38

need for them was so great, it thrilled him to administer them.

In his idleness, he had too much time for brooding. He was forever making promises to himself that in her presence were impossible to keep. He would think of the mound of her stomach and the moist, smaller mound below it, and these thoughts, coupled with some sense of her terrible lonesomeness, made idiots of his resolutions.

Then one day the parents of Anastasia Pratt received an unsigned letter apprising them not only of the girl's elaborate carnal generosities in the storeroom of the World movie theater, but of her visits to Joe as well. Mr. Pratt came to the house one evening intending to "beat the life out of that boy," but he was a small man and ended by doing something else: He went to the police. Joe never learned what transpired at the police station, but the next afternoon Sally telephoned him from downtown saying, "It's all over, precious, they're putting the poor girl in a nice home." "A nice home" was Sally Buck's euphemism for an insane asylum.

The ending of Anastasia Pratt's career caused considerable talk. Joe Buck's name, having been linked with it, achieved a certain notoriety. The stories that circulated were not always accurate. In one version, he had forced her to these multiple acts with others for his own financial gain; in another, he had made her pregnant; and it was also told that he was formed in a certain way that drove the girl mad.

Gradually aware of his new position in the town, Joe was ashamed and embarrassed. Soon everything about his life, his truancy, his idleness, his dependence on his grandmother, piled one upon the other and he developed an acute sense of his own worthlessness. He despised the

39

very thought of asking anyone for a job, and since nothing in his life pressed him to do so, he continued to avoid it. Sally Buck's shop was thriving and she showed no concern over him whatever. Apparently his lack of employment, even as it extended into his nineteenth year, and then into his twentieth, did not seem to her in any way remarkable. She continued to furnish him with the money that clothed and sustained him, and she paid him as little attention as ever. He kept the yard in shape and washed Sally's car occasionally, and once he painted the house and made some repairs on the roof. Now and again he would drift into a purely sexual connection with someone, always with the shameful certainty that he was somehow being exploited and made a fool of, and yet hopeful that one of these experiences might bring about a real and friendly alliance with someone. Bobby Desmond was a typical case. For a brief period, perhaps a week or so, having long since broken away from the pack at the magazine store, Bobby sought out Joe's company: took him for rides in his car, and stopped by the house now and then with a six-pack of beer. As it turned out, this young man merely wanted the experience of being used by Joe in the same way Anastasia Pratt had been used by him that night in the storeroom of the World. Joe, eager as always to oblige, gave the young man the experience he wanted. But three weeks later, when Bobby Desmond got married, Joe was disappointed not to be invited to the wedding. The persons, female and male alike, who were so eager to avail themselves of his splendid body never appeared to notice that it was inhabited by Joe Buck.

He did indeed give the impression of being absent even while his presence was clearly in evidence. A lone, lonesome childhood had taught him that today, whatever day he was in, was barren as a wasteland with nothing in it worth looking at, and it had made of his mind an inveterate wanderer, nearly always gypsying about in places and situations in which a worthwhile tomorrow might take place. Even while laboring over some lady in the hope of pleasuring her so keenly he would win her devotion forever—for this was what he sought in these early acts of love—even at such moments his mind would trot on ahead somewhere, perhaps savoring a future time in the life he would have made with her.

This, then, was the manner in which Joe drifted into his twenties, with nothing sufficiently remarkable taking place in his life to press him into the ways of manhood. And when he was twenty-three the government called him into the army. He was afraid he wouldn't do well. And he didn't. But he stayed out of trouble and wrote a lot of letters to Sally Buck.

> Dear Sally—
> It does not look like I am going to make corporal—Columbus Ga is not so hot and neither is the army ha—they have got me driveing trucks—what is new back in good old Albuquerque—how is the days there fast or slow—well I am getting sleepy and there is not much new so dont do anything I wouldnt do—love Joe
> PS they call me cowboy here

That was true: some sergeant one day called him cowboy and others took it up. He was pleased and began to walk in a new way; also he developed a habit of hooking his thumbs into his back pockets as if his trousers were a low-slung gun belt.

There was much complaining in the army and Joe

41

found he had as much to complain of as anyone else, and so he learned at last to take part in conversations. The young men clustered around the big table in the barracks said "shee-it" a great deal and some of them called each other "man." And one young soldier, who claimed he was from Cinci-goddam-nati, had this remarkable system of fitting cusswords into unexpected corners of his talk. Joe liked these mannerisms and adopted them for his own use. Bit by bit he was acquiring a personality, a style of his own.

All in all he was having a pretty good time, and the months passed more quickly than is usual in the army.

In October of his second year he wrote:

Dear Sally—

Well there is 59 days to go and then I will re-inlist ha (that is a big joke, a?)—did you die laughing?—yesterday was an inspection the brass has not got anything else to do so they have inspection—well that is all the news for now so be a good girl and keep the home fires burning for your favorite boyfriend and besides you are the only thing I miss so the hell with it, a?—incidentally I past the inspection it was easy—well so long—love Joe

This was his last letter to Sally, and he was never certain she received it. For back in Albuquerque something terrible had taken place.

His grandmother found a new beau who owned a big ranch. The man was a few years younger than Sally and this disparity in their ages seemed to necessitate the telling of a few white lies. For instance, she told him something that had not been entirely true for forty-five years: that she could ride horseback. People were to say later

42

that this beau should have known better than to allow Sally Buck to ride anything at all, as it should have been clear from one glance that the poor little thing was brittle as glass. But one Sunday afternoon, this lady, at the age of sixty-six, mounted a raspberry roan and rode off into the desert with her sweetheart.

That was the end of Joe Buck's fourth blonde. The horse threw her, and the old lady simply broke to pieces.

This news reached him late one afternoon while he was cleaning his truck at the motor pool. A chaplain's assistant came over to him and handed him a telegram from a woman who worked in Sally's shop.

DEAR JOE YOUR PRECIOUS GRANDMOTHER KILLED FALLING FROM HORSE GOD BLESS YOU DEEPEST SYMPATHY FUNERAL FRIDAY MARLITA BRONSON.

When Joe had read the telegram several times, the soldier from the chaplain's office asked him if he was all right. Joe didn't seem to understand the question. He went behind the truck and stayed there. After a few moments, the other soldier found Joe lying on his side under the truck, shaking from head to foot, the telegram stuffed into his mouth, his arms clasped about himself.

The young assistant didn't know what to do. "Are you all right, soldier?" he asked. But there was no answer. A little later he said, "Why don't you come out of there now?"

But Joe stayed where he was. His eyes were wild, and the assistant was alarmed. He went for help, bringing back two soldiers to remove Joe from underneath the truck and a doctor to give him an injection. Then they put him in the hospital and kept him under sedation for a few days and of course he was unable to attend Sally Buck's funeral.

After three weeks he went back to his duties. And when his time was up, Joe tried to re-enlist. But the army didn't seem to want any soldiers who reacted as he had to the death of a mere grandmother. They paid him off. He went back to Albuquerque, not quite realizing until he arrived that no one was there waiting for him. He checked into a hotel and went calling on Sally's friends. Sally had left no will. He learned she had a sister, one she'd never mentioned, up in Coeur d'Alene, Idaho. This old woman knew nothing of Joe either. She had come down, liquidated the assets of the dead beautician—including the house Joe Buck had lived in from the age of seven—and had gone back to Idaho with the proceeds, never to be heard from again.

Now at the age of twenty-five, with his head full of grief and worry, Joe felt the need to do some thinking. But he was unused to having any very wide variety of thoughts in his head, and there seemed to be severe limits as well to his imagination. There was nothing wrong with these faculties in him, but they were untrained and did not serve him well in emergencies.

He stayed on in the hotel for a few days, spending most of his time up in his room with the shades drawn. Night and day became confused and he didn't always remember to eat. He slept a good deal and had nightmares. Awake or sleeping, he pined for Sally Buck, sometimes calling out for her. Once he was certain she came into his room while he slept and sat on the edge of his bed. He awakened and there she was, fidgeting with her fingers as real as could be. He saw her face in profile. She was looking at the

44

night sky through the open window. He said, "Sally, what am I going to do?" But she gave no sign of having heard him. And then she said something, but it was unclear. She had said either "I'll get my house back" or "I can't ride horseback." Whichever it was, it was no help at all to Joe. But he was glad she'd shown herself to him once again.

One night he dreamed a dream that would become recurrent, a dream of an endless chain of people marching across the side of the world. From his vantage point in some chill and dark and silent corner he could see them coming up from over the eastern horizon, all joined at the bellybutton by a golden rope of light and walking to a rousing march beat, and he could see them moving along until they had gone out of sight behind the western horizon. There were people of all kinds, bus drivers and nuns, musicians and soldiers and ten-cent-store girls; there were Chinamen and pilots, hillbillies and fat men and red-headed women; you could find miners and bank clerks there, millionaires, store detectives, swamis, babies, grandmothers, thieves; look for any kind of person in this golden rope and there would be one, a whore, a dwarf, a saint, a crazy man, cop, teacher, reporter, pretty girl, bookkeeper, shortstop, ragpicker. There seemed to be every kind of person but his own. He made many attempts to join them, running up close to the marching stream of golden people, hoping to discover an opening big enough to slip into; but just as he would find one there would be a rapid closing of ranks, the chain would become tight and exclusive and impossible to break into, and the dreamer was forced to remain always on his chill and dark and silent edge.

After this dream, Joe could no longer remain in that hotel room. He dressed and went into the nighttime streets of Albuquerque, wondering how such familiar places could be so strange to him. "You may know us," said the buildings of the town, "but we don't know you." He walked over to the old neighborhood and stood outside Sally Buck's house. The place was empty now and all the windows were black. He went around to the back yard and knocked on the window of Sally's bedroom, half expecting some kind of an answer.

He waited and waited.

"The thing to do," he thought at length, "is get the hell out of here, away to someplace."

He went back to the hotel and placed his few belongings in a duffel bag, amazed that all of his years could be stuffed into something so small.

5

In Houston, Joe hoped to find a person named Natale, a barber he had known and liked in the army. But Natale had a long Italian surname, and Joe spent more than an hour in the bus station poring over the Houston telephone directory in unavailing efforts to find him. Before he gave up entirely he had dialed away a dollar's worth of dimes.

Then he went out onto the sidewalk for a first good look at Houston. "Shee-it," he thought, "this ain't no improvement on nothing. Don't look to me like this town needs any Joe Bucks in it. But they got one, goddam 'em."

He walked until he came to a hotel. It happened to be the one with the *O* missing in its sign, a cheap, dark place with poorly ventilated rooms and a bathroom floor always covered with water.

It was a cold January day. He sat on the edge of the bed wondering what to do about his predicament and not quite certain just what the predicament was. He saw a future for himself sitting on the edges of hotel-room beds trying to get his thoughts straight. In fifty years, with a long white beard reaching to the floor, he would surely find himself in just such a place, asking himself why it was that the world everywhere was as peculiar as the world in Albuquerque, and why it was he found himself shut out of it.

His only window gave on an airshaft, so that traffic sounds seemed to be heard only from a great distance. This silence, combined with his mood of uncertainty, put him under a kind of spell that lasted for several hours. Later when he would think about them these hours would remind him of a period in his childhood when the TV set had been out of order. Time had been an actual burden under which he was unable to move. It surrounded him like a solid mass through which movement was not only impossible but inconceivable. And now, during these hours in the H tel room, a chill entered him that had nothing to do with temperature or weather; it had more the quality of death about it.

He was saved from this spell by sleep, a long sleep, and when he awakened it was night. The memory of those damp and clammy hours was like the hand of a specter on the back of his neck. He put on his clothes, raced a comb

47

through his hair, and hurried out of that hotel so fast it was as if some slimy thing with warts all over it were chasing him into the streets.

Some blocks away could be seen a brightly lighted street. Joe walked toward it eagerly like that dreamer in the dark moving toward the golden chain where life was, and as he drew nearer, the silence gave way to traffic sounds. In a few moments he was standing in front of the Sunshine Cafeteria, the place with the yellow sunburst over its door.

Walking into the Sunshine, Joe felt himself to be embraced by all of its sudden light and flesh and color in the heart of a dark dead country. It was nearly full, and he had a sense of knowing personally everybody in the place.

There were couples; pairs; groups; silent persons and chatterers; solitary people, some women but mostly men, smoking cigarettes and staring out over empty coffee cups. There were a few travelers and some people on their way to and from night jobs, and there were the inevitable loiterers, the kind to be found everywhere on earth, and a number of that special breed known best in the U.S.A.

At first glance these young men may appear to loiter in packs, for often they occupy one table or group about a single parking meter, but chances are they are as unconnected to one another as they are to the prairies and cities and rivers of their homeland. You will find in the eyes and demeanor of these persons a kind of restless sadness that is probably incurable; they seem to be suffering some nameless common loss, as if something of worth had been snatched from them with such shocking irrevocability that they have forgotten even what it was.

Joe stood just inside the door for a moment, as if scanning this crowd for a familiar face. If he found such a face, he would go over to it and say, "Shee-it, man, where in hell you been?" And finding none, he was tempted to pick out some stranger to say it to, but that took nerve. He went up to the counter and ordered coffee and a hamburger, and while he was waiting it happened that he found a face he liked. It was looking at him from a mirrored column in the middle of the counter. Shee-it, man, he said to himself but not aloud, admiring the good-looking, dark-eyed, tousel-haired, white-toothed image that returned his sweet, crooked smile with such warmth and spontaneity. Where in hell *you* been? Who, me? he answered, Christ, I don't know *where* all! But I'm back! And he and the mirror had a good laugh.

And so Joe took to hanging around nights in this friendly place.

One night he fell into conversation with the busboy, a pretty, rather sissified Mexican.

"Poop, buddy-mine," said Joe, who had begun to worry over his financial condition, "I'm about busted. They give you any kind of money in here, hauling all them dishes?"

"Iss not make rich," the boy shrugged. "One dollar itch hour."

"Yeah, but hell, you can *eat* stuff. Right?" An idea was coming into bloom in Joe's head. "Isn't that right? Don't they let you eat stuff?"

The next day he got a job at the Sunshine. They put him to work on the afternoon shift, finishing at midnight. Joe liked the place so much that when midnight came he stayed on, eating a big meal and then smoking over a coffee cup throughout most of the night.

On his second night the Mexican busboy stopped at his

table, scanned him with his quick black eyes, and said, "At first I sought you wass hosty-ler."

"Oh yeah? Naw, naw, hell no."

The next time the boy passed his table, Joe said, "Hey, what is that?"

"Iss what?"

"That thing you thought?"

"Iss what seeng I sought?"

Joe said, "What you said I, uh, you know, before."

The boy frowned. "I am sorry my Eengleesh," he said, leaving with his tray. And on the next trip he stopped and said, "I wass *chure* you wass hosty-ler."

"That's it!" Joe said. "What is that?"

"A hosty-ler?" The Mexican boy at first was skeptical, then somehow convinced himself of Joe's innocence. "A hosty-ler iss *chick-chick-chick*," he said, making a grinding motion with his hips and rubbing his thumb and forefinger together in a way that indicated money. "*¿Comprende?*"

Joe had some loose images in his head but none that would assemble themselves into a firm clear thought.

"Ah, fooey," said the boy. "*¡Tu comprendes muy bien!*" And with a switch of the tail, he was off to another table, where a group of his friends were gathered.

This was a group Joe had noticed before with some interest: five young men. Four were of one general type that tended to laugh a great deal, chatter more than usual, and gesture often. They dressed with a kind of ostentatious boyishness, and their eyes darted about the place like birds unable to perch.

The fifth, however, was clearly of a different breed. He neither laughed nor spoke nor gestured; his attire seemed careless—old levis, a faded denim shirt, dirty white sneak-

50

ers. His hair, the color of sand, was loosely brushed to the side, and his eyes were for the most part still and remote. He listened to the chatter with some amusement but no real involvement, and somehow this detachment gave him superiority over the others. They were given sufferance so long as they continued to amuse him without making any demands upon him. He was clearly killing time and seemed to have no need of anyone at all.

The Mexican boy stopped at this table, said something and then went on toward the kitchen. The four turned to look at Joe, but the fifth did not. Instead he rose, went to the counter for a fresh cup of coffee, and came directly to Joe's table with it.

"May I sit down?"

Joe was flustered and pleased. "Oh hell yeah." He got to his feet and began to shuffle chairs unnecessarily, unhinged by his sudden role of host. The visitor put out his hand and said, "Perry."

"W-what's that?"

"My name, Perry, P-e-r-r-y."

"Oh yeah, oh yeah." He took the young man's hand and shook it. "Joe Buck," he said. "Want a cigarette?" They lit up and then Joe found Perry looking at him. His eyes were peculiar, humorous and touched with death: If a young person were to bring about his own untimely demise by some absurd and foolish blunder, these might be the eyes with which he would observe his own funeral.

Not knowing how to cope with these eyes upon him, Joe laughed and shrugged his shoulders, faking the situation. Perry smiled faintly and then stopped looking at him altogether. He simply leaned back in his chair, spread-legged, seeming to be totally relaxed and self-contained. He kept his eyes on the portion of street visible through the large front window of the Sunshine. There wasn't much doing out there; occasionally a pedestrian passed and now and then a taxicab cruised by.

Joe was impressed by his own good fortune. Here he was sitting at a table with another person for the first time since he'd left the army. He was eager to prolong the situation but uncertain what was expected of him. He thought of various ways in which he might initiate conversation, but if Perry had joined him in order to participate in his silence, Joe didn't want to spoil it all by talking.

He developed very quickly a deep and mysterious admiration for this stranger named Perry. If some wizard capable of magical transformations were to have approached him with the proposition that he and this sandy-headed personage in levis might exchange identities, he would have seized the opportunity with no questions asked. And he would have been unable to give any reason at all.

But it was this: Such people as Perry enjoy a special privilege. They walk into a place and their favor is sought and that's all there is to it. Often they are beautiful, but this is not always the case. The thing is that they are doomed and have accepted their doom with a kind of deadly grace unusual in persons so young.

And so, elated and uncomfortable, Joe sat in this young man's presence. After a few minutes Perry's former company, the colorful four, got up and started toward the door. A tall redheaded boy who seemed to be their leader led them past the table where Perry and Joe were seated. He said, "Good night, dear," and kept on moving. The second and third giggled, and the fourth, a short young man with a double chin, said, "Lotsa luck." Joe watched as they filed out of the place. But Perry did not. He turned to

52

Joe and looked at him briefly in a way that revealed nothing, and then continued to look out the window.

This night was the beginning of a mysterious and silent friendship that lasted for some weeks. Each night when Joe finished his work and had eaten his midnight meal, Perry would wander into the place from no one knew where and establish himself quietly at Joe's table.

At first there would be some minimum of talk between them, having to do with the fetching of coffee or the passing of sugar, but on many nights no words would pass between them at all. They would look out the window together, or sometimes they would observe an interesting table for a while, and occasionally their glances would cross and hold for a second or two, but mostly between them there was just this sitting together in the Sunshine through the nights with no other apparent connection at all. They shared the time and they shared the place, and who could have said just why?

There was no way of guessing when Perry might leave or where he would go. He would simply rise from the table after ten minutes or after a number of hours, sometimes nodding and sometimes not, and off he would go through the revolving door and past the windows out of sight.

Joe gradually conceived the notion that Perry was the keeper of some remarkable secret that with luck would one day be imparted to him. The secret would have to do with other aspects of Perry's life, where he came from at midnight and where he went at dawn. Somehow Joe would then be allowed to partake of these unknown activities; he would walk with Perry into the mysteries that lay beyond the revolving door of this cafeteria, and from then on Joe's own way of occupying the dark would change. The emptiness of his own existence, the long lonesome sleeps at the H tel, and the senseless hours of dish-clattering in the scullery would be altered in some way. Perry would choose to look upon him with his peculiar grace, he would make some simple gesture that would signal the beginning of this new time Joe foresaw, and the waiting, the initiation of coffee-drinking nights at this silent table in the otherwise noisy Sunshine, would enter upon a new phase or would cease altogether.

Joe's thoughts on these matters were not well formed; he did not even know them as thoughts. And he knew Perry only as a man knows his fate when he is visited by it: in his blood. Perry was the visitor and Joe, with no real thought to cover the matter, knew himself to be the host waiting for the visitor to state in his own good time the nature of his visit.

One night Perry turned unexpectedly to Joe and said, "What's the story?" But he did not seem really to be asking a question. He did, however, keep his eyes on Joe.

Joe shook his head. "Hell, man, I don't know," he said. But what he seemed to be saying was, "I am just waiting, that's all I know."

On another night, in a similar way, out of the blue, Perry said, "Do you make the scene?" This was somewhat more of a question, but Joe was at a loss to answer it.

"Make the scene," he said, faking it, "yeah, that's right, hell yes." He had no notion of what he was talking about.

On these few occasions when Perry did speak, his voice was deep and low, just a cut above a whisper and intimate as the grave.

One morning at dawn he said, "Are you for real, Joe?" and then he left the table and went out of the place, clearly not expecting to be answered at all.

And then one night he looked at Joe in that very first way, the long look of that first night.

Joe was nervous. It was time. For something. He was desperately anxious to know what was expected of him. He puffed on his cigarette, stalling, hoping for inspiration. He laughed and wheezed and shook his head knowingly and tapped the table with his finger tips. And then, suddenly, almost involuntarily, he stopped all this false activity and sat still, simply looking at the man across from him. His eyes clearly said, Help me, but he had no idea any message at all was being transmitted.

Perry nodded slightly. His eyes were sympathetic. Then the amusement in them became more pronounced than usual. And suddenly all that could be seen in them was the mystery that was nothing more or less than his own doom. He turned his gaze on the street once again.

It happened that at this moment, as if by some outlandish plan, the revolving door was spinning. A small man in a green necktie and brown tweed sport jacket was coming toward their table.

6

The man was young, about thirty, but nearly bald, and he had a high naked-looking forehead and burning beady eyes that were enlarged many times over by the thick lenses of his spectacles. He looked like a mad young scientist in a silent movie.

He stopped at the table where the two young men were seated. "Perry," he said.

Perry gave no sign of having heard his name spoken.

"Please, Perry, do you know how many times it's been this late?" His voice lapped the ear with something caramel-soft and caramel-sweet.

A long ash fell from Perry's cigarette onto his trousers. He brushed at it with his hand and went on smoking.

"*Please*, I said, Perry." No answer. "I just want to ask you if you know what time it is, that's all."

He changed his tack: took a chair from the next table, placed it in such a way that it faced Perry, then sat down with a deliberateness calculated to suggest that he could outwait any human being alive, folded his hands on his lap, and commenced to stare.

Perry after another long moment said to Joe, "Want some coffee?"

Before Joe could answer, Perry turned to the third man without actually looking at him directly and said, "Marvin."

The man would not break his game of staring. "Yes, Perry."

"Marvin, two cups of coffee."

The movie scientist leaned forward, tilting his head in a way that indicated pleading. All his gestures had this quality of standing for something not quite felt. "Oh, *Perry*," he said.

"One black, Marvin, and one with cream."

Marvin, by pressing his lips together and raising his thin black eyebrows, acquired an imposed-upon look. He sighed and went to the counter.

Joe smiled and said, "Hey, Perry, I bet you that fella's a brother o' yours, right?"

56

"Wrong."

Returning with the coffee, Marvin placed both cups in front of Perry. Some aspect of the situation seemed to prohibit him from acknowledging Joe's presence at the table.

Perry said, "Serve my friend, Marvin."

Marvin slid one of the cups across the table toward Joe.

"Thanks," Joe said. "Thank you a lot." He smiled at the big forehead and tipped an invisible hat to it, considering an absurd impulse to draw a picture on it.

The man resumed his seat and his impassive stare and said nothing.

"My friend thanked you, Marvin."

"He's welcome, Perry. You're welcome, sir."

Perry's voice did not alter; it was a warm narcotic bath of sound: "His name is Joe, Marvin."

"You're welcome, *Joe*."

A moment passed.

Perry said, "Marvin."

"Yes, Perry."

Perry put his hand forward, still not looking at the man. He seemed to place a high, benedictory value on his eyes and would not squander them on unworthy subjects. "Let me see your billfold, Marvin."

"Oh, Perry, please."

Perry's hand was still extended. "I meant immediately, of course, Marvin. I always mean immediately, unless I specify otherwise."

Marvin placed his billfold in Perry's hand. "Oh, *honestly*," he said.

Perry counted the money. There were four one-dollar bills. "How much is in your pocket, Marvin?"

"*What* pocket?" Marvin said, quickly removing a hand from the side pocket of his tweed jacket.

"That pocket," said Perry without pointing or even glancing in Marvin's direction.

Marvin then handed over a small wad of bills, which Perry held without counting. "How much is here?" he said.

"Tch." Marvin sighed. "Seventy," he said.

"You may have my portion then, Marvin." Perry handed back the billfold. "And I will have yours." He pocketed the seventy-dollar wad.

"Now I'd like the car keys, Marvin."

"No! I absolutely refuse! Please, Perry."

"Excuse me, Marvin. I didn't hear you. What did you say? You said something just now. Repeat it."

"Oh, how am I going to get home?"

"What's the matter, are your feet just killing you, Marvin?"

"Oh, Perry, why are you doing this? Is it to impress your friend? I'm sure your friend is very impressed."

"I had planned," said Perry, "to come to your home tomorrow afternoon. However, you're behaving so poorly, Marvin, it may be necessary to adjust my plans."

"What time?" Marvin said. "Late afternoon or early afternoon or what tomorrow?"

"The car keys, Marvin."

"I'll give them to you, I'll give them to you. But say what time."

"Are you suggesting a bargain, Marvin?"

"Oooh!"

"Don't whimper. You're whimpering, Marvin."

Marvin smiled and tried to laugh, but all he could manage was a twitch of the eyebrows and a few minor explosions of breath.

Joe by now had completed plans for the drawing he would never be able to place on Marvin's big blank forehead: a girl-child with long mascara'd eyelashes.

Marvin took the car keys from his pocket and placed them on the table before Perry.

"Here, *take* the things. Five o'clock?"

"Thank you, Marvin, for the use of your car, and for all your other kindnesses. I may sometimes fail to show my appreciation, but you do have it, from the heart." Perry rose from the table. "Come on, Joe."

Joe rose slowly from the table, confounded by what he had witnessed. He had the feeling that if Marvin would show his eyes everything would then be all right. But the spectacles clearly grew out of his face like flesh and horn and muscle and there was no removing them.

Marvin got up and grabbed Perry's arm. Perry stood stock-still, holding the offended arm aloof from his body, his back to Marvin. "Remove your hand, Marvin. And sit back down."

These commands were executed at once.

"What time then?" urged Marvin. "About five? Or after? Or what?"

Perry now turned for the first time to the little man with the many-times-magnified eyes and bestowed upon him a long ambiguous gaze: It looked like contempt, but then again it looked like tenderness. "Sometime tomorrow afternoon," he said. "Now I want you to sit still and stay that way till I've gone. Do you understand what I want?"

"Tch." Marvin sighed. "All *right*, Perry."

Perry would not remove his eyes until Marvin repeated what he had said, omitting the implication of resistance.

59

"All right, Perry." And, "Thank you!" he threw in for good measure.

Perry went through the revolving door, and Joe followed close behind. As they passed the window, Joe looked in at the little movie scientist. It was eerie to see him sitting there, in motionless obedience, his thick glasses catching the light of the cafeteria at an angle that made them look like two high-powered flashlights following Perry's departure.

7

They were in a parking lot, Perry leaning on the fender of a white MG, Joe standing before him, thumbs caught in his hip pockets, smiling uncertainly, wondering what in the world was about to take place. The night was cold and clear, and the stars, like the possibilities, seemed brighter and far more numerous than usual. Joe laughed. Perry smiled and looked at him and shook his head in the manner of one who is indulging a small child.

"Joe," he said. He made frequent and gentle use of a name, knowing that to its owner it is likely to be the most sacred word in the language, reaching not only the ear but the heart as well. "What're you laughing for, Joe?"

Joe shook his head, still smiling. "Beats me." He laughed some more, trying still to pretend he understood everything and yet fully aware he was merely making a fool of himself.

"We got to get you cooled, Joe, we got to get you tuned in. Would you like that?"

"Yeah, hell yeah, that's just what I need."

"You don't know what I'm talking about, do you, Joe?"

"Well now, tuned in, that's a— No, not exactly; I wouldn't say I knew exactly." He tried another little laugh, an immediate failure.

"No, you don't, Joe. You don't know anything much. But that's valuable. Otherwise you couldn't learn. You want to learn, don't you?"

"Oh yeah, you bet I do, Perry."

"Well then, isn't it a good thing you don't know much?"

Joe frowned, afraid to risk another laugh.

"Do you trust me, Joe?"

Joe nodded, quite vigorously. He meant for this nodding to express all of his respect and affection for Perry, and he went at it in earnest. And then he heard himself babbling something: "I sure do, Christ yes I do. But I'm just fairly new here in town, and uh—" He was trying to get some point over to this highly important new friend, but it wasn't coming out at all right. "I just got to town here, I'm a stranger, I come in from—" No, that wasn't it, not even close.

"You don't have to tell me where you came from, Joe. You're here, aren't you?"

"I'm what? Here? Yeah I am, by God." This was not the kind of conversation in which he'd learned to participate in the army. There it had been fairly safe to laugh and pull a certain face when you'd lost the thread, and that usually got you through. But with Perry here it was different: He kept pretty close track of things.

"I'm going to help you, but I want you to relax and trust me. Now listen, have you got a room near here?"

"A room! Yeah, I got a room in a hotel."

"Let's go there then. Where is it?"

"It's got an *O* missing."

"Where? I mean, do we walk or do we drive?"

"Either way, we can just—"

"How far is it, Joe?"

"I'd say it was a few blocks."

"Get in."

They parked the MG across the street from the place, walked past the desk clerk's cubbyhole and up the stairs to Joe's room.

Perry sat on the edge of the bed.

"I don't see a radio, Joe."

"Radio? Nope, no. I don't have a radio. Yet. I'm gonna get one, though."

"Make yourself at home, Joe. It's your room, isn't it? And you're with a friend, so relax."

Joe sat on a straight-backed wooden chair. "It make a lot of difference in here to have a radio."

"Yes it would. It's very bad not having one."

Joe said, "I believe I'd like to have me a transistor, you know about them and all?"

"Yes, I do."

"Mm-hm, well, I'm saving for one."

"Starting when?"

"Tomorrow." A moment passed, then Joe said, "What I want, I want one with some power in here, not one of them little dinkies." He looked around the place, scanning the dark walls quickly. "You understand what I mean?"

"Exactly," Perry said. "You want a radio with some power. You don't want one of those little dinkies."

Perry placed a thin, hand-rolled cigarette in his mouth and lighted it. He sucked some smoke out of it, making a hissing sound, then held his breath and handed it to Joe. Joe tried to imitate Perry, but he gave away his inexperience by emitting the smoke at once.

"You don't know what you're doing, Joe. You must learn from me and then you'll know. Now—" he held the cigarette in the air between them— "this is not tobacco, Joe, this is a special cigarette, containing the dried leaves and flowers of a hemp known botanically as *Cannabis sativa*. It's comparable to the high-powered non-dinky transistor radio you're saving up for starting tomorrow. No, that's not quite true. You and I are the radios, the *Cannabis sativa* is the, uh, juice, power. . . ."

He stopped talking and filled his lungs again, using sign language to get the technique across to Joe. Together they finished the cigarette and then they sat in silence for a few minutes and then they smoked another one. Joe got up to open the window. Perry told him not to. Then Joe realized he was enjoying his own movements in a new way, and this caused him to smile.

"That stuff *helps*," he said. "I believe it helps."

Perry took the tiny ends of the two cigarettes they had smoked and tore them to pieces, dropping the fragments into the sink and washing them down the drain. "Unlike tobacco, the butt of the *Cannabis sativa* must be disposed of entirely, Joe. There."

"Hey!" Joe said suddenly. "That was *marijuana!* That cigarette had marijuana in it!"

"That's right, Joe."

"Hell!" Joe was delighted. "No wonder I feel so nutty!

You sure are one sneaky devil, Perry." He went about the room testing his responses to movement, to seeing, to simply being, and he found them altered, heightened, and he felt more amused with himself than ever before.

Perry lay back on the bed. He took a long while adjusting himself, and when he was spread out comfortably, ankles crossed, hands behind his head, he said, "You comfortable there, Joe?"

"I'm fine," Joe said. But suddenly he wasn't fine at all. Something was wrong and he couldn't put his finger on it, but it was as if some nameless threat were creeping silently into the room from under the door and through the cracks in the window and he was at a loss to stop it, or even describe it.

"Is there anything you want, Joe?"

"Oh no, no, I'm fine."

"No, you're not. You're not fine, Joe."

"Huh?"

"You need help."

"Do I?"

"Oh, yes, definitely. And I, in concert with the *Cannabis sativa,* am here for just that purpose: to help you find out what you want and show you how to take it."

Joe felt as if his heart were filled with air; it might burst, and painfully, dangerously; he pressed on it with the palm of his hand. That didn't help at all. He picked up a book of matches and began to fool with it, trying to distract himself from the anxiety he felt. The matches were very real and definitely a relief; he bent them and twisted them and put them down and picked them up. Perry was still talking:

"It's not just tonight you don't know what to do with. Your whole life is a burden to you. You frown a lot, Joe.

And you pick things up and put them down." He looked pointedly at the book of matches. "You have plans for burning down the world. But you're losing a lot of motion, a lot of time. You've got to get cool. Find out what you want and rule out everything else, and then you'll be cool as can be. Now: What have you got to do?"

"Find out what I want?"

"Correct. And then?"

"Ummm."

"Rule out . . ." Perry coached.

"Rule out everything else."

"Right. Now again."

"Find out what I want, and rule out everything else."

"You're getting tuned in, Joe. That was lesson one. Here's *exercise* one: this room. What is there in it that you want? Just name it, anything at all, and I'll see to it you get it."

Joe started to scan the room with his eyes, and Perry said: "Look at me. Maybe that will help you, Joe. That's it. Now I'll ask you again: Is there anything at all you want?"

Joe studied Perry's face, straining to find a clue in it. But he found none.

"You know, Joe, there are people and quite a few hundred of them at that who would pay out considerable sums of money to be in your position right now: locked in a room with me and being asked what they want."

Joe was actually dizzy from the mental effort he was expending. Another long moment passed. Then suddenly Perry was off the bed and standing before Joe's chair, looking down at him. His movement from the bed had been so quick as to be almost violent. The quiet of the place and the mood Joe felt had been instantly annihilated, and now a strange young man had hold of his shirt front, was gripping him in a way that compelled him to look up into his face.

He was surprised to find no anger or violence in the man's eyes, as there had been in his movements. He was simply looking into Joe's face in a gently penetrating way, and when he had looked for a long moment, he said, "If we're going to be friends, Joe, there's just one rule . . ."

Joe felt he was living through some miracle: This stranger, a fine and handsome and knowledgeable and authoritative person, was turning his powers, his focus, his friendship, upon such an unworthy object as himself. Surely he had made some mistake in judgment, selecting Joe Buck for his attentions. When he discovered his error that would be the end of it. Meanwhile Joe was terrified of making some wrong gesture, speaking some stupid giveaway word that would hasten Perry's departure. He tried to think up ways of stalling off this inevitable blunder, little words and gestures that would nudge it gently forward in time. But he wasn't up to it. He knew he wasn't up to it. Perry was too wise, too far ahead of the game, he couldn't be fooled.

". . . and the rule is, no crap. There is to be no crap. None. I am sick of people who know what they want and won't take it, won't even speak up and name it. When I say to you, 'What do you want, Joe,' you answer. You just say whatever that thing is you want. You understand me?"

"Yeah. Yeah I do, Perry, I do."

"That's good." His face broke gradually into a smile, and then he released Joe's shirt front and sat on the edge of the bed, bridging with his eyes the few feet of space between himself and Joe. When Joe's eyes had joined his own, he said, "Say it now. Name the thing you want."

66

Stupid bastard, Joe said to himself, *say* something, talk up, can't you talk up? So stupid you don't know what you want? Say something, say anything, and that'll be a start.

"I, uh, I think I might, uh, be—um-uh . . ." He closed his eyes and frowned, inclined his head toward his body, as if what he wanted were trapped somewhere in his stomach, and might be conjured out of him by an act of will.

"Just say it," Perry encouraged him. "Whatever it is."

"Hopeless. I'm hopeless." Oh Jesus Christ! he thought, the truth is an ugly sonofabitch. He lifted his shoulders, wanting his face to disappear into his body.

When he opened his eyes, he half expected Perry to be on his way out the door. Instead he was looking at him as gently as ever, and with even more concern than before.

"Why? Tell me why you're hopeless, Joe."

"Shee-it, Perry, I may as well tell you, I am dumb. I am. I am one dumb sombitch. I don't know shee-it. I can't talk right, I can't think straight." He laughed, but his face was grave. He saw nothing funny at all. For he had hung some ugly, ungainly, unforgivable thing in the air between them and it had to be pushed away; he hammered at it with his laughter. But he couldn't get at it. The more he laughed, the bigger it got.

Suddenly he saw in his mind a beautiful picture: Sally Buck's gravestone, pure white and utterly blank, needing to be filled in, inscribed. The crayon in his head drew a quick sketch on the stone, a cartoon of himself, and that somehow made him easier: The picture was complete. He could look at Perry again.

"I keep thinkin'," he heard himself saying, somewhat to his surprise, "that what I'll do is I'll keep worshing them dishes and then they'll bring in some more and I'll worsh 'em, and then uh . . ."

"And then . . ."

"And then I'll come up here and sleep some, and then I'll worsh some more dishes and then I'll, um . . ."

"You'll what?"

"I'll, uh . . ." He put his arm forward and shook it, waving his hand back and forth, as if to indicate that the word was somewhere in the room.

"Just say it, Joe."

"Die."

Oh! Oh shit! What kind of thing to hang in the air is that? Kill it, kill it!

He tried one quick harsh blast of laughter. No, that wasn't going to get rid of the thing. Nothing would. It was too big, too ugly.

In his mind there was a shovel, and he placed the shovel in the hands of some shadowy creature, and this creature set about using the shovel to dig a grave next to Sally's. And then there was an open coffin sitting next to the new grave, and the coffin had a beautiful young person in it: himself. Oh, oh goddammit, he thought, is that all I get? Just a coffin for all my being young, a coffin for all my juice, and all my good looks? The sadness of it overwhelmed him, and suddenly he was crying, writhing on the floor of that H tel room looking at a stranger's dirty sneakers, gasping for breath. He felt the necessity of getting that stranger out of the room, and he said, "*Go,*" but that was all he could get out, for there was something inside of him now far bigger than his lungs and it was using up all the space where breathing was supposed to take place, and not only that, it was poking at his liver and into his heart and all his vital places, and it hurt like a handful of knives in him. The dirty sneakers had a person in them. What's it want? What's it want with me? What's this sombitch want with me? his mind demanded over and over again. Don't he know I'm, I'm, I'm . . .

The stranger took hold of his shoulders and pushed him onto his back with great force, and then Joe was being sat upon, straddled by him. These actions were sudden enough to drive out the big, sharp-edged, heavy horror that was in him. Now he breathed again, emitting sound with each exhalation of breath, and the groans comforted him: Only live people made such noises. His face was wet. Apparently he'd been crying; but he wasn't ashamed of it. It was the marijuana, that's all; it wasn't his fault.

He looked at Perry straddling him there, and at his face, hovering very near his own. And he heard him speak in his friendly, deep, sweet and dark narcotic voice, "Now I'll bet you feel a whole lot better, don't you, Joe?"

Pinned. He was pinned down, pinned down by somebody friendly, wise, calm. Good.

At last!

What now?

"So now," Perry continued, "all you got to do is let me know, give me a signal what you want. Otherwise, how can I give it to you?"

Who is this bird setting on my belly? Is he God? Is he Santy Claus? Is he magic? Give me what I want? Is he crazy? He ask me once again, just once more, I'll tell him, I'll tell him all right. Tell him I want me a blonde lady to fuck, and have her take care of me all my life, a blonde lady with long eyelashes and fat dimply knees, got to have meat on them knees, and wear a yellow dress with real tits inside, no foam rubber like poor old Sally, and be home a lot and bring me stuff to eat in front of the TV, and her

69

come up to me during the horseshit part and say to me, *Cowboy, I love you so,* and have her cry about how much she loves me. *Tch tch,* I'll say to her, *I never in my life seen anybody love somebody as much as you love me, how come is that anyway?* And then have her say, with her voice milky as her tits, *Why? Why I love you? Cause you're Cowboy Joe Buck and you do me so good, and you don't waste your juice trying to make a living when you don't know how anyway. And besides they's something special about a cowboy that loves as good as you and takes his time with it. So you just set back handsome and hard and tell me what you want from the kitchen. Jello? With cream on it? And how about a peach and a drumstick, sweetheart, for you to nibble while I sing you* Blue Moon. *And then we'll make love here on the floor and when it's over you sing me git along little dogie git along git along git along little dogie git along* . . .

8

that's nothing unusual," Perry said. "Marijuana often induces hunger." They were sitting at the counter of an all-night eating place somewhere on the highway, Perry smoking and drinking coffee, Joe finishing the last of two hamburgers.

"Want another one?" Perry said.

Joe shook his head, his mouth too full to speak. He felt

wonderful, like a baby who has cried his lungs out and then been spanked and fed. He felt inexpressible warmth toward Perry.

"Who's Sally?" Perry asked.

"Sally! How you know about Sally?"

"You said her name a lot, while you were having that crying jag. Is she an old girl friend?"

"Yep! An old girl friend." *Lie!* That's a fine way to do, he told you he likes the truth! Yeah, but a grown man can't go telling somebody he been babbling about his gramaw.

"What would you like to do now, Joe? It's only four A.M."

"Me? What I want to do? *Hell* with what I want to do! What do *you* want to do?"

"No, no, this is your night, Joe. You say what you'd like to do."

"I'd like to do what *you'd* like to do."

"No. You say."

"But Perry, I don't know shee-it about stuff to do and all."

"Yes you do. You know what you like. Eveybody does."

"Well, I, uh, I'll tell you what we used to do in the army. That's all I know about and it don't amount to nothing, but what we'd do, we'd go into Columbus and pick us up a whore, and that was all they was to it. Never nothing special."

"Is that what you want now?"

"Now? Shoot! You mean *now?*"

"Yes, now. Do you want a woman now?"

"Aw, hell, I don't have to have a woman. Shoot, I'm just fine as I am, I don't need anything like that." Joe stirred his coffee in silence for a moment. Then he looked at Perry and said: "Why? You want one?"

"Never mind about me. You want a woman, right?"

"Well . . ."

"You do, don't you?"

"Oh, I suppose if they was something right here pulling at my elbow, I'd just as leave grab onto it, but I, uh, don't want you to go to no trouble." And then, hopefully, he added: "Unless you want one, too."

Perry said, "No."

"Well then, to the devil with it—uhm, unless you mean they's something close *by*. Where it wouldn't be too much trouble. And we could just, uh—"

Perry rose. "Come on."

He started to hand the cashier a five-dollar bill but Joe tore it from his hand and gave the woman a ten. Then he took the five and pushed it into Perry's hip pocket. Perry smiled and said nothing.

On the edge of the parking lot was an outdoor telephone booth. Perry left the door open. Joe leaned against the side of the booth, listening. After a moment of dialing and waiting, Perry said:

"Juanita? This is Perry. *Perry!* That's right. Now listen, Juanita, this is what I want you to do for me. Juanita, don't talk so loud, you're hurting my ear. Hold the phone away from you, you're blasting me. Now listen, is Dolores there? No, I don't want to talk to her. You just wake her up, Juanita. I said, *wake her up!* I'm bringing someone nice for her, a very handsome young— Keep still, Juanita, just listen. Wake her up and give her a good bath, and we'll be around in about half an hour."

He hung up. Joe was standing there with his mouth open, shaking his head back and forth slowly, unable truly to grasp his good fortune. He was like a child to whom a guardian angel has chosen to make a material

72

appearance. "Perry, you goddam sombitch!" he said, his voice trembling with love.

In the car, on the freeway, Perry said, "You know, Joe, you've wrecked my evening."

Joe was alarmed. "What? What'd I do?"

"Well, you see, a great deal of my pleasure comes from spending Marvin's money on other people. And you wouldn't let me pick up that tab back there."

Joe laughed, relieved.

"No," Perry said, "I'm serious. Don't ever do that again."

"Say, Perry, is that uh, Marvin fella, is he some relative or other?"

"Oh no, he's just my employer. I'm employed by Marvin."

"Oh! Oh, I see. He's your *boss.*" For a moment this seemed to clear the matter up. But as Joe reviewed in his mind the scene that had taken place between the two, he realized this new information only increased his confusion. "Boss, huh?"

"Yes, that's right. I'm employed by Marvin to perform a highly specialized service. I'm supposed to remind him how loathsome he is, and my remuneration is based upon the extent to which I succeed. I held my first such position in the East some years ago, and I learned something invaluable. I learned to look beneath what people say they want and give them what they're really screaming for under their breath.

"Light this for me, will you?" He handed Joe a cigarette. Joe leaned forward, huddling against the windshield, and lighted the cigarette. He placed it between Perry's lips. Perry puffed on it, then removed it from his mouth and continued to speak:

"For instance, you'll find that people who have the most to say about their great appetite for tenderness are really just asking for terror. Only they don't quite know how to pronounce it, I suppose. I'm not talking about people who simply want tenderness and shut up about it. I'm talking about the ones that babble about it endlessly. You can bet that any form of kindness, or even just decent treatment, would make them sick. On the other hand, you can't really give them straight terror either, even though they worship it, because they're too chickenhearted to take what they want. You learn to be terribly cool, and measure everything out with teaspoons, and call it by other names.

"Nothing can be simply what it is. Even while they're groveling in full horror, they have to think it's love. So you touch them on the head occasionally. But not too often. And then pretend it never happened. The same with terror: Don't deliver too much. Just promise it with your eyes and punctuate with small wounds: Never draw blood.

"Now with Marvin, I think I'm doing extremely well. Initially—I mean before he met me—he looked upon himself as something about the size and value of a worm. But he couldn't bear such an exalted position, it was too burdensome, he just couldn't wear the mantle, he was desperate. And now, in just a few short months, I've reduced him to the point where he's just sort of an underfed maggot, and he's delighted with the progress we've made. Couldn't you tell? Didn't he seem pleased?

"But this won't last, I'm afraid. Marvin's too ambitious. Ultimately, he'll want me to step on him entirely, just lower my heel, so to speak, and grind him out of existence altogether. However, I haven't actually signed on for that.

I'm much better at these intermediate stages where some subtlety is required; I'm no good with hammers and bread knives and such. Besides, Marvin can't afford to be murdered, not on his salary. I suppose if he's lucky, somebody might lose control some day and do the thing for free. But not me. I know my work."

"I'll say you do," Joe said. "You sure do know a lot. How old is a fella like you anyway, Perry?"

"Twenty-nine—going on a hundred."

"Hell, I'm twenty-five," Joe said, "And I've just pissed away my life, Perry, I swear I have. For instance, I didn't really get the whole drift of what you was talking about just now. What do you think of that?"

"I'd say that was pretty amazing, Joe. But that's what I like about you, your virginity."

"Oh no," Joe said, "I'm afraid I'm no virgin, Perry. I am awful goddam dumb, but I've fucked aplenty."

"I'm not talking about that kind of virginity."

"Oh! Well then, tell me the kind you're talking about then. Come on, Perry, 'cause I got to learn this shee-it."

Perry looked at Joe for such a long while that Joe began to be uneasy about the progress of the car along the highway. Then Perry looked away again, shook his head slowly back and forth, as if his eyes had just beheld something unearthly, and said, almost under his breath: "You will, you will."

In an excess of affectionate good will and gratitude, Joe placed his hand on Perry's shoulder and squeezed it. "You're the best buddy I ever had." This statement seemed incomplete, inadequate. Joe felt a deep impulse to get at the whole truth, to keep talking until he had done some justice to what he felt for Perry.

"Listen, you're not just my best buddy, because listen I

75

been in the fucking army and all that crap, and I've known plenty of guys, but they wasn't none of them done me like this. I mean, you driving me all the way out here to get me laid, and that hamburger back there. And all that don't count for *poop!* Well, yes, it does, it counts for something all right, but the main thing is—you *talk* to me, goddammit, and you say Joe this and Joe that. And I never heard of *any*body *any*where *any* time having that kind of, uh, well, shoot, *friend,* goddammit, *friend!* You see what I'm getting at here?"

"Yes, Joe, But I want you to shut up now. Okay?"

Joe withdrew his arm slowly, and looked straight ahead. He stopped breathing for a moment and said, "I said too much, didn't I."

"Oh no, no you didn't." Perry said. "But now I want you to shut up. That's all."

"Okay, Perry," Joe said. "That's the least I can do."

9

the little sports car turned off the freeway into a helter-skelter arrangement of trailer parks, building-supply places, old houses and small factories known as Newville, Texas. And then it drove onto an undelineated field on which there were no trees or bushes, no vegetation at all, nothing but bare earth surrounding a big old frame house. No path led to this house and no driveway: Its placement in that setting seemed haphazard, as if it were the abandoned toy of some god-sized child who tomorrow might choose to wind up its bulldozer and do away with the object completely.

Perry parked the MG alongside the place.

As they climbed the front steps, a porch light went on, the door opened, and there, holding the screen for them, stood a tall and ungainly person named Tombaby Barefoot.

Tombaby Barefoot was a light-haired, pale, oddly constructed halfbreed. He had a small head and no shoulders to speak of, but from his stomach to the ground he was big and thick and heavy. He wore a gray sweatshirt with HARVARD printed on it, faded and torn levis, sneakers, and a pair of golden earrings.

"Hey Perry," he said. His voice was soft and high, his accent Texan.

From inside the house came an angry growl: "Turn off that porch light, Princess."

Tombaby smiled. "Mother wants you to fall on your asses, isn't she sweet?" He shook hands with Perry and then with Joe Buck.

Perry said, "Joe, meet Tombaby Barefoot."

"Pleased," said the big pale epicene Indian.

"How do, Tombaby," said Joe.

Tombaby Barefoot led the way through a hall and into the living room. He moved like a cow with loose knee joints and seemed always on the point of collapsing into a pile of thighs and elbows. Inside the door, he stepped aside. "Welcome to the palace of Mother Goddam," he said.

The room was furnished with thick oversized stuff from Grand Rapids in a style known as modern in the nineteen

77

thirties. On the mantlepiece, and flanking a sequined vase that contained the American flag, were framed photographs of unrecognizable but famous-looking people (all signed), and on the striped, dark-pink walls hung a number of framed prints—fragments from the ceiling of the Sistine Chapel, for the most part details of bosoms, backsides, and hands.

Squatting Buddha-like on the center cushion of a couch on the far side of the room was a small, middle-aged hag in a red satin kimono. Her enormous watery eyes were pale blue, rimmed with feverish red and sleepless black. These eyes seemed a monstrous liability to the rest of her organism; rapacious, incessantly active, they seemed not to belong to any small woman, but to some great nightmare foe. Across her mouth was a quick deadly slash of purple paint, and jutting from it a cigarette butt with a hot red coal on the end of it.

"Perry!" she shouted in a surprising man's voice.

"Evening, Juanita," Perry said.

"*Evening* my ass," she said. And then to Joe, "Hello, son."

While Joe was being introduced to this woman, whose name was Juanita Collins Harmeyer Barefoot, her son disassembled himself into a rocking chair and folded his hands across his stomach.

"Up up up!," Juanita commanded, gesturing. "Tend bar, Princess, tend bar. Bourbon all around."

Tombaby rose with less effort than one might have expected. "Bourbon all around," he said.

As he left the room, he walked past a remarkable article leaning on the wall next to the dining room archway: an eight-foot stuffed toy in the image of a giraffe. Joe, in his own mind, allowed Tombaby to climb onto this

78

toy giraffe and ride away, not just into the dining room but clear out of Texas, but then the giraffe grew weak under its burden and there was a dreadful collapse with many skinned knees and broken limbs. And while he was coping with this crisis in his imagination, he and Perry in reality took seats in big chairs that faced Juanita across a mirror-covered cocktail table.

"I," she said to Perry, "went thoo one bitch of a commotion here for you tonight."

Perry smiled. "You always do, Juanita."

"Look!" She thrust forward a hag's hand, tobacco-stained, dirty, its nails bitten to the quick. But what she meant to display was a pair of fresh scratches on the back of the hand. "She done that to me when I woke her up, the goddam animal." Then suddenly Juanita tossed her big eyes into Joe Buck's face: "You better like animals, hear?"

Joe grinned at her. But he was sick. What he saw as she spoke was a cage with a creature half lady half tiger padding back and forth in it, starved. But he didn't want it, didn't want any kind of animal at all. What he wanted was something soft and fat and gentle, full of rounding sweet places to hide in.

" 'Cause that's what you gonna get," Juanita said. She turned to Perry. "You think this is bad?" she asked, meaning the scratched hand. "Last week she bit me. Drew blood."

Tombaby Barefoot returned with a bottle of Old Overholt and a handful of jelly glasses. "Tell about what you done to her, Mother, we'd love to hear that."

Juanita asked Perry: "What'd he say? Something smart? D'he say something smart?" And to the halfbreed, "That's it, Mumbles, just keep it up, keep it up."

Tombaby handed a glass of whiskey to Perry and another to Joe. He took a sip from a third glass, and started toward his rocking chair with it.

Juanita picked up a heavy cut-glass candy dish from the cocktail table. "Princess!" she barked threateningly, taking aim with the candy dish.

"Oh!" Tombaby feigned surprise. " 'Scuse me, Mother, I forgot all about you." He placed his glass on the table in front of her and poured another drink for himself.

Juanita put down the dish and picked up the glass. "And git some music. What're we runnin' here, a cat house or a funeral parlor?"

"Well, now, that's a question," Tombaby said. "If you're the main attraction, Mother, I'd be halfway inclined to think it might be a cross between—"

"*Shut up!*" Juanita's voice rattled the place.

Tombaby left the room.

"I always like to make it clear to strangers," Juanita told Joe, "that this big-assed rooster with the dimple where his dick ought to be, yeah, that's right, and a sack o' gumdrops for balls, well, he ain't no son of mine, not by a damsite. He nothing but the mistake of some goddam broken-down night-shift nurse at the General Jones Hospital in Shreveport. She switched kids on me. You think I'm joking about a thing like that? Listen, I ermember the night, plain as day too, the night I got planted with that kid, I ermember things everybody else is forgot, I got total *re*call; I ermember where it was, and how I was lyin', and how it felt, and what happened after, Darlington Barefoot and me, lyin' out on his porch, on top of the world, drink in one hand, lookin' at the moon in the other. Ermember the whole shebang, like it was ten minse ago. Don't tell me poor Tombaby is what you get to ermember a time like 'at with. Besides, my kid had black black hair when he come out of me. I know, I was wide awake, I seen him come out, and he was black-headed. What else, being son of Darlington Barefoot of Brownsville, was he gonna have for hair, pink? Shit! And what'd they shove at me next morning to feed but this mess, all mouth and rear end. Lemme tell you, my titties dried up in horror on the spot. Looka here!" She pulled apart the red kimono and showed two stringy breasts. "Think I'm jokin'? That day to this, not a drop of milk come out of these things: dry!"

"The whole point of that story," said Tombaby Barefoot, returning from the dining room, where he had caused the sound of the Ink Spots to pervade the place with *Someone's Rockin' My Dreamboat*, "is to show her poor ole boobs. If she waits for a demand—well, you can just about imagine I'm sure how *long* a wait that'd *entail*."

Juanita's eyebrows were cocked in imitation of a listening attitude. "I caught every syllable of that insult, peahead. My notebook is crammed full. God help you, God *help* you!"

"No, Mother, you misunderstood me. All I said was they'd like to see your vagina next. Ready? Here's your music: Ta-*taaaaa!*"

"What he say, what he say? Tell me, Perry."

"Oh," said Perry, enunciating carefully, "he said he hoped Dolores would be ready pretty soon. So do I."

"Yeah, I'll bet. Well, Darlington Barefoot took one look at this thing—and smell? It was born with a caul, had to hold my nose every time I come near it. Anyway, Barefoot had one look at it and he was on his way, took off like greased lightning. Can you blame the man? I mean, look at it his way: His daddy, *Darlington's* daddy, was a brave, a goddam *brave!* So what was he gonna do, take this gland case, Miss Jane Withers here, back to his tribe and say meet the kid? Fat chance!"

"Therefore," said Tombaby, "Mother, who was already flat on her back, had no difficulty at all in making a living—except that she was forced to specialize in faulty-vision types: drunks, the blind, et cetera." He winked at her coyly and waved his hand. "I was *telling* them," he said, raising his voice, "how *hard* you've always *worked* to sup*port* me."

A quick red flash and flutter of motion on the couch, and a glass of bourbon landed in the rocking chair. But the rocking chair had been vacated by the big blond half-breed. He picked up the glass, unbroken but empty now, and turned to his mother. "Would you care for a drink?"

Juanita said to Joe, "Want to know why I put up with him? 'Cause I love him just like he was my own. *Call* me a damn fool, I don't mind, I make no bones about it."

"I love you too, Mother," said Tombaby. "And I love, let's see, snakes and policemen and war and big hairy spiders and, um, oh, what else! Oh, I know! Cancer of the rectum!"

"Whatever he's sayin', matter how sassy it sounds, it's based on 'fection and erspect. Right, Tombaby?"

Now the Ink Spot with the falsetto was asking: *"When evening shadows creep, do I lose any sleep over you?"* And somewhere in the back of the house, a door slammed.

"Dolores just rang for you," said the Indian to his mother.

"Go light a fire under her. Tell her I said *ahora mismó.*"

Tombaby left the room, and while he was gone Juanita said, "That poor thing, Perry, what's to become of him? I worry so! Every time he goes to N'Orleans or Dallas, or anywhere atall, and tries to make a livin', some police-

82

man chases his ass back home to mama. Enough to break y'heart. So naturally I put him to work here, do you suppose I'm too soft? He just come back from Pensacola. Was gone three months this time, I thought Christ maybe I'm rid of him. But he come draggin' ass back last week. Don't know *what* happen in Pensacola, he won't even *talk* about it. He's ugly, he's a fag, he's put together like Donald Duck, and nobody can stand the sight of him. 'Cept me. So what am I gonna do? I sent him to beauty school: He can't make a curl to save his life, can hardly wipe his own twat. Imagine all the hell I've had and him not even my own! I'll tell you what's wrong, if you want to know: Inferior blood is what it is, inferior blood, and they's not a goddam thing you can do about inferior blood." She took a tissue from the box on the table and blew her nose hard. "Oh, I know, you're not supposed to cry in this business. Well, I'm sentimental, dammitall, and I do as I please, and nobody don't like it can take a flying leap at the moon."

Juanita finished the liquor in Tombaby's glass, and while the stuff was working inside of her she hunched her shoulders forward, held her head back, and pressed her lips together, eyes closed. Then like a priestess of some weird cult she took a deep breath and pointed in quick succession to various parts of herself, head, throat, chest, stomach, saying: "Pain here, pain here, pain here, pain here. Who cares? Not me. Pain don't bother me. Reach me that bottle, Perry."

Tombaby Barefoot came simpering into the room and settled into his rocking chair. "Dolores wanted to know," he reported with relish, "how *old* the señor was. I said roughly seventy-three. She's in there crying."

Juanita made him repeat this until she had heard it.

Then she disentangled her legs and got to her feet. In the process, Joe caught a glimpse of her knees, noting a similarity to those of his grandmother, with this difference: in Juanita's there was nothing very sad in all that boniness.

She said to Joe: "Listen, I'm gonna be rude as hell, I'm gonna take Perry into the kitchen and tell him something secret, hear?"

Eager to be agreeable, Joe gave a little wave of the hand and arranged his face in a way that he hoped would convey to her an impression of long familiarity with the necessity for telling secrets in whorehouse kitchens.

Juanita on her way out of the room stopped at his chair to look him over at close range. Then she nodded, still looking at him, and said: "Quite a horse, quite a horse. If I had me one like this, I'd head East with it, New York City. Hear tell it's all fags there, fags and money and hungry women. Young stud like this in the stable, I'd clean up good." She shrugged and walked toward the door. "But look what I got, will you?" Juanita jabbed the air with her thumb in the direction of Tombaby Barefoot. Then she and Perry went through the dining room into the back of the house.

Joe knew good and well that the woman who had just left the room was a frightful person. She had said things appalling enough to shrivel the balls of Tombaby Barefoot a dozen times over, and she was clearly selfish and callous and disagreeable in all possible ways. He knew too that in Tombaby here, hands folded grandmotherlike across his stomach, was a cold skinny black tongue connected to a heartful of poison. And the house itself, with so many darknesses beyond the darknesses he could see, was fearsome as a nest of vipers. But still he would have moved into it with these persons on a second's notice. For

84

they were not one, alone in the place, but two, sharing the horrors of it and of one another; and he saw clearly—without knowing what name to give it (love? hate?) or how it came to be or what it could lead to—some kind of priceless safety in their connection with one another.

Joe felt the soft eyes of the halfbreed upon him. He lifted his bourbon glass and said, "Well, here you go, Tombaby."

Tombaby had no drink. His hands were fidgeting with one another on his stomach and he was looking at Joe with a damp smile on his mouth. "Oh yes, here I go," he said, and he kept on smiling, kept on looking.

After a moment in which the Andrews Sisters sang *The Shrine of Saint Cecilia*, Juanita appeared in the doorway. "Son?" She was beckoning to Joe with her hand. "Come on, come on! We got somethin' for you."

10
●

Joe followed Juanita through the dining room and into a long dark hallway. They stopped at a closed door at the end of the hall. Juanita hit the door with the back of her hand. "All right, Dolores."

She looked at Joe. "Go ahead, son, enjoy yourself." She turned the knob and gave him a gentle shove forward.

In a corner of the room stood a girl of no more than seventeen, short, dark, clean-faced. She wore a long blue robe held tight about her body as if for protection. She looked at Joe with a mixture of fear and hostility and seemed to be trying to think of ways to keep him at bay.

Joe closed the door and took a step toward her. The girl stiffened as he approached.

He said, "What's the matter, miss?" But the girl said nothing.

Puzzled, Joe started to leave the room, but when his hand was on the doorknob, the girl said, "No!"

He turned to look at her again. The girl studied his face for a moment, and then the fear and hostility gradually drained from it, leaving nothing, just resignation. She turned her back to him and began slowly to untie the robe. When she had stepped out of it, she walked quickly to the bed in a way that made Joe feel he was stealing something from her. The girl lay flat on her back, stared at the ceiling. She was motionless.

After a moment, Joe walked over to the bed and looked at her face. She wouldn't turn her eyes to him.

He tried not to look at her body, feeling it had not truly been offered to him, but his eyes were not entirely under his control. They traveled quickly over the bed, saw a kind of sweet plumpness, olive-tinted cream in color, with many soft round places, two of them tipped with perfect rosettes, and one, the softest of all, dark-tufted, mysterious.

He held his hands in front of himself.

"Say, miss, I, uh . . ."

He wanted to say something to this girl, something important, something deeper than a thought, a fact about himself: that making love was the one special use he had found for his manhood, and therefore he could not pridelessly climb onto someone just to take his pleasure, too much would be lost. But such facts, scarcely understood by their owners, do not easily yield themselves up in the form of speech. "I don't partic'ly think—what I mean, 'less *you're* in the mood, why don't we just—"

"No speak," she said. "No onnastan."

Joe walked around the foot of the bed to the place where she had stepped out of her robe. He picked it up and placed it over her body. The girl looked at him, astonished. He shook his head back and forth several times, trying to convey gently to her his reluctance. She studied his face for trickery. Joe offered her a cigarette. She declined and he lighted one for himself.

The girl looked at him for a long time, then she lifted her head, resting on her elbow, and looked at him some more. "Hey," she said, and patted the place next to her on the bed. Joe walked over and sat with her. She took his cigarette and rubbed it on the bedside stand, leaving another black mark on the maple finish.

She took Joe's hand and kissed it and smiled. Joe kissed her hand. Then she took his again and kissed each of the fingers in turn. Joe returned the gesture and then he kissed the palm of her hand. They looked into one another's eyes for a long time, and then the girl began to frown and there were tears on her eyelashes. Apparently she had things to say, too, things that were not going to get said, not on this night, not to Joe Buck, maybe never to anyone. He bent over her and touched the tears away with his tongue. Then he withdrew his face from hers and smiled at her, showing all those fine white teeth, and the girl began to laugh. She pulled at his clothes.

In a moment they were both on the bed, holding, being held, exploring, caressing, touching, sampling, kissing. And then there was a certain preliminary moment, a very quiet moment, a gentle, dangerous, important moment in which neither of them breathed. Until they breathed together. And this was followed by the deepest embrace of all, and then there took place the easy, easy, easy beginnings of a giving and a taking and a taking and a giving that caused the girl's eyes to lose their power of focus. And at a certain moment he waited, and waited and waited, causing her to call out to him in her own tongue words of love which he nonetheless understood, and when he knew he had waited long enough he began to build for her the finest thing of which he was capable.

And then suddenly he stopped moving.

The girl clutched his shoulders.

Joe's head was cocked to one side, listening for something. And then he withdrew himself from her, so quickly that the girl called out in pain, and he jumped from the bed and looked toward a closet in the corner of the room. The door was ajar.

The girl sat up in bed: "Hey! Hey! You crazy?"

But Joe remained standing there, and after a moment the door was pushed all the way open from within. He saw that it was not a closet at all but an adjoining room.

Seated on a stool was Perry. Behind him stood Juanita, and towering above both of them was Tombaby Barefoot.

Perry was smiling.

"Go ahead, Joe," he said, "Don't let *us* stop you."

Within seconds, Perry was on the floor of the bedroom and Joe sat astride his chest, still naked, and working hard with his fists, bent on obliterating that smile. The girl screamed, but Perry himself offered no resistance whatever. In fact he looked directly into Joe's eyes in a way that was clearly calculated to provoke him further. Juanita began barking out short unintelligible phrases made

88

up of ugly words and Spanish ones. Joe, stopping for a moment, held his fist over Perry's face. "Don't smile any more," he begged. "Quit it now. Please." But Perry would not quit and the blows continued. The girl was now behind Joe, pulling at his shoulders with all her strength, and then Juanita and Tombaby were surrounding him, too, and there were hands all over Joe's naked body as he was drawn away from the bleeding man on the floor. Joe struggled to free himself and then a fist caught him in the stomach. This fist belonged to Juanita. It took Joe's breath. On the edge of the bed, he doubled over, trying to pull some air into him. Surrounding his lowered head were a number of legs that made a kind of cell around him. Still he felt hands all over him and some of them were soft damp hands and they glided all over his back and along his thighs. Combining with the pain in his stomach these hands sickened him, and he began to retch and vomit. But nothing came out. Still the hands continued and one of them began to manipulate him in a surprising way that caused in him a kind of nightmare panic, and when he was able to achieve a little air, he used it to gird himself for further struggle. But at this point, a voice, Juanita's, said in a loud whisper, "You want it, Tombaby, they's only one way you gonna have it."

Now there was a crash in which everything was at once obliterated, and instantly re-created, but in a totally different perspective:

The room had become a hole, shaped something like a well, and Joe was lying in the bottom of it, looking up. No, it was only his head that was on the bottom. Everything else, even his own body lying on the bed, was above him. And beyond his toes, way up near the top of everything, were people standing: the halfbreed and the hag.

89

They were arguing but their voices were muted, almost inaudible. It was as if his ears were submerged in something liquid that deadened his hearing. Now the woman floated out of view and Joe Buck seemed to be alone with a big yellow-looking thing leaning over the edge of the bed. It was reaching down with both hands toward Joe. And then the opening at the top of the hole was completely covered over by this fat form darkening everything so that it was no longer possible to see. Joe felt the air had been cut off, but when he gasped, he found there was still some left for breathing. He was desperate for light and began to try to work his neck muscles in a way that might pull his head up into the light.

Gradually he became aware that some effort was being made up above, someone was trying to release him from the anguish and the darkness. It was as if some giant force were being applied at the top of the well, drawing Joe slowly upward, upward, upward, using his sex as a handle. As he knew himself to be closer and closer to freedom, the constriction he felt became more and more intolerable. He fought hard to cooperate with the force that was drawing him upward, straining every muscle in order to help. And then, just as it became clear what exactly was being enacted upon him, something broke deep inside of him, and he felt that he had fought too hard and lost everything in the effort; he felt his life spurting out of him uncontrollably, and in a way it was shamefully pleasurable to be at the end of the battle. But he had not won anything, and there was no longer anything up at the top of the hole and he was still way down in the bottom of it where "Perry pushed me," he said in his own mind. "My friend, Perry, he shove me down a hole."

11

Shove *me* down no hole! I may be shee-it, but f'm now on, anybody look like they gonna flush me down better look out!"

Joe was fierce in the mirror. Two days had passed and he had not left his room. He was pale and he had hunger cramps and something was wrong with the back of his head. But even in this sorry shape he was able with no effort at all to hold a certain new idea in his head: that there was in this world only one person who had his and only his interests at heart. "Cowboy," he said to his image, addressing it with a kind of excited enthusiasm that looked a great deal like love, "I'm gonna take care of you, I'm gonna work my butt off for you, I'm gonna coddle you to death. See this crapper they call a room? You gonna get out of here one of these days. Your head ain't broke for good, hm-mm, not by a long shot." He liked the new determination in his voice, and there was something new in his eyes, something wild and dangerous, and he was delighted to see it there.

Joe had in these days alone stumbled upon this new kind of fuel to operate on. He had taken a lot of angers, large and small, old and recent—the one against Perry was of no special importance, it merely sparked the others —and together they made something bracing, almost intoxicating: fury itself. He had taken out all of his years, like things stored in a trunk, and picked them over for memories that would help sustain this fierce new power, and it seemed that everything his mind lit upon was perfectly usable material, supporting the view that the world's indifference to him stemmed from downright hostility. He didn't know what it was based on, but there seemed to be something about him that no one wanted to be kin to. This feeling, always just below the surface, was one of many he did not know how to consider in his mind: the feeling of being a person with no real place in the world, an alien even under the red-white-and-blue of his birth, one who did not belong even in his own neighborhood.

He had gone about always, even in these most familiar places of his life, with a slight frown of uneasiness, his head cocked for some clue to the true meaning of the language he heard spoken but which was clearly not his own, walking softly as if unsure of the very ground of this peculiar planet. And now, thinking it all over, carefully but inexpertly, there seemed to him to have been from the very beginning a campaign afoot to make him aware always and always and always of his own alien status. And the awful conclusion he reached was that nearly everyone he knew or had ever known was part of this conspiracy. Even the many persons with whom he had enjoyed a certain sexual popularity—especially these persons—had refused any contact with his other aspects: They took their pleasure and they ran like the wind, no doubt laughing at the earnestness with which he had gone about gratifying them. And so of course they had a very special place in his new fury, but it was in no way exclusive to others. He ticked off in his mind the persons and groups and institutions he felt this anger against—old teachers, the army, his little pink boss at the cafeteria, Adrian Schmidt's magazine-store mob, and so on. By far the greater number had no name. They included just about everyone he'd gone to school with, scores of clerks and public servants and strangers who had dealt with him brusquely or condescendingly or who had ignored him altogether. The list flourished until it included buildings and banks and libraries whose workings he did not understand and whose employees always seemed to treat him as if he had come to rob the place or to defile it in some way. At length he realized the entire city of Albuquerque was in this category, and this thought invited his mind to think in broader terms: if Houston were no better than Albuquerque, it was a safe bet that Hong Kong and Des Moines and London town were no better than Houston. Following this logic, the map of the entire world was quickly filled in with the color of his fury.

But in this sweeping view he felt something had been glossed over or left out; some first-class sonofabitch was playing hide-and-seek in his memory. But who? Or what?

And all at once he thought of Sally Buck.

Sally Buck on the telephone: *"Joe, how you doin', honey, that's nice, listen, I got me a late appointment, and I'll be s'tired when I get outa here, I might just step around the corner to the Horse and Saddle for a beer or two."*

"Handsome? How you feelin'? Listen, y'gramaw's goin' t'Santa Fe for over the Fourth, looks like I got me a new beau, how's that for an ole lady, huh? You be all right here in town, won't you."

Sally Buck standing in the doorway of her bedroom:

"Believe I'll just hit the hay, sweetheart, get a decent

*night sleep for a change, did you have a nice day, better
tell me all about it in the mornin', I'm too tired to follow
what y'sayin'."*

Sally Buck in her beauty shop:

*"Listen, sugar, this waitin' room is for ladies and you
know how they are, you take that magazine along home if
you want, and don't play too hard now."*

*"Hey, toots, they's no point in you waitin' around for
me. I might have to stop off at Molly 'n' Ed's anyhow.
Can't you tuck y'self in like a big fella?"*

*"Report card? Didn't I just sign one last week? You
mean it's been six weeks! Lord, how time flies, give it here,
where do I do it, on the back? There! Now run along,
baby, I got me a head in there waitin' for a set."*

Sally Buck. He couldn't remember why he'd ever loved
her so much: silly, pinch-faced old chatterbox, never sat
still, always dabbing at her nose with perfume so you
couldn't smell the liquor (but you could anyway), or pulling dollar bills out of her pocketbook to buy off old promises she'd made, forever fooling with a compact or picking
lint off her dress whenever you tried to tell something to
her. All he could think of in her favor was how spindly her
legs were and how sad it was to look at her big bony knees
when she crossed them. But even as a ghost in that Albuquerque hotel room, she couldn't give a little real attention to him, just sat there fretting about getting her house
back or riding horseback or some damn thing. Ride on,
Sally, old fool, he thought, ride on to the devil. Set his
head in curls while you're at it. Shee-it.

And *who*, questioned his mind, straining after a sense of
fairness that would make his case even tighter, *who* had
ever looked upon him as a creature worth giving the time
of day to? Who? Just say who. There came to mind two

94

faces and a cowboy song. The faces he would not allow:
The owner of one was in the loony bin, and the other had
not been a flesh-and-blood person for nearly two thousand
years, if then. And that left *git along little dogie git along
git along* . . .

Woodsy Niles!

Woodsy Niles was clearly an exception. But what good
was he here and now? The memory picture of him was too
shiny, too brilliant to look upon with any trust, it was
nothing but the tobacco-scented, guitar-strumming, grin-
ning-devil souvenir of a long-ago, long-ago summer; and
so rare, much too rare to find a place for in any useful
view of the world. And so the crazy, shining, blue-bearded
face of Woodsy Niles and the big bony knees of Sally
Buck he placed out of the range of his thinking: They
were dangerous to him, they caused the anger to run out
of him. And somehow he had come to know that if he
was going to manage in the world, he'd need all the anger he could keep hold of.

Joe found himself working faster and harder in the scullery of the Sunshine Cafeteria. There was a kind of fever
in the way he loaded the dishes into the trays and threw
the trays onto the conveyor belt. It was as if he had to
feed just so many millions of dishes into the steaming jaws
of that machine, and then it would be appeased and belch
up enough money to . . .

He wasn't certain what the money was for. He only
knew he had to get some of it together in order to cause
something to happen. He went about with the single eye
of a man with a plan. But he didn't quite know what the
plan was.

Three mornings a week he spent in a gymnasium,

where he performed strenuous exercises, punched a bag, and swam the length of the pool eight times. He watched his body acquire new strength and agility. He massaged his scalp and fooled with his hair a lot, and he became obsessed with the acquisition of a Western wardrobe, carrying with him night and day a feeling, a belief, that everything would change for the better when he had created himself in a certain new image. He knew what the image was, that of a cowboy, but he never did press himself too far on the question of how that image would make his life different. There is an Indian legend that at a certain time in the life of a young man he is given a dream in which he sees a mask, and when he awakens he must set to work carving a real mask in that dream image. This is the mask he must wear into battle in order to be victorious. It was as if Joe Buck had had such a dream, and his life was given over to the carving of the mask.

He wasted little time these days in longing for the company of others or in any kind of brooding. If he had no kin in the world, who was there to yearn for?

But he did do a lot of aimless wandering at night when he left the cafeteria. To Joe it was not aimless at all. Ask him what he was doing, and he would have brushed the question aside, as if his purpose were to be found somewhere deeper than questions and answers could penetrate. But he was clearly searching the town for something. He kept his eyes wide open and alert, scanning the nighttime streets of downtown Houston like a warrior scout. Very little of what he saw seemed worth remembering. Most of what passed his eye left no more of a mark on him than images leave on the face of a mirror.

But there were, from his many nights of wandering and looking, three pictures that had somehow fallen through to a level in him deeper than the surface, and these, in memory, showed themselves to him over and over again:

One was a cutout image of a young Hollywood actor floodlighted on top of a movie marquee. He stood there with his suntanned snarl in full color, two stories bigger than life, legs apart, pelvis thrust forward, and he was in the act of turning a big gun on you. The barrel of it was coming at you thick and gleaming, and it was about to go off.

The second article in this nighttime collection of images was a brief scene on a street corner. A long white convertible was stopped for a red light. The woman in the driver's seat was looking at a tall, handsome young man in Western clothes standing at the curb. Her motor died under her. But she kept on looking at the young man. After a moment she said, "I can't get it started without help." And the young man said, "I'll *bet* you can't, honey."

The third picture to remain in him from these walks was the only one he couldn't enjoy looking at later. But whether or not he liked it, it was one of the three and would not be discarded. This was a large poster depicting that bearded young man in whose eyes resides all the sorrow of history. Above his head was a message attributed to him in a large Gothic typeface, and on the bottom of the poster, scrawled there in raspberry-colored lipstick, were the words FUCK THEE.

And these were the things Joe Buck found as he was seeking to find his way.

part two

1

The power of a Greyhound bus impressed itself upon Joe at once, and during the first hundred eastbound miles he gave his attention over to it almost entirely: the sound the changing gears made, the breathing of the brakes, and, on the open road, the deep bass hum of a thing that was not exhausted by the miles but seemed to thrive on them. There was an empty seat in the front opposite the driver, and Joe sat up there smoking for a while, fascinated by what was taking place between the bus and the highway, the way the highway seemed to enter it underneath, all these miles disappearing into an enormous machine and the machine all the while seeming to get leaner and more fit. Before returning to his own seat, Joe wanted to make some remark to the driver. "It's a powerful mothah, ain't it?" But the driver didn't look up.

Walking back toward his own seat, Joe felt like a circus performer dancing on horseback. This great being through whose center he moved had something in common with himself, but Joe was little better equipped to think about it than was the bus itself. He felt it, though, some kind of masterful participation in the world of time and space, a moving forward into destiny.

Back in his own seat, he smiled at this new sense of himself and blew a kiss at his new boots, and before long his eyes were closed and he was sleeping the deep black sleep of a creature who has not yet been born.

The first half of Joe's big trip East was passed in this way. Sometimes his eyes were open, but even at such intervals he dreamed himself into whatever landscape he was passing through, still so confident of himself and his future that he gave them scarcely a passing thought.

It was on the afternoon of the second day, the day on which at five P.M. his arrival was to take place, that Joe became somewhat fretful. Perfection had begun to arouse his suspicions. It occurred to him that he might be embroiled in some colossal confidence game in which he was both victim and perpetrator. For instance: Exactly what in hell was he going to do in New York City? He kept glancing above him, taking reassurance from the presence of his black-and-white horsehide suitcase and all the fine articles it contained, and every few minutes he touched the hip on which his money rode. He searched the faces of other passengers, wondering if someone among them was a potential ally or if they were all strangers like himself, uneasy at the prospect of arrival in the richest and tallest of all cities.

The last rest stop was at a Howard Johnson's in Pennsylvania. Joe took his suitcase with him into the men's room and spent the twenty minutes grooming himself for his arrival in New York City. He shaved, splashed himself with Florida Water, changed into a fresh shirt, and gave a quick spit-shine to his boots. Even though there were other men using the facilities, Joe could not resist using the mirror in his own peculiar way. He walked away from it, prepared his expression, his attitude, then spun around to surprise his image. What he saw was tremendously

102

comforting to him. When he click-click-clicked out of that men's room, other passengers were already returning to the bus. Two very young girls, occupants of seats near the front of the bus who had been keenly aware of Joe Buck's presence throughout the trip, were climbing aboard just ahead of him. One of them, stimulated by his proximity, giggled breathlessly. Joe was as pleased as he could be. As he passed their seat, he tipped his Stetson and allowed them full benefit of the sweet, crooked smile he had developed. Their reaction was wild and hysterical: For miles, in a kind of heavenly hell of painful titillation, the girls stifled screams, hid behind damp handkerchiefs and struck each other. Joe was reassured and couldn't remember what he'd been worried about. What to do when he got to New York? Shee-it, what could be simpler? Head for Times Square and follow his nose.

Suddenly up ahead was the Manhattan skyline, buildings like markers in a crowded graveyard. Joe's hand moved to his crotch, and under his breath he said, "I'm gonna take hold o' this thing and I'm gonna swing it like a lasso and I'm gonna rope in this whole fuckin' island."

2

at the Times Square Palace Hotel, Joe was conducted to his room by a shriveled old bellhop who called him "sir" a number of times and carried his suitcase for him. Joe gave him a dollar and then closed the door and examined the room. It was twice as expensive as the place in Houston, but many times more pleasant, and it had a private bath as well. The walls had been freshly greened; the bedspread was spotlessly clean, tan in color; the furniture was maple. Over the bed was a water color of the Manhattan skyline, and next to the bed a telephone on a stand. Joe believed himself to be in a first-class situation.

He unpacked, placing his radio on the bedside table. Then he lighted a cigarette and sat at a small desk in front of the window, looking back and forth in amazement at his two new worlds, 42nd Street out there, throbbing and rich and noisy, and this place inside where his hat would hang and where his head would rest.

He sat for a long time studying the bureau, and for one crazy moment he found himself unable to believe that his personal belongings were still there, even though he himself had just placed them there. For that brief moment he was convinced that when something was out of sight it lost its existence altogether.

He hurried across the room and looked into the mirror. It was a relief to find that he himself was still there, but he was not entirely certain until he had waved and smiled at his image and blown a cloud of smoke at it. Then he checked the drawers of the bureau and the closet. Reassured, he crossed the room again, stopping to smile once more at his reflection in the mirror, saying: "Now you take it easy, cowboy. You're all settled in here, about to get rich." He performed a little hip dance, mimicking copulation, and returned to the desk to finish smoking his cigarette.

"New York City," he said, looking at the street. A fat, incredibly sloppy old woman, sitting on the sidewalk un-

104

der a movie marquee across the street, poured something from a bottle onto her filthy, naked feet and rubbed them with her free hand. No one paid much attention to her. A policeman watched with some interest but no concern and then moved on.

"Your room," he said to his radio. He went over and turned it on, hoping its sounds would give him the feeling of having truly arrived in this new place.

A woman's high-pitched, somewhat hysterical voice was saying: "And that's my system!" Then she giggled. A man's voice with a special electronic fervor in it said: "Well! *That* beats anything *I've* ever heard! When you have insomnia, you simply get out of *bed?*" "*Yes!*" shrieked the woman, losing control of herself. "*What* on earth do you *do?*" the man urged. "I turn on my *lights!*" she said breathlessly. "And I get dressed! And I do my work, maybe even cook something! Or *bake!*" Seemingly overcome, the woman was unable to continue speaking. The man said, "Aren't you very *tired* the next day?" "*Oh, no!*" the woman swore, suddenly in dead earnest as if she had been accused of something dreadful, like malingering. "*Hon*estly, I'm not; *honestly!*"

Joe felt sorry for the lady but at the same time he was delighted by what he'd heard. For it seemed to bear out all those rumors about Eastern women. Aloud, he said, "What's wrong with you, lady, is perfickly clear to me. Get *me* over t'that radio station, I'll put you in shape."

"Of course," the woman said, "I'll probably col*lapse* right here at this microphone!" Then she gave way to utter, breathless hysteria.

"Well!" said the announcer, chuckling fatuously, "I hope you won't collapse until you've *sung* for us!"

He played a record on which the woman, in a quieter

mood and through an echo chamber, sang *My Foolish Heart*.

While she sang Joe opened the desk drawer. He found a ballpoint pen and two post cards picturing this very hotel. After some study he was able to determine which of the windows was his own. Encircling it with the pen, he turned the card over and wrote "Dear" in the message space. Then he stopped writing, wondering dear *who*. Unable to think of a name to place there, he tore the card in half and dropped it out the window.

The lady on the radio sang that this time it wasn't fascination, this time it was *love*.

Joe picked up the second card, encircling his own window again, and wrote: "This is me," across the sky. And on the message side, skipping the *dear* part entirely, he wrote: "Well I am settled in here—new york is not so much but I have got my own place and very clean too—" In the space intended for an addressee, he printed the word SHIT. Then he tore the card in half and said, "I'm fucked if I come to this town to write post cards." Just as he threw the pieces of the card out the window, he thought of someone to whom he might have addressed it: his Negro colleague in the scullery of the Sunshine Cafeteria. He put his head out the window and saw the fragments still floating toward the street. For a moment it looked as if one of them might drop right into the cap of a loitering sailor, but the sailor moved on, joining a stream of early-evening pedestrians.

3
•

Joe adjusted his pace so that he and the rich lady might arrive at the corner at the same moment. With luck, the light would be red and they would wait there together and somehow a conversation would begin in which the rich lady would be afforded an opportunity to place a bid on his wares. Park Avenue was not what he had expected: Of the few persons walking here at twilight, not one had given him a second glance. His faith in himself and in his project was a delicate thing at best, and he had now to be especially agile in avoiding any doubt that might bump up against it and wreck it entirely.

For instance, there was no single aspect of this rich lady he followed that might suggest any hunger for what he had to offer. But he knew that if he pondered even for a moment her flawless, elegant self-sufficiency, evident in every detail of her appearance and in every step she took, his own resolve would be lost to him at once.

She was a small-boned, brown-haired lady of medium height. As she preceded him down Park Avenue, Joe admired her ankles. They were slender, beautifully formed, and they seemed to say: "We are not very strong, but we are strong enough—and rich."

At the corner of 39th Street, waiting for the light, Joe removed his hat and held it over his heart. "Beg pardon, ma'am," he said, putting many facial muscles to work on a powerful smile. "I'm new here in town, just in from Houston Texas, and lookin' for the Statue of Liberty."

The rich lady continued to present him with a perfect view of her profile, a fine, delicate, pretty thing to behold, but she gave no sign at all that she had heard him speak.

When the light was red, the rich lady crossed Park Avenue. Joe followed. On the east side of the street she stopped and turned to him, saying: "Were you joking? About the Statue of Liberty?" Her tone was direct, neither friendly nor hostile.

"Joking? No, ma'am. *Oh*, no! I mean business!"

"Do forgive me, then," she said, clearly unconvinced, but going along with it for reasons of her own. "I thought you were making some sort of—never mind." She smiled and Joe was touched suddenly by the very special beauty of a lady at the far, far end of her youth—old age just under the surface of her skin, but not yet emerged, not yet—and by the still-young blue of eyes that were more deeply sympathetic than truly young eyes could ever be.

She faced south. "I've never actually seen it, except from the boat. But what you do, let me see, you take the subway, I'm almost sure of this, the Seventh Avenue Subway, and you get off at the end of the line. Oh, but I'm not really certain. You'd better ask someone else, play it safe, don't you think?"

Joe was so taken with the lady he hardly listened to the words she spoke, but each of them, as formed by her lips, seemed to him a miracle of beauty. "You sure are a pretty lady," he said, surprising himself.

The lady turned to him quickly, taken aback and blushing in a way that thrilled him.

"Oh!" she said, trying to frown—but she was clearly not

108

a frowner. "You're not looking for the Statue of Liberty at all!"

"No, ma'am," he said, "I'm not."

"Why, that's—that's perfectly dreadful. Aren't you ashamed of yourself?"

She began to smile, increasing the number of lines in her face and intensifying the blue and the twinkle and the sympathy of her eyes. This face, especially these remarkable eyes, seemed to be saying: "You and I are wonderful people who understand all the beautiful things of the world that are lost to others, but now that we have had this greatly amusing and secret moment, it is time for us to part."

Aloud, she simply said goodbye. And walked away from him.

He watched her leave, noting that her trim rear end was now intensely conscious of itself. This pleased him. It also caused a disturbance in his stomach. He had always been an appreciator of the walking-away of certain women, the way they had of switching the fanny from side to side in such a carefully measured way and yet holding the head so high you were supposed to believe the thoughts in it were seven thousand miles north of the Arctic Ocean, and as cool. But now, along with the enjoyment, Joe Buck felt this weakness, an anxious churning deep in his body; he had to tighten the muscles in his thighs in order to remain standing, and his toes gripped the soles of his boots.

"Cute lady," he said aloud but very softly as he watched her proceed up 37th Street. "Rich, too," he said, following her slowly on the opposite side of the street and admiring her more with every step she took. "Too bad she ain't the buying kind," he said, watching her turn and walk up the steps of a great brownstone house.

He watched her open the front door. And he watched her enter the place. And then he made a sound that was not a word at all, as something cold and awful touched his heart: Her door had closed.

He sat on a nearby stoop and continued watching the place, wondering at the nature of his sudden new suffering. And then the dark windows on the parlor floor silently and softly exploded into light. This light was the color of amber and warm as flesh, but Joe had no notion of why it hurt him so to look at it. He only knew for certain that the twilight had ended and it was time for a good long drink of liquor.

He forced himself to his feet and began to walk. And pretty soon he came upon another kind of rich lady altogether.

4

The second rich lady was walking a white French poodle on Lexington Avenue in the Thirties. Joe found her looking at some yellow pompoms in front of a florist's window.

The poodle was so small it looked like a windup toy; but the lady herself was very large. She was like some movie star you'd read about who had wrecked her career with food. She was brunette, her eyelashes stuck out a good three-quarters of an inch, and there was a lot of paint on her face and fingernails. Altogether this ornamentation gave her the look of a marionette inhabited not by a mere hand but by an entire person: you saw those little green eyes peering out of this big doll and wondered who in the world the tiny person inside could be.

While she studied the pompoms, Joe pretended to look at the roses until it was clear to him that the lady was keenly aware of his presence.

"Hurry up, Baby," she said in animated irritation, addressing the dog, who was crouching and straining under the florist's table. "Do-um goody-goods for mama. Go on, do-um goody-goods."

Joe held his Stetson over his heart. "Beg pardon, ma'am," he said, "I'm brand spankin' new in town, come from Houston Texas, and hopin' to get a look at the Statue o' Liberty."

The woman looked at him, eyebrows raised and mouth open in disbelief. "You're hopin' to get a look at *what?*"

"The Statue of Liberty," he said, putting out a smile to dazzle the moon. He had a way of twitching his mouth slightly that made the smile appear to be involuntary; this somehow increased immeasurably its worth.

The rich lady met his eye and held it like a man. "It's up in Central Park takin' a leak," she said. "If you hurry, you'll make the supper show. Now get lost." Her voice was harsh and loud.

But then, just as she walked away, Joe's second rich lady winked at him. And she smiled in a distinctly provocative way. Perplexed, he watched her shimmy away up Lexington Avenue in her tight black dress and pink

111

high-heeled shoes, the little dog racing to keep pace with her.

At the traffic light she looked back, held the cowboy's eye for the count of four, smiled, and then stooped to pick up the dog and disappeared around the corner, mouthing elaborate baby talk at the tiny beast trapped in the crook of her arm.

Joe hurried to the corner, where he could see her waiting for him under the canopy of an apartment house. The lady, confident that he was following, proceeded into the building.

In a moment, Joe passed through a pair of solid-gold doors—perhaps not solid-gold, but covered with some gold-colored metal that made you feel once you'd passed through them that money was no longer a problem. He stepped into a carpeted elevator, where the rich lady was looking straight ahead of her as if she had no notion of his existence. But the minute those doors had made their soft, expensive little *kllooosh* sound of closing, Joe's lips were being licked by the long tongue of the rich lady, who was also rubbing her stomach against his. Then, even though she was a very large person, she smiled as if she were very small, and said, "Hi." Joe shivered.

The poodle yapped, there was another *kllooosh*, and they stepped off the elevator into a private apartment with fluffy white carpets.

The rich lady took hold of his hand. "I got to make a couple phoney-phones," she said, pulling him along behind her toward a white-and-gold desk where there was a telephone. Dialing with one hand, she unbuttoned Joe's trousers with the other and began to work with the zipper.

112

The entire episode was taking place with a speed and style far more amazing than Joe's best fantasies.

"Cass Trehune," said the rich lady into the telephone, her left hand by now busy inside Joe's trousers. "Any messages? Who is this? Imelda? Hello, sweetheart. Anything for me? Needleman, right. Got it. How long ago? I said *when*. Okay, what is it, the Murray Hill five? No, no, never mind, I've got it. I've *got* it. Imelda, I've *got* the damn thing, honey, you know? *Thanks!* Bye."

Still holding the receiver, she disengaged the connection with her thumb. Then she looked down to examine what she had found with her left hand. "*Ye gods!*" she said, impressed, and hung onto it as she dialed the Murray Hill number.

"Mr. Needleman, please."

There was a pause in which she let go of Joe, lifted her skirt, turned around and backed against the front of him, guiding his arms around her waist.

"Oh, hello, Mr. Palmbaum, what are *you* doing there? Fine thanks. Sen*sa*tional in fact. Put Morey on, would you?" There was another pause: She put her ear in Joe's mouth. "Oh stop oh God," she said, "I can't stand that, I just die. *Morey?*" Her voice went soft and sweet: It seemed to be luring some small child into a gas chamber with promises of candy. "Aw, Morey. Hi-ee. I got your call. I was walking Baby. No, sweety, I haven't been out but just that once. I mean, himth got to do himth goody-goodth, right? Well, yes, as a matter of fact I did walk him once earlier. About three. But, sweety, I checked with the service and there wasn't a thing, honest. Well, you didn't leave a message, did you? All *right!* That's what I *said!* Oh, now you're making me mad. Mad and sick. I'm gonna hang up and then I'm gonna heave all over this rug. Morey, you make me *quite annoyed,* do you know that? All you think is just one thing about me, so how would you like to go screw yourself?"

She giggled and continued: "Of course I don't mean it, old goosey. Now looky, when can you get here?" She turned her face toward Joe and put her tongue deep into his mouth. There was no passion in the act; she seemed more to be motivated by some clinical curiosity about the shape of his back teeth. Then, withdrawing the probe quickly, she spoke again into the telephone. "Okay, if you say so, but I'm *very* disappointed." She winked at Joe and showed him a hand on which fingers were crossed. "What I'll do, Morey," she said, "I'll nap for an hour or so, then maybe fix a little TV dinner here and take a long time getting dressed, *you* know, kill time. Right? All righty, doll, midnight at Jilly's, here's a big wet one."

She made an obscene sound into the mouthpiece and concluded the call in baby talk. "No, you can only have *one!* And I love *you* terrible much, too."

Then she hung up and turned her full and considerable attentions onto Joe Buck.

The event that followed took place in three rooms, and most of it was witnessed by the little white poodle. Commencing at the desk, the action moved on to a cocktail table, two chairs and a pouf. Then, as it proceeded to the kitchen drainboard, the poodle lost interest and left the room. A few minutes later, Joe and the rich lady repaired to the bedroom. Finding the bed occupied by the dog, they made use of the floor.

Soon they fell asleep there on the fluffy white carpet, and while they napped, darkness fell.

Joe awakened to an odd sensation: It seemed to him the

114

dog was nibbling at his toes. Gently he withdrew his foot. Then he felt a human hand on his ankle. He opened his eyes and found the nibbler to be the rich lady herself. He sat up and reached for her, but she rose playfully to her feet and ran naked out onto the terrace. He followed, amazed anew at the size of the woman and delighted to discover that the place of his first employment was an actual penthouse. He chased her about the terrace until she allowed herself to be caught leaning breathless against a low wall that protected her from a drop of some fifteen stories.

"Sssh!" she said, looking upward, her forefinger against her lips. "Star light star bright first star I see tonight wish I may wish I might have the wish I wish tonight; *there!*" Now she was bending over the wall, her belly resting on top of it in a way that invited Joe to step up behind her.

"Oh, oh, *ooh*," she said, "I'm so afraid, I'm so afraid, I'm so afraid of *heights*."

Joe had one of her buttocks in each of his hands, enjoying their doughy pliability. "I won't let you git away from me," he said, taking one slow, deep, final step toward the rich lady.

"Ye gods!" she cried out. "What are you doing, that's a terrible thing to do, I've never heard of such a . . ." And then she stopped talking.

Joe took one long north-to-south look at the great island of Manhattan, and then he happened to look upon himself, here on the roof of one of its tall buildings, under the stars, naked, joined to a woman, and he was moved deeply by a sudden keen awareness of the moment. It was as if he himself were one person and the one he dreamed of being were another, and these two had been traveling separate paths until here and now, on this terrace and on this night, the two were merged. He paused in his activity to contemplate the marvel of this meeting with himself, and his eyes filled over with tears. He was having a moment of happiness.

And then the rich lady moved in a way that caused his attention to return to the matter at hand.

5

now Joe's first assumption about Cass Trehune's financial condition had been based somewhat recklessly upon two factors: the tininess of her dog—it must cost a fortune to keep the little thing breathing—and the number and size of the rhinestones at her wrists, which he mistook for diamonds. The estimate had been further sustained by another shaky notion: that anyone living in a penthouse had to have even more money than an archbishop.

Therefore, at a few minutes past eleven, while Cass was showering in preparation for her midnight rendezvous with Mr. Needleman, Joe consulted himself in the bedroom mirror.

"Say, Cass," he rehearsed aloud, "I want to tell you I've had as good a time here tonight as I've *ever* had! And that's a goddam fact. It's why I hate to bring up this *bus*iness thing, ha ha."

Judging this to be a fairly poor beginning, he stopped

and began on a new tack. "*Hey!* You beautiful thing!" He leaned with both hands on the dressing table and swung his eyes onto the image in the glass. "Can you let me have twenty?" "Oh, *sure,* baby!" said a little voice in his mind, "Take fifty! Although God knows you're worth a hundred."

He pursed his lips and sent a kiss into the mirror, and then smiled at it again.

Cass came tiptoeing in from the bathroom, fully made up but still naked. In some curious mood of after-bath modesty, she held a towel front of her. "Don't look," she said, heading for the closet.

"Say, Cass," said the cowboy, "I, uh, sure have enjoyed bein' here tonight."

"Me, too, lover," came the voice from behind the closet door.

"Believe it's as fine a time as I've had in my *life!*"

A moment later, a tower of black bugle beads and ivory came backing toward him. "Zip this thing, will you, Tex?"

Joe zipped her dress for her. Then he said, "You know, Cass, I'm in, uh, well, to tell you the truth, I'm in *busi*ness."

"Oh, poor you," she said, seated at the dressing table, spraying her hair with lacquer. "Morey's got *ter*rible ulcers."

"Mm." Joe thought for a while. Then he said, "Well, I don't know what kind of business Morey's in, but I'm in a different business myself."

Cass seemed preoccupied. "You're plenty different'n Morey," she said, "in lots o' other ways, too. Believe you me." She studied herself in the glass. Finding some flaw in her mouth, she picked up a lipstick tube.

"Matter of fact," Joe said, wondering whether or not he could get the next words out, "I'm a—hustler."

There!

"Hm," she said, stretching her upper lip across her teeth and smearing it with orange. "Herson zodda meg a livig."

"Beg pardon?"

She relaxed her mouth and replaced the cap on the lipstick. "Said, a person's got to make a living."

Joe laughed. "You sure you heard what I said?"

Cass gave no answer to this. But Joe was encouraged when she rose from the dressing table and went to a chest of drawers where she took out a gold lamé evening bag. "Scuse me, hon," she said. "'Fraid I'm only half here. Maybe you ought to run on along."

She opened the evening bag. Joe was thrilled. He sat on the edge of the bed and tried to hide his pleasure by fooling with the tops of his boots. From the corner of his eye, he saw her come toward him and stop, lowering the bag to a level with his eyes.

It was wide open, and it was empty.

"Tex," she said, "could you let me have a little coin for the taxi-waxi? I didn't get to the bank this afternoon." She cupped his chin in her hand and looked down at him seductively. "You're *such* a doll!" she said. "I hate money, don't you? God, it's been fun. Why don't you take this phone number anyway?"

The shock went deep, but Joe's recovery was quick. He laughed weakly and said, "Funny thing you mentioning money. I'ze about to ask you for some." He started to cover this request with another small laugh, but the sound froze in his throat along with the air in the room and everything else in the place. There was a long dangerous moment of locked eyes.

118

Finally, in an impassioned whisper, the woman, still holding his chin, said, "*You* want money from *me*, hunh? You asking me for money, is that it? Is that what you're doing, asking me for money?" For Joe an act of speech would have been impossible, but apparently Cass found some answer in his eyes. "You prick!" she said, hurting his chin. "You bastard! You sonofabitch! You think you're dealing with some old slut? Look at me: thirty-one! You think 'cause you're hung you can get away with this crap? Well, you're out of your mind. I am a gorgeous chick, thirty-one, that's right, you said it! I'd like to kill you in cold blood."

Tears suddenly squirted from her eyes. Then she screamed and threw herself on the bed, saying *I've never in my life* and other phrases that could not be understood because some of her fingers were in her mouth.

Joe got to his feet. He had no notion of what to say or do. He lit a cigarette, put the match in an ash tray, and pulled a lot of smoke into his lungs. He stood over the woman, studying her body for some clue as to how he might behave. Her bare shoulders heaved with sobs, giving her the look of a beached whale in its death throes. It amazed him that sadness could so increase a person's bulk.

"Hey," Joe said, sitting on the bed next to her. "Hey, *Cass!*" He put his hand on her back, rocking her gently to and fro. "Did you think I meant that? About the money? Why, that wasn't nothing but a big *joke!* Shoot, and here I thought you had a wonderful sense of humor, shows how wrong I was."

Then he got up, pretending to dismiss her. "Ah! You just putting on. You not crying atall. Now how much taxi fare you want?" He took out his money, the entire wad.

119

"What d'you need, sweetheart? Five? Ten? Come on, now, name it, damn ya."

He bent over, holding the money in front of her face. "Open y'eyes! Look here! Would I be askin' you for money with a wad like that riding on my ass? Use your head! Christ, I'm from Houston Texas, lady, my daddy's an oilman! I never had to borrow nothing in my life. Now will you quit bawlin'?"

The sounds of her misery increased. He gave her a handful of tissues from the bedside stand. She clutched these to her face, but still the weeping continued.

Then very quietly, into her ear, he said, "Hey." He touched her cheek. "You *are* a gorgeous-lookin' piece, Cass. Gets a guy all horny just *lookin'* at you."

She opened her eyes. Joe nodded. "It's a fact," he said.

Then he took a twenty-dollar bill and pushed it into the crevice between her breasts: "*There* you go."

Cass Trehune sat up and blew her nose.

6

Leaving Cass's place, Joe went to a nearby saloon for a drink of liquor. He was tired and his brain was fogged. His thoughts kept going back to that terrible woman in the Texas whorehouse, Tombaby's mother. He didn't know why this hag's face kept flitting through his mind, but it did, over and over again.

He took a second drink of liquor, hoping the stuff would rinse his brain, help him to think more clearly. Then he walked for a while, looking at the street signs but giving no real thought to the direction he was taking. At midnight he found himself in another saloon, a great warehouse-sized place called Everett's on Broadway near 40th Street. A TV set and a juke box, braying at one another like electronic lunatics, bounced their noises off the gritty tiled floor and against the high tin ceiling of the place, setting up an ungodly racket, but none of the twenty or more customers at the bar appeared to notice.

Joe swallowed two more straight shots of rye, chasing them down with beer. Then he lit a cigarette and cast his eyes about in search of a mirror in which he might begin to see something that made sense to him. Juanita Barefoot had by this time moved into his mind on what seemed to be a permanent basis. She squatted there gesturing at him like a devil chairing a meeting in hell. He could see her mouth going, could hear even the sound of her voice, but the words themselves were indistinct. He found a small mirror on the cigarette machine, and, buying an unneeded package of Camels, he looked into his weary eyes, thinking still of Juanita. She was the one put this entire goddam New York notion in his head in the first place, so if she had any advice to pass out . . .

Advice.

He had to have some advice, that was all there was to it. The thought became an obsession: He wouldn't do another thing in this town until he'd found someone who knew the ropes and could give him some guidance.

Returning to the bar in this new frame of mind, Joe found he was being looked at by a person who had arrived in his absence. This was a skinny, child-sized man of

121

about twenty-one or twenty-two who had taken the seat next to him.

Catching Joe's attention, he grinned and made a small wave of the hand.

"Excuse me for starin'," he said in a New York accent, "I was just admirin' that colossal shirt." His head bobbed in approval. "Yeah, that is one hell of a shirt. I'll bet you paid a pretty price for it, am I right?" He spoke in a gravelly whisper in which Joe heard a definite note of conspiracy. Without even considering the matter, he was certain this kind of speech went hand in hand with a knowledge of the underworld.

"Oh, it ain't *cheap*," Joe said modestly. He put his fists on his hips and looked down, appraising himself. "I mean, yeah, I'd say this was an all right shirt. Don't like to, uh, you know, have a lot of cheap stuff on my back. Right?"

Suddenly Joe knew exactly where he would get the advice he needed.

He thrust his hand forward, saying, "Joe Buck from Houston Texas. Gonna buy you a drink, what d'you say to that?"

They shook hands. The dirty, curly-haired little blond runt introduced himself as Rico Rizzo of the Bronx. He had an air about him that suggested a knowledge of everything worth knowing. And he knew how to listen: His big brown eyes were tough and wise and sympathetic, and he had big ears that stuck straight out as if invisible hands were cupped behind them for maximum hearing power.

As they talked, Joe kept Rizzo supplied with drinks and smokes. Feeling himself to be the host in this situation, he was eager to honor his guest in every possible way and insisted upon doing the pouring of all beer and the lighting of all cigarettes.

Joe believed he was making a remarkable discovery about the nature of liquor. It had given him not only this social ease but some new power over his tongue as well: He laid open to Rizzo even the most subtle aspects of his dilemma in a fashion that held his listener rapt. And when Rizzo indicated an interest in Joe's present financial condition, the details were summoned up with the exactitude of an accountant, even to the fact that he had exactly ninety-one dollars left. In cash. In his hip pocket. The left one.

Rizzo thought they ought to count it. Just to be sure.

At this point in the conversation Joe's new friend was distracted by the entrance of two young men into the place. They came in and established themselves on stools at the front end of the bar. Rizzo showed some interest in avoiding contact with these persons. He suggested to Joe that they move to a booth.

Following Rizzo to the back of the barroom, Joe noticed two things about him. First, that he was a cripple. His left leg was small and misshapen, probably the result of some childhood disease. His entire body dipped to the side with each step so that his walk had a kind of rolling motion to it like the progress of a lopsided wheel. The second thing Joe noticed was that the big ears sticking out of Rizzo's head did not seem at all to be the property of a man. Suddenly the runt was a twelve-year-old, and Joe had to restrain an impulse to reach out and tweak an ear or tug on a handful of that filthy hair.

As they sat down—at a booth next to the blaring juke box—Joe watched Rizzo take his left leg in both hands

123

and lift it into place under the table. His teeth were clenched and his face went pale with the effort.

For Joe this was a precarious moment: the awareness that his new friend was in pain, probably lived in a constant state of pain, threatened to wreck entirely this brilliant hour they'd been having. Liquor had given Joe special seeing powers, and he saw now a truth about life heretofore hidden from him: that always, in even the finest hour, there lurked this potential sudden ugliness. You could be going along just great with somebody and a new piece of information would turn everything blue and sad. This, and the knowledge that there was nothing he could do to right the bad leg, induced in Joe an anger that was fierce. So fierce he was unable to maintain for long his focus upon the object of it. And there he was with all this fury and no one to throw it at, when suddenly his eye happened to catch hold of the juke box. He began to shout obscene names at the noises it made and he saw in his mind's eye a quick movie of a tall cowboy kicking hell out of all those colored lights. He rose, on his way to bringing this image into reality, when something in Rizzo's face stopped him: surprise and a flicker of fear.

Joe smiled a kind of puzzled apology and went to the men's room. On the way, he realized the liquor was having some undesirable side effects: nausea, dizziness. He had to hurry to the toilet in order not to be sick on the floor.

Later, at the sink, he rinsed his mouth out and gave himself a talking-to out loud in the mirror, surprised to hear, coming from himself, the voice of Juanita Barefoot, much deeper than his own: *"Let's cool them drinks, cowboy: They's work to do."*

"Shut up, old witch, I know what I'm doin'," he said, trying hard to sound like himself.

Returning to the table, he said, "I believe I've about had enough of that liquor. Yeah."

Rizzo, filled with some other thought, was nodding and looking at Joe through narrowed eyes.

"I got this thing figured out now," he said, pulling each word past the bed of gravel in his throat. "You're in luck, Joe. Gimme cigarette."

Joe quickly handed him a Camel and lighted it for him. Feeling that he was about to experience an important moment, he took one for himself, sucked deep on it and leaned forward.

Rizzo let out a cloud of smoke. Then he did some more nodding, looking always at Joe Buck. He said "Mm-hmm," said it three or four times, each time seeing Joe's face in some new way.

"What you need," he said at last, "is Mr. O'Daniel."

At this point the juke box set forth on some new rampage and Joe missed entirely the name of the thing he needed.

Rizzo was busy removing a piece of tobacco from his tongue and studying it, caught between his thumb and forefinger.

Joe grabbed him by the wrist. "I need what, I need what?" he shouted.

"Mr. O'Daniel," Rizzo repeated.

"Mr. O'*Who?*"

"*Mr. O'Daniel.*"

"Talk louder!"

"Management," Rizzo shouted. "You need management, you know what management is?"

"I'm listenin'."

"Okay now, look." Rizzo leaned forward and somehow miraculously Joe was able to hear every word he said. "With these chicks, the ones that want to buy it, most of 'em are older, rich and very dignified, social-register types. Follow me? So they can't, uh, can't be seen trotting down to Times Square picking out the merchandise. Don't that make sense? They got to have a middleman, an agent, a representative. You with me, Joe?"

"Yeah. *Yeah!*" Joe nodded vigorously, putting his head in position again, the ear near Rizzo's mouth.

"So all right already," Rizzo concluded. "Mr. O'Daniel is the guy!" He threw his hands into the air, palms up. "That's *it.*"

Joe felt all his muscles relax. He rested against the back of the booth. The seat was hard, but it felt like down. He shook his head, smiled and said, "Shee-it." Then he laughed happily.

"Matter of fact," Rizzo said, "I placed a fella with him about two weeks ago. He's doin' *fabu*lous today. Lots of new clothes. Drives a car. Goes to the bank every goddam day of his life—to make de*pos*its, naturally. And far as I know he's not that much of a stud, either. Just a very ordinary guy."

Joe sat forward again. "I wish to hell I'd bumped into you this afternoon."

"Yeah, it is a shame, a guy like you passin' out twenty-dollar bills to fat ladies, it's *crazy*. Not that I blame *you*. Christ, I'm just as bad as you. *Worse!* A woman cries around me, I give her anything she wants. One tear, I start carvin' the heart right out of my chest for her."

"I'd call *that*," said a new voice, "a very minor operation."

The two young men they'd seen entering the place ear-

126

lier were standing next to the booth. The taller of the two was the speaker: a shiny-faced, blue-eyed boy who looked as if he might be a farmer, but his eyebrows had been plucked into a careful, narrow line, confusing that initial impression.

"Cutting that little thing out of you," he said, "would be no more serious than lancing a boil."

Rizzo said, "Let's get out of here, Joe."

But he made no move to go because the young men were blocking his way.

"In fact," the tall boy continued, "just sit comfy there and I'll do it right here with my fingernail file. You won't even need to use your Blue Cross. What'd'ya think of that plan, Ratso?"

"The name is Rizzo."

"That's what I said, Ratso."

At this point, Joe Buck got to his feet. His movements had in them a slow mixture of menace and benevolence he'd learned from Western movies.

"Hey," he said, smiling at the tall young man in a way that said: *I'm not a real killer, but then again if I'm pressed* . . .

Both boys looked at him with considerable respect. And Joe Buck simply shook his head back and forth slowly, magnificently, suggesting an immediate cessation of all hostilities.

Rizzo said, "That's okay, Joe, I'm used to these types't pick on cripples. The sewers are full of 'em."

"Excuse me," said the farmer-looking boy, addressing himself with great politeness to the cowboy. "May I ask one thing?"

Joe lowered his eyelids in a slow, strong assent.

"It's just this: If you sit over here, and he"—pointing at

127

Rizzo—"sits way over there, how's he going to get his hand into your pocket? Oh, well," he shrugged, dismissing the subject, "I'm sure he's got that all figured out." He turned to Rizzo. "G'night, sweets."

The two young men left the place.

Rizzo looked at Joe with his eyes wide open, a sober expression on his face. "Well," he said, "now I suppose you think I'm *dishonest!*"

Before Joe could answer, Rizzo continued: "Well, I am! So if you wanta cut out on me, it's a free country."

"Hell," Joe said immediately, "I ain't going nowhere. I don't walk out on a buddy just 'cause I find out he's got some little bitty teensy something wrong." Now Joe saw in his mind once more a brief picture of Juanita Barefoot: She was looking at the sky and yawning. "Besides," Joe went on, paying no attention to the hag in his mind, "You know the ropes. And what I got to do, I got to get hold of them ropes, get out of this pickle I'm in."

Rizzo relaxed a little. He licked his lips quickly and said, "I suppose that's a sensible way to look at it."

Joe leaned across the table. "Will you take me to this bird right now, this Mr. O'Hoozit?"

"*Now?*" Rizzo showed surprise. "This time of night?" He frowned, seeming to turn the question over in his mind. "Well, I suppose I could, but—" He looked at Joe directly, challenging him: "Look, you tell me why I should. 'Cause you're a nice guy? 'Cause you bought me drinks? Well, that's great, but you know how long it's apt to take me to find this bum? First, I'll have to walk a lot, and with this gimp, it takes time and it's no picnic. Meanwhile, I'm not doin' my*self* any good: I'm tired, my pocket's not gettin' any fuller. You with me there? And tomorrow, while you're layin' up in some Fifth Avenue townhouse gettin' your back scratched by some rich broad, who knows where Rizzo'll be! The Automat prob'ly!"

"Hey now!" Joe was indignant. "You hold it, you just hold it *right there*. You think I'm the kind of sombitch is gonna take everything I make and *keep* it? You think I'm not gonna let you have a piece of it? Why, shee-it, you talk like a man with a tin ass." Joe waved his hand in the air between them as if to dispel all this nonsense at once.

"Thanks, Joe," said Rizzo. "I said you're a nice guy and you just proved it. But, uh . . ." He shook his head. "I don't do nothing on spec. It's a matter of principle. Y'understand?"

"I didn't say nothing about no speck," Joe declared flatly. "I said I was gonna give you a *piece*. So you just name what cut you want."

"No no no, Joe, what I mean is, I don't trust nobody to give me nothin' *later*. No offense, you look like an honest guy, you got an honest face. But so have I. Right? Have I got an honest face?"

"Hell yeah you got an honest face!"

"There!" Rizzo snapped his finger and pointed at Joe's nose. "You proved my point: I got an honest face—but I'm crooked as hell. So why should I trust you? Can you answer me that?"

Joe thought for a moment, frowning with the effort. He put out his cigarette and reached into his hip pocket. "I'll give you something now, right this goddam minute!"

"Oh, *wait* a minute, Joe," Rizzo said. "Use your head." He put on a sad, pained look, as if what he was about to say caused him great agony. Shaking his head, he spoke in a high, small voice: "You shouldn't be trusting me. Don't you see?" With this, he made himself very small and

129

looked up into Joe's face with his eyes so wide open the lids looked like they might tear at the edges. "It would be so easy to clip you," he said.

"Oh, hell, you think I'm worried about that?" Joe waved the thought away. Then he spread his money out on the table. "What d'you suppose'd be a fair amount?"

Rizzo leaned in, ready to do business. "I leave it up to you, Joe."

"Well, let's be hardass about this thing and figure it out right. What am I apt to clear from a night with one of these rich ladies?"

"A *night?* Did you say a *night?* Baby," Rizzo said, "Mr. O'Daniel don't bother booking no one-night stands. What he's gonna find you, he's gonna find you a *position* for chrissake. Now the first dame may or may not work out permanent. Who knows, maybe the second one won't, or even the third. For a permanent setup you got to hit it off just right. But the audition alone is gonna net you fifty, a hundred, maybe more. That's just for the goddam au*di*-tion."

"Audition?"

"The trial, the trial run, the trial night."

Joe was impressed. "Fifty or a hundred? Dollars?" He tapped the table where his money was. "Here. How much you want? Ten?"

Rizzo made a deprecating little laugh; then, smiling indulgently, he said: "Oh, Joe, please. D'you know what I could make in the time it's gonna take me to find this guy? Oh well, I'm easy. Listen, I'll tell you what I'll do: I'll take the ten." He stuck the bill into his pocket, handling it as if it were a thing of no value whatever. "But when I hand you over to Mr. O'Daniel, I'll have to have another ten. Is that fair?" There was a pause. "All right, if it's not fair, forget it."

"Answer me something," Joe said. "What's the chances of this bird putting me to work *tonight?*"

"Chances? It's got nothing to do with chances. You will be working tonight. Fact. That's *it.* Period. You just don't understand New York, Joe. You don't grasp the situation we got here. You know this expression: a seller's market?"

Joe shook his head.

"It means like, the demand is far greater than the supply. Y'get that?"

Joe frowned.

"Well, let me put it this way: There's more women than studs, so you can have all the work you want."

Joe was on his feet at once.

7

Walking up Broadway toward Times Square, Joe observed that Rizzo's leg served him well enough in an open stretch. He would catch hold of a certain target with his eye—the next corner, say—and then set himself in motion, falling at once into a kind of crazy-wheel rhythm that rolled him toward his objective at such a hell-bent pace one wondered if he'd be able to stop himself at the traffic light.

At 42nd Street, Rizzo said, "We'll try his hotel first.

With fantastic luck, I mean fan*tas*tic luck, we'll find him in his room. Come on." They wove their way through the traffic of people whose complexions appeared never to have seen the real sun, only this topsy-turvy daylight of neon and electricity, a kind of light that penetrated the first layer of skin, even cosmetics, illuminating only the troubled colors under the surface: weary blue, sick green, narcotic gray, sleepless white, dead purple.

"Not that he'll *be* there," Rizzo mumbled. "What I expect, I expect I'll have to drag this leg in and out of every bar in the West Forties; and frankly, I don't know why I bother, I don't need a buck that bad."

As they entered the lobby of the Times Square Palace Hotel, Joe said, "Shee-it, man, this is where I *live!*"

Rizzo brought himself to a halt. He looked at Joe carefully. "You live here?" he said in a small, high voice.

Joe nodded. "Yeah."

"Uh. Do you know anybody *else* that lives here? By any chance?"

"I don't guess. I only checked in today."

"You sure?"

"Hell yeah, I'm sure."

"Well, what do you know." Rizzo's smile was weak. "Coincidence, huh?"

He picked up the house phone. "Mr. O'Daniel, please. I want to talk to Mr. O'Daniel."

During the pause, he winked at Joe, showing him a circle formed by his forefinger and thumb.

"Mr. O'Daniel? How do you do, sir. This is Enrico Rizzo speaking. . . . Oh, but I remember *you*. Yes, sir. . . . Yes sir, many times, it was unforgettable. . . . Mr. O'Daniel, I've got a young man here, a very fine young cowboy. And he's, uh, he's ready to, uh—well,

132

frankly, sir, he's just in from the West and he needs your help—needs it bad. . . . You think you could work out something for him tonight? I've never seen anybody so . . . I was gonna say, he's anxious, anxious to get started. . . . OH, that's wonderful. . . . Yes sir, if you could, I uh—"

He held his hand over the mouthpiece and whispered to Joe: "He's *dying* to get you started tonight. I guess he's up to here with orders, and nobody to send. You sure you want to?"

Joe nodded with such vigor that the entire upper half of his body was used in the gesture.

Into the telephone, Rizzo said, "Yes sir, three seventeen. Thank you sir, thank you very much."

Rizzo hung up the telephone. "He's *very* exited to meet you already."

"W-w-what'll I do? Just go on up?"

"Room three seventeen. Let's see how you look." Rizzo stepped back, appraising Joe from head to foot. "Fine, you look fine. Now, I'm gonna have to have that other ten. Right?"

"Listen, kid." Joe handed Rizzo a ten-dollar bill. Then he took hold of his arm with both hands, one at the wrist, one at the elbow. "I want you to know I appreciate this, and furthermore, when things work out—well, I won't forget you. You can bet your bottom dollar on that, and I mean it."

"Nah, you don't owe me a thing. Look, I'm glad to help already." With a flick of the finger, the money disappeared into Rizzo's side pocket.

"No, no," Joe insisted. "I want to know where I can find you. 'Cause, dammit, I'm gonna make this thing right with you. Now what's your *add*ress?"

"C'mon, quit it, will you?"

"I want your *ad*dress," Joe insisted.

"All right, I'm at the Sherry-Netherland Hotel, now get your ass up there. He's *wait*in'!"

Joe released Rizzo's arm. He closed his eyes and pressed his temples with his forefingers, saying, "Cherry Neverlin, Cherry Neverlin, Cherry Neverlin. I got it!" When he opened his eyes, he saw Rizzo passing through the glass door and scuttling toward the street at his usual break-neck speed.

Joe used the mirror next to the elevator door. Finding himself somewhat pale, he leaned forward from the waist, dangling his head and arms toward the floor, hoping to bring some color into his face. Then he combed his hair, stuck in his shirt, fiddled for a moment with his cuffs, made a few reassuring clicks with his boots on the tile floor, smiled at himself and boarded the elevator.

The minute the door opened, Joe began to feel like a small child. For the man in Room 317 was clearly some-body's father; he was the age of a father, old but not *really* old, and he was wearing a fancy, cheap, worn-out bathrobe that looked like a long ago Father's Day present.

Mr. O'Daniel was fat, and the great sagging pouches in his face were those of a man on a diet or one who has recently been sick. His eyes were his most commanding feature. With dark-colored sacs below them and heavy brows above, they were the faded blue of an old sea cap-tain, half blind from questioning the horizon. Standing there in his bathrobe with lips slightly parted and looking at Joe with these searching eyes, he might even have been a survivor of a shipwreck who has not yet heard the fate

134

of his children: *Are they alive?* his eyes demanded. *Are you one of them?*

Joe acted as if he were trying to answer some such question when he said, "How do you do, sir, my name is Joe Buck."

Mr. O'Daniel nodded. He repeated Joe's name and nodded again. His eyes said, *This is an ungodly hour to get home, but thank God you're alive.*

Aloud, he said, "Joe Buck."

Joe felt he was being appraised and tried to squeeze a lot of worth into his face.

"They tell me you're a cowboy, is that the truth?"

"No, sir." Joe surprised himself by telling the truth. Then, somehow inspired to show a touch of humor, he added: "I'm no cowboy, but I'm a first-class fucker."

This didn't earn the response he'd hoped for. Mr. O'Daniel was plainly shocked. "Son." His voice was firm. "They's no reason to use that kind of talk. Now come on in here."

Joe felt at once the dreariness of the room, noticed the dirty green walls, the single window giving on an airless airshaft, with the smell of dampness coming from it and of something that had died at the bottom of it.

It never once occurred to him that Mr. O'Daniel would be staying in such a room out of poverty: Undoubtedly he had some sly motive relating to his profession.

"But then again," said the fatherly man, sitting on the edge of the bed, "why not? It seems to me you're in the mood for plain talk. That's why you come up here in the first place, or I miss my guess."

Joe said, "Yes sir." He felt he only half understood what Mr. O'Daniel was getting at, but it seemed important, especially in view of that first blunder, to appear intelligent and agreeable.

"You're—uh." Mr. O'Daniel was still appraising him. "You're a little different than a lot of the boys't come to me. With most of 'em, they seem to be, well, troubled, confused. Whereas I'd say you knew exactly what you wanted." The man's voice had some old-fashioned element in it—a riverboat orator's elongated vowels, a medicine man's persuasion—but mostly he sounded like a plain person from Chillicothe or some such place.

"You bet I do, sir."

"Well, I'll bet you got *one* thing in common with them other boys: I'll bet you're *lonesome!*" Mr. O'Daniel seemed almost angry now. "Am I right? You're lonesome, aren't you?"

"Well, I, uh . . ." Joe stalled for time. He wasn't certain what was expected of him. "Not *too*. I mean, you know, a *little*."

"There! I knew it, didn't I? *That's always the excuse:* 'I'm lonesome.' " He mimicked a whining person. " 'I'm lonesome, so I'm a drunk.' 'I'm lonesome, so I'm a drug fiend.' 'I'm lonesome, so I'm a thief, a fornicator, a whoremonger.' *Poop!* I say *Poop!* I've heard it all. And it always boils down to *lonesome, I was lonesome!* Well, I'm sick of it, sick to death!"

Suddenly Joe felt he had a grasp of the situation: the man was no doubt a whopper of a pimp, as Rizzo had promised, but he was also a little bit crazy. Joe wished he had been forewarned.

"Now the Beatitudes is very clear," said Mr. O'Daniel, looking at the ceiling and beginning to recite: " '*Blessèd are the poor in spirit: for theirs is the kingdom of Heaven. Blessèd are they that mourn . . .*' "

I wonder, Joe thought, if maybe he wouldn't appreciate

136

if I said a little something to bring his mind back to business, poor old fella. . . .

"'Blessèd are they which are persecuted for righteousness' sake: for theirs is the kingdom of heaven.' There!" said Mr. O'Daniel, proceeding like a man who has already proved his point and can now afford magnanimity: "Did you hear anything in there about *the lonesome?* Even one word? Oh, you heard about the poor in spirit, the meek, the merciful, and you heard about them that do hunger after righteousness. Sure you did. *But.*" He leaned forward on the edge of the bed, elbows resting on his knees, fingers woven together in a tense snarl of thick X's, eyes aflame with confusion, looking at Joe. "You didn't hear a purr, not a *purrrrr!* about the lonesome. And you know why? "Cause they's no Beatitude for the lonesome. The Book don't say they are blessèd. *Not once!*"

Mr. O'Daniel seemed to have worked himself up into another anger: "Lonesomeness is something you *take! You take it!* You hear me, dammit, I say *you take it, you take it!*"

He sat straight up and hugged himself with both arms like a person taken with a sudden chill. The news had arrived, the word on those children in the shipwreck: All drowned.

"They go do this, and they go do that, and they go do the other thing, and they live the life o' Riley, and they whatnot, and they follow every little whim, and they think its fine fine fine, oh just *fine*—because they was *lone*-some! Hm-mm. Hm-mm. Hm-mm. It's not fine atall."

His voice was suddenly tired: The oration was over. Rising from the bed, he began to pace the room, speaking quickly and quietly: "Read Matthew five it's all in Matthew five. Six won't hurt you either, read Matthew six, now let's get down to business. A cowboy, huh?"

Happy to return to the matter at hand, Joe said, "Yes sir, I'm a cowboy."

"Well, we need cowboys, we need everybody we can get." Mr. O'Daniel looked him over again, then nodded. "A nice-lookin' fella like you, young, strong, presentable, they's no end to what you can do in this work."

Joe was relieved and grateful to be accepted. He burst into a smile and began to relax in the presence of this crazy, fatherly, important person.

"Son, do you know what I think we ought to do?"

"Whatever it is," Joe said, "I'm ready."

"Yes, I believe you are." A heavy hand fell upon Joe's shoulder, and he was gripped by a pair of blue, moist, benign, searching, questioning eyes. "You know, I've got a hunch, Joe Buck. *Just* a hunch: But I think it's gonna be easier for you than most."

"I got that same hunch, sir." Joe nodded and smiled some more. "I think it's gonna be like money from home."

"Money from home." Mr. O'Daniel, impressed by this expression, repeated it over and over again. He looked at Joe as if he had discovered a major poet. "There, you see? That's another part of your power, your strength. You put things in very earthy terms an ordinary man can understand. Son, I'm warnin' you, I'm gonna *use* you! I'm gonna run you ragged! Are you ready for hard, hard work?"

Joe made a fist and drove it into the air. Then he threw his hands up in a gesture that meant: What more can I tell you?

Now Mr. O'Daniel was smiling, too. "You're a wonderful boy," he said. "And I think you and me's gonna have us

138

some fun, dammit! It don't have to be joyless, you know, not atall. Now!" He put his hands up, like a politician waiting for attention. Then, speaking almost in a whisper, he said: "Why don't we git right down on our knees? How does that strike you?"

There followed a moment in which no word was spoken, no motion was made, no breath was taken. Joe knew now what he had begun to know at the moment the door of the room had been opened to him.

The knowledge had been like something sickly green trickling slowly, irrevocably, into his bloodstream, too deadly to acknowledge. And now, even though he knew—and knew for certain—it was still too soon to act as if he knew.

Therefore, after this long moment, he said, "Get down —where?" His lips were dry, his voice small and puny.

Mr. O'Daniel said, "Right here. Why not? This is a church, isn't it? Every square *inch* of this earth of ours is a church. I've prayed in saloons, I've prayed in the streets. I'm not ashamed to pray anywhere. You want to know something?"

"What, sir?"

"I've prayed on the toilet! *He* don't care where. What He wants is that prayer!"

Joe nodded, and not knowing what else to do, he decided to get down on his knees and pray awhile. But he couldn't concentrate on it.

8

he reviewed in his mind the swindle that had taken place. It didn't seem believable to him, so he went through it all again, and a third time. Then he heard Mr. O'Daniel's words about getting Jesus into his heart and suddenly the reality of what had happened got through to him.

He rose without a word and ran from the room, determined to right the situation. He didn't even look back when Mr. O'Daniel called down the hallway after him: "Boy? Boy? Don't be frightened, don't be frightened, boy!" He didn't wait for the elevator either, but ran down the stairs two at a time, and out onto 42nd Street, all the way over to Sixth Avenue and back again to Eighth, knowing even as he searched that the odds against finding Rizzo were overwhelming. Even as he was trying to remember the name of Rizzo's hotel, he knew it was useless to do so. Joe didn't want his twenty dollars back, not any more; what he wanted now was some kind of revenge that would make him feel less of a fool. Standing on Times Square, looking up Broadway toward Duffy Square, he had this fantasy:

A grotesque little form wheels around the corner and slips into the doorway of a cigar store. Joe runs across the street and traps him there. Rizzo has no contrition whatever; instead he sneers at the man he has bilked. Joe takes out a knife and holds it up to Rizzo's throat, intending to perform a neat, fatal slitting operation. But even in fantasy he cannot get the knife to penetrate the boy's skin. He drops the knife and chokes Rizzo to death with his bare hands. The murder draws a crowd, the police come and—

At this point the fantasy ended: Joe saw a photograph of himself on the front page of a newspaper. He stopped and blinked his eyes and looked at it again. He wasn't imagining the newspaper, it was as real as his own boots, and there was the newsdealer with his little green shed and the stacks of newspapers. On the front page of one of the tabloids was a photograph of a young man being led away between two policemen. Joe thought, *"It can't be me, I didn't kill nobody!"*

But there was the photograph.

He bought a copy of the newspaper and hurried into the pizza place with it. Examining the photograph in this light he discovered that the young man, while close enough to himself in appearance to pass as a double, was in actuality someone else: a West Virginia mass murderer who had done in eleven members of his own family with a shotgun in a falling-out over a harmonica.

Joe was considerably shaken by this experience of seeing his own likeness led away by the police in such an official-looking document as a newspaper. He left the restaurant in search of a mirror and found one on the front of the place.

"Didn't kill nobody," he said to it. "Not gonna kill nobody."

He shook his head gravely at the image in the mirror, and then he walked away from it, hearing the clicking of

141

his own heels: a distant sound now, and one without much meaning to him.

A few minutes later, in his room, he looked into another mirror, the one over the bureau, and he studied his face as if he had just now met himself for the first time.

Not the kind of person't kills people, he thought. But in his eyes there was a question being asked. He saw the question, but he thought, no sir, not even rats. Not even Ratso. Thats' what them fags called him, Ratso. Ratso Rizzo. To hell with Ratso Rizzo. That night he fell asleep with all the lights on.

The next morning Joe experienced several awakenings from sleep, putting off the final one until afternoon. Even then he lay for a while in an imitation of sleep, unable to fool himself into thinking it was real.

But that day and for the next several days he did enjoy a kind of somnambulism: walked and talked and performed all the ordinary creature functions—scratching, eating, going to the bathroom, etc., without actually using his head much at all. He knew his money was running out at a rate that made the matter urgent, but he did not truly feel the urgency at all, not even at the end of the following week when he received from the manager of the hotel a special note on the subject of his bill.

In bed at night he dreamed of every form of peril imaginable: He was a passenger in cars gone berserk, an object of monstrous pursuits, a dweller in high, dangerous places, an exhausted swimmer in endless oceans. But in his waking hours he went about in this numb state, insulated from his own situation by layers and layers of unrelated thoughts and fantasies and tiny preoccupations.

He wandered endlessly in and out of the side streets of

142

Broadway, his head tilted toward the little transistor radio he held at his shoulder, feeling himself contained in some fragile safety by his participation in the unseen worlds of broadcasting. He liked talk stations best, and he often entered into the conversation.

"Are you telling *me*," he one day heard asked by a person of indeterminate gender and a very full nose, "that *ev*erything was simply falling off *ev*erything?" "No no no!" answered a petulant, pompous old man, "everything was *not* falling off everything. That would have been an earthquake syndrome! I'm talking about *pol*tergeists, *pol*tergeists!"

"Know what I'm talkin' about, genulman?" said Joe Buck. "I'm saying' *shee-it!* And I'm the boss." Click. He switched stations.

"Here ye, here ye," said a singsong, thin, ancient voice, "next time you feel rheumatic or sciatic or any of the symptoms of old age, don't complain. Just think of all those who do not have the privilege of growing old in this wonderful world." "Well!" said a candy-voiced man, "that's a pretty doggone grand recipe for better living! What d'you say, folks, is that pretty doggone good for a great-grandmother?"

"Oh yeah, hell yeah," Joe said, speaking through the applause, "but don't go 'way, Granny, I want you to answer me somethin' else. I heard a rumor about you, and I'ze wonderin' if it's any truth to it: Can you really take it standin' up, honey? Is that so? *Well*, I'd say *that* was pretty doggone good for a great-gramaw, yesir-goddam-ree-bob."

And so on.

One day at Riker's a glob of catsup spilled onto his beige leather jacket and left an ugly stain. Joe set about developing certain ways of standing and walking that would conceal this flaw in his grooming. Then he conceived the notion of getting some more catsup and painting what would appear to be a deliberate design over the stain. He got as far as stealing some catsup and taking it into the men's room of a cafeteria, but he was unable to decide upon a pattern. This indecision consumed the better part of an afternoon. It was typical of the kind of paralysis into which his mind had fallen.

One evening early in September something happened that jarred him into a keen state of alarm: He came back to his hotel and found he had been locked out of his room.

"Oh, we keep your things all nice and safe for you in the basement," said the clerk, in answer to Joe's inquiry about his black-and-white horsehide suitcase. "And when you pay your bill, we hand them right over to you."

Joe tried to bargain with the man, even offered him all of his belongings if he could just keep the suitcase itself and the packet of letters Sally had written him in the army.

"Oh no," the man told him, "we keep it all, yes, we keep the whole thing, that's the way we do."

Now Joe had the worrisome problem of finding a place to sleep. But that wasn't the worst of it. They had kept his horsehide suitcase.

He went into the subway arcade under Times Square, where there were many mirrors on the vending machines. He had to look into his own face to discover whether or not this new turn of events was actual or imagined. One glance told him what he needed to know.

"All right, cowboy," he said to the dazed young man in

the glass. "Enough of this shee-it. You know what you got to do?"

He nodded at himself.

"But do I *got* to?"

"Want your suitcase?"

He nodded again.

"Then go do it."

9

all the streetboys on the corner of Eighth Avenue and 42nd Street got looked at often enough. That wasn't the trick. The trick was adjusting your mind and therefore your entire attitude, physical movements, eyes, etc., to just the right degree of interest-disinterest that would make them come up and talk to you: give them the nerve to, and yet not cause them to lose interest. At that point another skill entered into it: what to say, what not to say, when to close the deal, when to hold out for more.

Joe was inexperienced in these arts and had no special gift for them to begin with. Also, he was unable to give the thing his full concentration: The sadness of what he was doing had gotten through to him, a sense of what this night was the first phase of, a leaden, paralyzing knowledge that in this pursuit success was in a way even worse than failure. But then there was the suitcase to be redeemed.

Standing there leaning on the window of the drugstore he tried to think about the suitcase and the letters in a new way, tried to see them as valueless objects. With the letters, he succeeded. He knew them by heart anyway and had long since drawn all the value off of them; in so many times of reading and feeling them, they'd actually gone fairly dead on him.

But the suitcase was another matter. It had become worth a king's ransom the moment the hotel locked its door on it. He tried to think why he cared about it so. In his mind he opened it and looked inside and though he found nothing there but darkness, this was the very thing that gave it its inestimable value, some special quality of darkness, sweet and warm and elusive. Most of all, perhaps, the suitcase was somehow a place to be: he kept slipping inside of it, in his mind, and pulling the lid down over himself. Gradually he thought he recognized certain smells in it: horsehide to start with, and then manure and all the ranch smells of boyhood Sundays, chocolate candy too and chewing tobacco, the Rio Grande, Sally Buck's pocketbook, somebody's '36 Ford. There was no telling how this suitcase, purchased in Houston a few months ago, could have trapped all that sweetness and value, but it had. And so there was nothing in the world more important than getting his hands on it again.

In two and a half hours of waiting, Joe talked with only two prospects. He found himself telling them about his suitcase, and this seemed to cause in them a certain alarm that made them lose interest. Or perhaps twenty-seven dollars—the amount the hotel people claimed he owed them—was too large a sum to ask.

By the time he spoke with a third person, a fat, bespectacled, frightened college student who looked no more than seventeen, Joe was ready to accept a compromise amount, but the student surprised him by offering the entire sum. Joe was both sickened and relieved to have come to some terms at last. Having by this time learned suspicion, he said, "Where'd a kid like you get that kind of money?" "From my mother," was the answer.

There followed a quarter hour in which this youngster with his schoolbooks led the tall cowboy through the streets of Hell's Kitchen, where he claimed to know of *a place*. On a side street beyond Tenth Avenue, the student turned and entered a tenement building.

The lower halls stunk so dreadfully one would swear demented old women boiled cat pee behind every closed door. But as they rose to the fifth floor, and then to the sixth and finally to the roof itself, all that stink was gradually replaced by good air, soft and September-sweet. And here on this roof, on perhaps the most beautiful night of the year, under the pretty amber light of a harvest moon, an urgent and sorrowful labor took place while Joe Buck stood and waited, trying to concentrate on other matters. And then the tall, fat child vomited at his feet while the cowboy held his head for him.

Joe said, "I'm awful damn sorry, kid, I can't help it if it makes you sick. You gonna have to gimme that money like we said." And the kid answered, "I don't have it, I was lying, what're you going to do to me?"

Joe looked at him hard, restraining an impulse to hit him across the face. "Turn your pockets inside out," he demanded.

147

The boy turned his pockets out, cooperating with a kind of frenzied eagerness that was obviously more pleasurable to him than the earlier act had been. But there was nothing of value in his pockets: a worn-out dime-store billfold with photographs of his family, a dirty handkerchief, two subway tokens; that was all. But he was wearing a wrist watch.

"How much is that thing worth?" Joe pointed at the watch.

The question put the boy into a panic. He began to whimper. "I can't go home without my watch, my mother gave it to me, she gave it to me for confirmation. She'd die, she'd just die, and she'd kill me!" He got to his knees. "Please, not the watch, please! Take my books, take my books."

Joe walked away, and even from the stairs he could hear the child saying over and over again how sorry he was, *so sorry, really so sorry, honestly I am.*

Joe believed him.

He walked for a long time with no particular aim, but hoping to come upon a place where there would be no other people, not an easy thing to come by in New York City—unless you have money to pay for it.

Eventually he headed west, remembering that there was a river over there somewhere, a river connected to other rivers and other waterways, probably even to the old Rio Grande. He thought he might sit on the edge of it, dangle his feet over the water. But when he'd walked as far west as you could go, it became clear that the river was barricaded by the buildings of the steamship companies: You couldn't get at the water. So he walked south under the West Side Highway, and pretty soon he came

148

upon a parking lot nearly full of big trailer trucks. He went into this maze of trucks and, finding one with an open tailgate, he hoisted himself up and sat with his feet dangling over the edge, imagining it in motion. Then he decided to lie down and look up at the sky. After a while he took off his boots and sniffed them: They'd begun to smell bad. Joe realized he wouldn't be able to take proper care of his boots for some time to come.

And while he thought about such things as the condition of his feet and the color of the sky and wondered idly how dirty the floor of the truck was, there as an awareness entering him too momentous to acknowledge: he was a nothing person, a person of no time and no place and no worth to anyone at all. This knowledge, too terrible to be accommodated in his mind, found other corners and crevices of his being to fit itself into, and while it did so, Joe went on with his musings, wondering for instance if anyone had ever counted the stars or considered the possibility that they were made of solid silver to explain that shimmering; shimmering silver; and who were those three silver-headed women anyway, those long-ago blondes of his childhood before Sally Buck: Were they just a houseful of whores, is that what they were?

The little radio, resting on his chest and rocking slightly with each ta-bloomp ta-bloomp ta-bloomp of his heart, suddenly claimed his attention. Thank god they didn't get his radio, he thought, the sonsabitches didn't get that, no-sir-goddam-ree-bob, it was right here. But feeling it necessary to conserve the battery, he couldn't turn it on. He did, however, sniff the leather casing around it, and then he crossed his arms over it.

For a while, lying there looking at the stars and at the moon, he lost his sense of things as they are. He was wide awake but it was as if he were merely dreaming of himself and this truck.

The truck wasn't quite real, it could have been any remote midnight place, a cave on the dark side of an unheard-of satellite, and he, lying in it, was nameless and not a person at all, just some elemental being with no actual kinship to anything.

The yellow globe out there in space seemed to be the earth, so that the scene as he saw it now was like the one in which his old dream took place, the dream of all the people marching in a ring around the world.

But it was different in one respect: There were no people to be seen anywhere at all.

10

having no sense at all of where he might be headed, Joe Buck simply meandered deeper and deeper into September.

Soon there would be a question of cold weather and even sooner a question of money running out. Meanwhile he was warm enough, and as for money, he doled out to himself in bits that remaining seven dollars, cautious as a widow, allowing himself only necessities and denying himself many of these. He learned cheap ways to eat: the Automat gave you baked beans or macoroni and cheese for only twenty cents, you could go to the A & P and fill your pockets with raisins and carrots for a quarter, apples could be stolen on Ninth Avenue—plums and peaches too—and there were Jewish bakers not at all jealous of their onion rolls and bagels. Lean to start with, Joe lost only a few pounds and remained fit enough in body. But blue began to show under the skin surrounding his eyes, and the eyes seemed to sit deeper in his head; this was a result of sleeping poorly in uncomfortable places, trucks or movie theaters, or on benches at Pennsylvania Station or at the Port Authority bus terminal. There was about his face now a quality of almost saintly sadness. He avoided himself in the mirror: Such a look seemed to him the sign of a shameful kind of failing. But he worked as hard as ever at his grooming and kept himself even cleaner than before. Carrying soap and a disassembled razor in his pocket and a toothbrush in his sock, he used the public facilities of the cafeterias and saloons. He washed his private parts regularly too, and almost every day he found an opportunity to take off his boots and lift his feet into a wash bowl. When other men happened upon him using the rest rooms in these ways, Joe bore his embarrassment by concentrating ever harder on the need to be clean. For somehow he had come to see his survival in terms of soap and water.

All in all, he was busy as a gypsy. He would seem to be squandering a good deal of time—hanging around a ten-cent store, say, admiring the mountains of clean socks and contemplating the theft of a pair, or leaning on a barber pole weighing the need for a haircut against other possible expenditures. But nearly always he was engaged upon some small pursuit that had become important to him.

Thoughts of going to work visited his head, but having

nothing much in common with their host they left quickly without making a very favorable impression. And yet Joe did have some interest in work, perhaps even his own kind of longing for it. In his walks the one thing that would never fail to catch his interest would be the sight of other men at their labor. He would watch the pizza making in a Broadway window as if it were some intricate form of entertainment whose meaning he could not quite grasp. Why did a man work? For money. What did he spend it on? Rent, food, a family. It was as simple as could be. And therefore all the more baffling. For the fact was that Joe's mind had fallen into that state of wondering in which all the usual kinds of sense are rendered hollow. Always, beyond the answers he could give himself, there seemed to be another more important one hiding in some corner of his mind. And this, if ever it would show itself, would prove to be like a light that made everything else truly worth while.

One rainy night—which would prove to be his last night of solitude for some time to come—Joe allowed himself sixty-five cents for a place to sleep: a 42nd Street movie theater. It was showing a science fantasy picture in which certain people of the earth found themselves on a distant planet under the control of A Voice. A Voice from nowhere at all. This film played over and over again through the night, and Joe's dreaming always accommodated perfectly the action on the screen.

For instance, at certain intervals, The Voice would call out *earthling! earthling!* and Joe would always awaken as surely as if it had said *Joe Buck! Joe Buck!* When he'd had all the sleep he could get, he stayed on to see who The Voice belonged to, half hoping its identity might make something else come clear to him. But of course it turned out to be nothing but some outlandish machine they'd put together to show in a moving picture.

But that day in his wanderings he had some strange and enjoyable new view of the way in which people, even himself, were connected to the planet earth, the way they had come from it and were part of it and peculiar to it and lived off of it and busied themselves upon it, so that when his attention was drawn to anyone, an old woman in the street, for instance, or some running child or a jeweler in his window, he would say under his breath *earthling, earthling,* and doing so he saw their features, their limbs and their skin and their hair through this wondersome new faculty developed in the night.

Once, in this same mood—and quite by surprise, since he hadn't been looking for a mirror at all—he came upon himself. This took place in a building entrance on Eighth Avenue. A big-eyed, handsome person, tall as a scarecrow and with the dark, purposeful look of a tireless hunter, was coming at him. In seconds, of course, he knew the image to be his own, but still, out of a kind of curious hoping for some unnamable connection to take place, he felt the need to stop for a moment and call out to himself under his breath, *earthling! earthling!* But it didn't work at all; nothing about himself was any different than before: Say *earthling* all he wanted to, he was still who he was.

He walked on to 42nd Street, and there in front of the bank on the corner was Mr. O'Daniel, scolding a gathering of people for its lonesome sins.

"Yes, I have traveled the length and the breadth of this great country," he said, gesturing with his right hand and supporting an American flag in his left, "and I have found the most shocking conditions. I have found the streets of this nation filled with lonesome people, young boys, middle-aged men, girls and women of all descriptions, all of them gripped by the bleakest solitude. And I've seen school grounds that had in 'em children at play. And mine eyes was blinded by what they seen. I seen in the eyes of them children the seeds of the same terrible sins: The lonesomeness is been planted in them, and if it's not stopped, I say if it's not stopped, this country is gonna make Sodom and Gomorrah look like a Sunday-school picnic. Do you hear me? I say *read* your Beatitudes!"

Joe saw that Mr. O'Daniel was wound up good and showed no signs of running down. He walked on, hearing these last words:

" 'Ye are the salt of the earth: but if the salt have lost its savour, wherewith shall it be salted?' Jesus said that. And I say, Jesus! Help us! Before the lonesomeness taketh away all our savour and they's nothing left."

Joe kept walking and the voice became indistinguishable from the other street noises. Then he turned around for a last look, watching the evangelist give what was now a dumb show, and he noticed that the speaker was not actually looking at the people gathered there on the sidewalk. His gaze was well over their heads, as if ready to apprehend an arrival that had not yet taken place. It looked to Joe as if the man were making all that noise for another than the apparent reason: He seemed to be hollering and waving his flag in just the way of a lost person trying to make his whereabouts known to someone far, far away. But who? Some lady? A child? And where could he hope they would come from? New Jersey? Eighth Avenue? From out of the West? Or the sky?

Altogether it was a disturbing spectacle, this crazy-eyed, fatherly-looking searcher flailing his arms that way and seeking a visitation from nowhere. It made Joe shudder. He muttered the word *earthling* and set about again on his own aimless, gypsy business, eager to forget the matter.

And on that very afternoon, something happened that would change his entire life: He encountered, in his walking, the crippled swindler, Ratso Rizzo.

11

Passing the 8th Street Nedick's in Greenwich Village, he found a pair of large brown eyes looking at him from behind a coffee mug at the window counter.

Seeing Joe, Ratso closed his eyes quickly and remained as motionless as a person praying for invisibility.

But Joe, having wandered homeless and a stranger for three weeks, a long time by the clocks of limbo, was thrilled to see a face that was known to him. His whole being stopped short, accustoming itself to this keen, unexpected pleasure, and it took more than a moment to remember that Ratso Rizzo was an enemy. Joe went straight for the door and entered the place.

When Joe's hand landed on his shoulder, Ratso trembled, shriveling even farther into himself. "Don't hit me," he said, "I'm a cripple."

"Oh, I ain't gonna *hit* you," Joe said. "I'm gonna strangle you to death." The anger in his voice was the anger of an actor, for so acute had been his pleasure at seeing someone he knew, it would not leave him entirely. "Only first, I want you to turn your pockets inside out for me. Go ahead, start with that one."

Ratso complied without a whimper. The search yielded:

64 cents

2½ sticks of Dentyne chewing gum

7 Raleigh's cork-tips, crushed flat

1 book of matches

2 pawn tickets

"What's in your sock?" Joe asked, remembering to snarl.

"Not a cent, I swear to God." Ratso raised his right hand and cast a quick glance toward heaven. "I swear on my mother's eyes."

"If I found out you was holdin' out on me," Joe said, "I'd kill you quick as look at you." He pushed the contents of the pockets across the counter toward Ratso. "Here, take this shee-it, I don't want it."

"You keep the sixty-four cents, Joe. Go 'head, it's yours, I want you to have it."

"Agh, them nickels is all sticky, what you do, slobber on 'em? I don't want to touch 'em. Put 'em back in your pocket."

At this point, having nothing to gain, Joe felt he should walk away from the filthy little rat altogether. But somehow he couldn't get his feet in motion. He was in a new quandary: Reason told him he was in the presence of an archenemy, and yet he had no appetite whatever for vengeance. Too much time alone had done something peculiar to his heart: A confused and unreliable organ at best, it now held something akin to joy.

Ratso was talking rapidly about that first night, saying I swear to God this and I didn't realize that, probably trying to lie his way out of the swindle he'd perpetrated.

Joe said, "You want some free medical advice, you'll shut y'goddam mouth about that night, hear?"

"Okay, right, right, okay!" Rizzo said. "Another subject: Where y'livin'? Y'still at the hotel?"

This question caused Joe to remember something he had been avoiding for days: his black-and-white horsehide suitcase locked up in that hotel room. Clearer than reality, it stood out now in his mind quivering with some quality of life it had never before possessed. At this moment he knew he would never see it again, and all the inappropriate joy he felt at seeing Ratso Rizzo turned suddenly to pain. He had to clench his teeth to keep his face in proper shape, and then he turned and hurried out of that Nedick's and across Sixth Avenue, headed uptown.

As he approached 9th Street, a voice called his name. He turned and found Ratso hurrying toward him, his body gyrating grotesquely with each step and his balance so precarious he seemed to be running the risk of a bad fall. Joe wanted to be alone, but he knew if he increased his pace, the runt would only hurry faster. In his present mood he had no stomach for such a spectacle; he slowed down.

When Ratso caught up with him, Joe said, "Listen, pissant, keep away from me. Now I mean it."

"Where you staying, Joe? You got a place?"

"You hear what I tole you?"

" 'Cause I have. I got a place."

"I mean it, Ratso. I ain't just talking. You come near me again, I'm gonna snatch you ball-headed."

"I'm inviting you, goddammit," said Ratso. "I mean I'm in*vit*ing you."

"You inviting shee-it."

"I *am*."

"Where is it?"

"Come on, I'll show you already."

They started to walk uptown together. Joe said, "I don't want to stay with you. You think I'm soft in the brain, stay with you?"

Ratso paid no attention to these protests. "It's got no heat," he said, "but by the time cold weather comes, I'll be in Florida. So what do I care, right?"

"I'd have to be out of my goddam mind," Joe said. "You'd sell the teeth right out o' my head while I'ze sleepin'."

"Actually, I don't have no beds either. But I got enough blankets to smother a horse."

"That how you gonna do it, eh, you crooked little turd? Smother me to death? Just you try it."

"An' I don't bother with no electric. To hell with it, I got candles. Right?"

Bit by bit, Joe began to understand Ratso's living conditions.

In New York there are always a large number of tenement buildings being emptied for eventual demolition. One by one the families are moved out, and as they leave, the owner, a great corporation, has a large white X taped across each window of the evacuated space. Ratso had been living in a series of these X-flats—as he called them—since he'd left home at the age of sixteen. In need of a place, he would walk the streets in search of a building on whose windows these white X's had begun to appear. Sometimes he had to break a lock, but more often the door had been left wide open. And occasionally he would even find that the departing tenant had left behind a few sticks of furniture for him. He would move his own meager belongings into the place and use it as his home until the management became aware of his presence, or until the last legitimate tenant had left and the water had been turned off.

His current dwelling was in a largely Puerto Rican block in the West Twenties. He took Joe there, led him up two flights of stairs to an otherwise vacant floor and down the hall to a little flat in the rear.

The late afternoon sun still gave some light to the room, and Joe found the place more welcoming than anything he'd slept in in weeks. Ratso's only furniture was a table and chair, but he had enough blankets to supply a rooming house. Joe's eyes were drawn to a thick stack of them in one corner near the window: every kind of blanket imaginable, comforters, quilts, army blankets, Indian blankets, all spread out neatly on the floor, making a good soft bed.

Ratso was eager to demonstrate the graces of his situation. He offered Joe a chair and then set to work with a saucepan of water and some canned heat to brew up powdered coffee for his guest. Joe headed for the chair but walked right past it and lowered himself onto the bed of blankets. He started mumbling something about how hard it was, but before he got the sentence out he had fallen into a deep dreamless sleep.

Some hours later, he awakened lost. He knew himself to be lying face to the wall in a strange, nearly dark room where a candle flame cast weird shadows on the walls and ceiling. But where? He turned slowly and found himself

159

on a makeshift bed on the floor. Next to him, clad in corduroys, was a pair of poorly matched legs that he began to recognize.

Ratso was sitting there in the candlelight leaning against the wall, smoking, examining Joe's radio.

Joe sat up and snatched the radio from him. He turned it on to make certain it was undamaged. Then he switched it off again and held it close to his body.

"Where's my boots?" he said.

They were under the table. Ratso pointed at them.

"How'd they get off me?"

"I *took* 'em off ya."

Joe looked at the boots again, and then at Ratso. "What for?"

"So's you could sleep is all. I mean, *cripes!*"

Joe got to his feet and went to the table where his boots were. "I believe the smart thing for me is haul ass out of here." He sat on a chair and began pulling on the boots.

"Why? Why why why?" Ratso said. "What'sa matta?"

Joe held one of the boots between his forefinger and thumb, swinging it back and forth slowly, and in a sense he held Ratso in a similar fashion with his eyes. It was as if he were weighing one thing against the other.

Ratso was a thief, Joe thought, and only dangerous if you had something worth stealing. Now if he were to spend the night here, he could put the radio under his pillow—and as for the boots, what good would they be to somebody whose feet were of two different sizes? And what else could the kid be after? He didn't seem to be a fag. Looking at him now, Joe saw nothing more frightening than a puny crippled kid sitting on a pile of old blankets on the floor of a tenement flat afraid of being left alone. So why not stay? He didn't know a reason, but it seemed to him like every time he did something that

160

looked simple, it ended up costing him his ass. Still, it wouldn't hurt to get one good night's sleep. But first he would scare hell out of the little sonofabitch on general principles.

Joe said, "Listen, I'm gonna tell you something, Ratso. Only first gimme cigarette."

Ratso gave him one of the crushed Raleighs and held the candle for him to light it with.

Then Joe looked squarely at Ratso and said: "It's this I want to tell you. For your own good. Now, um, you want me to stay here tonight, is that the idea?"

Ratso shrugged. "I ain't forcing you. I mean, like, you know, I ain't *forcing* you." His voice was lacking in conviction, and when he shrugged to demonstrate the quality of his indifference, his shoulders hardly moved at all. Joe knew that in spite of his actual words Ratso was pleading with him to stay, but still he felt the need to assert his control over the situation.

"Oh. Oh, I see." He put his foot inside his boot. "Hell, I had the 'pression you wanted me to stay here with you. But, uh, seems like I had the wrong 'pression."

"All right, I do," Ratso growled. "I want you to stay, you're invited. I tole you that already."

"You know what you're in for?"

"What?"

"If I stay? 'Cause I'm a very dangerous person, you didn't know that, did you? About all I think of is ways to kill people." He studied Ratso's face for a reaction. Ratso simply looked at him, betraying nothing. Joe continued: "It's a truth. Somebody does me bad like you done, all I do is think up ways to kill 'em. So now you been warned. Y'hear me, Ratso?"

"I hear you."

"You don't say that like you mean it. Maybe I better

161

'press you further."

"All right, I'm impressed already! You're dangerous, you're a killer!"

Joe nodded. "You goddam well better believe it." After a moment, he added, "So if you still want me to stay here for a day or two—I mean, is that what you want? or not?

Ratso frowned and growled, "*Yeah! Goddammit!*"

Joe held up his hand, satisfied. "Easy, easy." He dropped the boot and moved toward the pile of blankets. "Just want to be sure is all. 'Cause I'm not takin' any favors off anybody. Can't afford it."

When he was back on the blankets again, he looked around the place, accustoming himself to his new whereabouts.They smoked in silence for a moment. Then Ratso said, "You ever kill anybody?"

"Not yet," Joe said. "But I tore up this one fella something awful." He told the story of the night he gave Perry a beating in the whorehouse of Juanita Barefoot. "I couldn't control m'self. I get mad, I don't know m'own strength. If they had'en pull me off, that sombitch be a goner today. Same with you. I come after you with a knife that night. You didn't know that, did you? I'ze all set to use it, too." He stopped for a moment, thinking of a way to enrich the tale. "I spent the whole night in jail. It had'n been for them cops, they'd be one dead Ratso along about now."

"Ha! You think I'd mind that?"

"So," Joe went on, "ever' time you pass a cop f'm now on—you blow him a kiss, hear?"

He put out his cigarette on a jar lid Ratso maintained for this purpose.

"And while you're at it, Ratso," he said, lying down, "move the hell over. Y'crowdin' me."

Ratso moved over as far as he could, and then he said, "Joe?"

"Yeah?"

"In my own place, do me a favor, will you?"

"Nope. No favors. I ain't doin' no favors."

"No, I mean, look, in my own goddam place—this is my place, am I wrong?"

"My favor days is all over," Joe said.

"Well, it's just, in my own goddam place, my name is not Ratso. You know? I mean it so happens my name is Enrico Salvatore. Enrico Salvatore Rizzo."

"Shee-it, man, I can't say all that."

"All right! *Rico* then! At least call me Rico in my own fucking place!"

"Go to sleep," Joe said.

"Okay, though?" the kid persisted.

Joe lifted his head and barked out: *"Rico! Rico! Rico!* Is that enough?" He turned his face to the wall. Then he said, "And keep your meathooks off my radio."

After a moment Ratso said, "Night," in a small, throaty voice. But Joe was far from ready to exchange any such niceties with this person. He pretended to be asleep.

12

This day in late September marked the beginning of Joe Buck's alliance with Ratso Rizzo. The pair of them became a familiar sight on certain New

York streets that fall, the little blond runt, laboring like a broken grasshopper to keep pace with the six-foot tarnished cowboy, the two of them frowning their way through time like children with salt shakers stalking a bird, urgently intent on their task of finding something of worth in the streets of Manhattan.

Ratso chewed his fingernails, consumed all the coffee and tobacco he could get hold of, and lay awake nights frowning and gnawing at his lips. For he was the natural leader of the two, and upon his head rested the responsibility for thinking up new schemes for their survival.

Joe Buck, in the fashion of a follower, simply expressed his across-the-board pessimism about whatever was suggested, and then went along with it. Once, for instance, Ratso heard about a town in Jersey where the parking meters were said to be vulnerable to the common screwdriver. Joe Buck was skeptical and said so, often, but still he submitted to hocking his radio in order to raise bus fare for the trip across the river. When they got there it became clear at once that Ratso's information was out of date: the town had all new meters of a make no screwdriver could ever disturb. In the face of such a disappointment, Joe Buck was capable of behaving with magnanimity, at least to the extent of keeping his mouth shut while Ratso made excuses for the failure.

But on the whole this person with the sunburst on his boots remained cranky and disagreeable in his behavior toward the little blond runt. He realized it, too. Joe knew good and well he had become a pain in the neck, and what's more he was none too concerned about it. But there was a reason for his unconcern: He was happy.

For the first time in his life he felt himself released from the necessity of grinning and posturing and yearning for the attention of others. Nowadays he had, in the person of Ratso Rizzo, someone who needed his presence in an urgent, almost frantic way that was a balm to something in him that had long been exposed and enflamed and itching to be soothed. God alone knew how or why, but he had somehow actually stumbled upon a creature who seemed to worship him. Joe Buck had never before known such power and was therefore ill equipped to administer it. All he could do was taste it over and over again like a sugar-starved child on a sudden mountain of candy: cuss and frown and complain and bitch, and watch Ratso take it. For that's the way in which power is usually tasted, in the abuse of it. It was delicious and sickening and he couldn't stop himself. The only thing the runt seemed to demand was the privilege of occupying whatever space he could find in the tall cowboy's shadow. And casting such a shadow had become Joe Buck's special pleasure.

He enjoyed listening to Ratso, too. As they walked through the city, or shared a cup of coffee in a lunch stand or cafeteria, or shivered together in the progressively colder doorways of the waning year, he heard Ratso's views on many subjects. Bit by bit, he was able to piece together a picture of Ratso's early years in the Bronx.

Ratso was the thirteenth child of tired immigrant parents. He remembered his father as a hard-working brick-layer who in his off hours went to sleep whenever he found something even vaguely horizontal to lie upon. His mother, a burnt-out child bearer, usually sick, managed the family like a kindly, befuddled queen, issuing contradictory mandates from her bedroom. Occasionally she would pull a housecoat about her body and move through the flat trying to sort out the confusion she had wrought. On one such tour she found the seven-year-old

Ratso under the kitchen stove in an advanced stage of pneumonia. Surviving this, he contracted infantile paralysis a few weeks later, and by the time he was discharged from the hospital the following year his mother was dead and gone. His three sisters and two of his nine brothers had left home, either for marriage or for other purposes. Of the eight remaining boys, none took any interest in cooking or housework; nor had Papa Rizzo ever given any special attention to the running of a family. When he thought of the job at all, it was in terms of supplying food. Therefore once a week he stocked the shelves with saltines and cans of pork and beans, the refrigerator with cheese and cold cuts and milk. For six days the boys would grab what they could, and on the seventh Papa Rizzo gave them a real Sunday dinner at a neighborhood spaghetti place. Occasionally in an earlier time—usually at Easter or on Mother's Day—he had hosted such dinners in this same restaurant, and the owner had always made him feel proud of his enormous brood by calling attention to the fact that he required the biggest table in the place. *"Ecco, che arriva Rizzo!"* he would say. *"Prende la tavola piu grande del locale!"* Even now, with only eight sons left, it was necessary to shove two regular tables together. But after the first month or so, these Sunday dinners were ill-attended, for the old bricklayer had developed a foul temper and took to using them as occasions for scolding and shouting. The boys, one by one, having learned to forage in ways they found easier than listening to the ravings of a disagreeable old man, wandered away from home altogether. Finally one Sunday afternoon at the family dinner there was only Ratso. When the owner led them to a table for two, the old man was shocked, and then embarrassed, and then chastened.

166

He ate in silence, behaving with an almost ceremonial kindness toward the skinny, crippled, thirteen-year-old runt of his progeny. He also drank a good deal of wine, and then there came a moment in which he broke the silence and ended the meal by landing one tremendous wallop of his bare fist on the little formica-covered table, shouting his own name and reminding the world at large, and God, too, that he was accustomed to larger tables than this: "*Sono Rizzo! Io prendo la tavola piu grande del locale!*" The owner came over and the two old men wept together and embraced each other. Then Ratso led his father home. Entering the flat, the old man drew back and let out a dreadful howl. It was as if he had suddenly awakened from the longest of all of his naps and found his family wiped out by bandits and the walls of the flat all splattered with blood. Looking past Ratso as if the boy didn't exist, the bricklayer started to sob, asking over and over again the whereabouts of his sons. "*Dove sono i miei ragazzi terribili?*" Gradually, and perhaps only by default, Ratso became the favorite, and for a while life was better for him than for the others. He was given an allowance and was never scolded. The Sunday dinners continued. There was not much talk at the small table, but a silent intimacy had grown between them and the atmosphere was affectionate and peaceful. Papa Rizzo, by now a fat, benign, baldheaded old bear in his late sixties, drank a quart of Chianti all by himself, and on the way home from the restaurant he would find a number of opportunities to place his hand upon the head of his last remaining son, or, waiting for a traffic light, to wrap a heavy arm around his shoulder. On one such afternoon of a summer Sunday, Ratso was undermined by the great burden of weight his father placed upon him, and they both fell to the sidewalk. When Ratso was able to disengage himself, he found that the old man had died on him, right there in the crowded sunlight of the Bronx River Parkway.

From then on, Ratso was on his own. He was sixteen, with no special training for life. But he did have a quick natural intelligence, and, like most persons raised in large families, he was a good, fast liar. With these assets, he took to the streets.

Ratso could talk about the Bronx, and he could talk about Manhattan, and he could talk about nearly anything under the sun. But his best subject was Florida, and though he had never been there, he spoke more positively and with greater authority on this topic than on any other. He often studied folders in color put out by transportation companies or perused a stack of travel clippings collected from newspapers; he also owned a book called *Florida and the Caribbean*. In this splendid place (he claimed) the two basic items necessary for the sustenance of life—sunshine and coconut milk—were in such abundance that the only problem was in coping with their excess. For all that sunshine you needed wide-brimmed hats, special glasses and creams. As for coconuts, there were so many of these lying about in the streets that each Florida town had to commission great fleets of giant trucks to gather them up just so traffic could get through. And of course coconuts were the one complete food: This was common knowledge. Anytime you got hungry, all you had to do was pick one up and stab it with a pocketknife, then hold it up to your mouth. Ratso was unable to tell about this without demonstrating with an invisible coconut. "Here your only problem is," he would say to Joe, sucking at the air between phrases, "—you want to know what your only problem is here, diet-wise? It's the warm

168

milk running down your face and neck. Yeah, sometimes you got to exert yourself, you got to reach up and wipe off your chin. Tough, huh? You think you could stand that? I could. I could stand it." As for fishing, he made this sound so simple Joe actually got the impression you didn't need a rod and reel or even a pole. Without examining the picture too carefully for probability, he had formed a kind of cartoon image of the two of them standing near the water saying *here fishy-fishy,* at which point a pair of enormous finned creatures would jump into their arms precooked. A silly, happy thought, and he could smell the fish plain as day. Sometimes to keep this pleasant discussion going, Joe might feed a question: "But shee-it man, where in hell would you sleep? They got no X-flats down there, you can bet your smart ass on that." But Ratso had an answer for everything. At this cue he would begin to tell of the endless miles of public beaches on which had been built hundreds of pagodas and pergolas and gazebos; under these, on sun-warmed sand or softly padded benches, protected from rain and wind, one slept the sleep of Eden.

Most often under discussion, however, was the subject of their financial problem. Ratso was inclined to belittle any so-called honest solution. Neither of them was sufficiently presentable to get a job that would pay them at a worthwhile rate, nor had either of them been trained for such work. Besides, any course of action involving full-time employment did not seem worthy of being called a solution; such talk Ratso considered frivolous and had no patience with. Of course, living by one's wits was just as problematical in its own way as legitimate work: Competition was overwhelming, one had constantly to be on the lookout for a new angle and, finding one, to be ready for its sudden obsolescence. ("For example, them goddam parking meters; right?") As for Joe Buck's earning potential, it was Ratso's considered opinion that he had not a hope in hell of making a living from women. Such a profession was extremely specialized, requiring a wardrobe, polish, and a front. The cowboy gambit wouldn't work on New York women. Not only was this costume an almost purely homosexual lure, it was severely specialized even within that group, attracting to it almost exclusively a very small masochistic element. ("Never mind *what* that is, you wouldn't believe it if I told you.") Sometimes, against his own better judgment, but in an extremity of hunger, he would arrange for Joe a fast five- or ten-dollar transaction in which little more was required of the cowboy than standing still for a few minutes with his trousers undone. But these unhappy conjunctions usually left Joe in a depressed and disturbed state of mind. He felt as though something invisible and dangerous had been exchanged, something that was neither stated in the bargain nor understood by either of the parties to it, and it left him sad and perplexed and with an anger he couldn't find any reasonable place for. Ratso agreed this was a poor way to earn a dollar. He claimed that prostitution had always been the hardest profession in the world as well as the most competitive—and even worse in today's world, where the commodity was being given away free in such liberal quantities. The only way to do really well at it was to rob the patron, but this required an adroitness and a sense of timing Ratso felt was lacking in his cowboy friend, and he did not encourage him to enter this extension of the market. Ratso did credit himself with the needed wit and cunning for it, but his chances of success were severely limited by the condition of his leg. ("Now you take your average fag: Very few of 'em want a cripple.")

Ratso had a specialty better suited to him: He was a pickpocket. But he wasn't very good at it. Too often he would be caught in the act by someone twice his size who could have hauled him off to a policeman with no trouble at all, and Ratso would then have to undergo the indignity of pleading for mercy on the basis of his crippled leg. He was more skilled at a variation of this form of theft, but this variation required a greater investment of time and was apt to be less lucrative as well: He would sit in a bar and strike up a conversation with a stranger, then watch for the moment at which he could steal the person's money. Sometimes he would lose up to an hour and come away with nothing more than a little change in his pocket and a beer or two under his belt.

Joe was disgusted by this kind of operation ("Makes me *puke!*") and would have nothing to do with the gains from it. Ratso would have to invent some cock-and-bull story to explain this kind of money, otherwise Joe would refuse to swallow so much as a hamburger purchased with it and would go around for days with a face as long as time.

But Joe was still in the first flush of his friendship with Ratso Rizzo, and during these weeks nothing that happened seemed quite so terrible to him as the prospect of being once again a totally alone person. Even though he had stepped free of those lone years and had entered upon this new time, they still existed somewhere, shadowing even the present like some creature of nightmares, black

171

and ruthless and many-armed, ready to snatch him back into more and more and more solitude.

The pair drifted along through October and into the foul November weather with nothing very remarkable taking place in their lives.

The sameness of their days, and the feeling of being trapped with no real prospect of things getting better, caused in Joe a growing restlessness, an agitation that was often downright painful. It was as if Manhattan were his cell and the cell was shrinking at a nightmare rate, and he was doomed to pace back and forth in it in ever smaller steps until finally it would press in upon him altogether.

They suffered one cold after another. Ratso especially: His voice had taken on a basso profundo rattle that Joe found comical in one so small. He gulped cold remedies and cough syrup in such quantities he went about light-headed and drowsy, and he had no appetite for real food. Now and then he got down a few spoonfuls of soup or a Hershey bar. And of course coffee. He could always drink a cup of coffee and smoke a cigarette. Whenever he watched Ratso smoke, Joe got the feeling there must be some special life-giving substance in the tobacco that only Ratso knew how to extract.

November was a cruel month for persons who hovered as much in doorways as they did, a cold month and a damp one, and windy, too. And it seemed that as the weather worsened, they were more and more in the streets. The temptation, of course, was to stretch the nights out as long as possible, lingering in the shelter of the X-flat. But each in his own way had developed a kind of fear of the place, and the extra hours spent there were hateful ones. Threatening, too. Somehow they knew that

172

if you settled for this kind of hiding there was no telling what would become of you. No wizard was on his way there to knock on the door and offer them magic to change their fortunes, or even food for that matter. And they knew it, and so it was all right to lie down in such shabby, make-do safety in the nighttime for real sleep. But to be awake there in the daylight, when the shadow of that big white X fell across the room like a message, was to indulge in a comfort so sinister as to be actually tiring. Nor was this matter ever discussed. It didn't need to be. For in any kind of foul weather, no matter how sick they felt and no matter how grimly attractive the place seemed by contrast with their poor, poor prospects on the streets, they were out of there by noon.

Signs of Christmas appeared in the store windows and in the streets. But such a holiday had nothing to do with either of them. The sameness went on and on. Ratso appeared one day with a big sheepskin-lined greatcoat, offering it to Joe for a present. He claimed it had been given to him by an overstocked dealer in exchange for a small favor, but Joe had reason to believe it'd been stolen at the movies. He said you couldn't go around stealing winter coats unless you knew for certain the owner had another one somewhere, and he ended up making Ratso feel so bad about the matter he simply hid the thing away in a cupboard. Joe went on wearing his catsup-stained yellow leather jacket. He claimed not to feel the cold, but he shivered a lot just the same and was always finding excuses to duck into stores and vestibules and theaters.

At certain odd moments Joe knew that the restlessness he felt had nothing at all to do with the sameness of his days. Somewhere in him was the knowledge that there was no such thing as sameness: You might do the same

173

things and cover the same streets and even think the same worrisome thoughts, but inside, deep where you couldn't see them, things were changing and changing and changing and working up to the point where they would come together and show. And then before long you would be saying that something had happened, and your life would suddenly be so different to you you would hardly even recognize it as your own.

But Joe's was not the kind of mind that could take hold of such a thought with any good firm grip and keep it. It would appear to him for a moment or a split second and then recede as if it had a life and a rhythm all its own. So that, to Joe, his own anxiety seemed most often to be a fear of nothingness. Only at these odd, unexpected moments would it be a fear of *something*.

And then there came a night in early December when this waiting time ended altogether.

13

h_im?" said the boy.

"Just a second, let me look," said the girl. She tapped Joe on the shoulder.

It was a December night. He was having coffee in the 8th Street Nedick's when he heard these voices behind him. He turned and found himself being studied by two childlike young people dressed in identical costumes:

black turtleneck sweaters and tight black jeans. They seemed to be brother and sister, perhaps even twins. There was no great difference in their apparent genders. Her hair was short for a girl and his long for a boy. Both were blond, gray-eyed, and gently pretty; neither wore any makeup.

The girl was clearly the bolder of the two. She took hold of Joe's chin and examined his eyes. "Oh yes, *definitely*," she said to her brother. "Definitely him."

The boy smiled in a meaningless way and handed Joe a small piece of thin orange paper rolled into a scroll and held together by a gummed silver star.

Then the boy and the girl left the place. Joe, caught by something peculiarly calm and deliberate in their manner, watched until they were out of sight before opening the scroll. A message had been printed on it by hand in black ink:

You are expected to appear before midnight at the kingdom of hell which is located in a filthy loft on the northwest corner of Broadway and Harmony Street. There you will be poisoned.

Hansel and Gretel
MacAlbertson

Joe went outside and looked in all directions, but there was no sign of the MacAlbertsons. He looked at the note again, read *before midnight,* and then consulted the clock on the red brick tower next door to the women's prison: it was eleven o'clock. He lit a cigarette and contemplated the good fortune of being handed something by these strange blond youngsters. The traffic light changed. Pedestrians trying to cross the street bumped against him in their effort to avoid old snow piled up at the curb.

Joe read the note over and over again. He realized he'd need help in interpreting the thing. Ratso was probably working a certain Sixth Avenue saloon. Joe crossed the street, headed in the direction the saloon, when he caught sight of Ratso under the green awning of a newspaper vender. He was wearing the controversial sheepskin coat, and when he saw Joe coming there was a defiant look in his eye. For his part, Joe was pleased to see the thing getting some wear. He handed the orange scroll to Ratso.

"If you want to read something," he said, "read that." Then he explained to Ratso how the note came to be in his possession. "In that whole place," he said, "they only give one to me." He tried to hide the pride he felt.

Ratso pulled the great collar up about his ears and started to move. "Let's *go,*" he said.

"Whay-whay-whay-*where?*" Joe said, following close beside him. "I mean what *is* the damn thing? Is it some kind of a adver*tise*ment, or a religion, or a what? 'Cause we don't know what the hell we're walkin' into."

"It's a Halloween party."

"Halloween? This ain't Halloween. This here's December."

"So what do you care? It's a party, and we're invited."

We? Joe wondered. "It don't say nothing on there about you," he said.

"Agh!" Ratso waved the thought away.

"Man," Joe said, "they sure look me over 'fore they hand me that thing."

They were walking east on 8th Street, headed toward Broadway.

176

Yeah, Joe thought, they sure look me over good, and the one says, Him? and the other'n says, Oh yeah, definitely. Now I wonder how come they picked me? Is it my boots and my hat? Something about my face? Just sexiness in general? Or what?

The thought of his sexiness, a suddenly remembered asset, caused him to smile and laugh out loud. They were passing a bakery that had an amber-tinted mirror in its window. Joe swung his face quickly toward the mirror, hoping to catch some of the good of that smile. He caught a little of it.

Then he said to Ratso, "You know, it wasn't too long ago I was setting in Sally Buck's living room looking at the TV."

"Yeah? So?" Ratso looked at him. "I mean, *so?*"

"Well, that was in Albuquerque, can't you see? Way in the hell somewhere else. And what am I now? I'm in New York, ain't I? Getting picked out for all these goddam—I don't know, can't you understand what I'm talkin' about?"

"Nope."

Joe's thought was so clear to himself he felt Ratso's failure of comprehension had to be deliberate.

"Well," he said, "I see you're out to fix this party tonight, fix it good, cranky little wop bastard, you."

Ratso caught hold of Joe's arm and hung on it. "What? What'd I say?"

"Never mind," Joe said. "They may not let you in anyhow."

"You want to bet?"

A group of college people loitered in front of the Eighth Street Bookshop. Joe wished they all knew where he was headed. But there was no sensible way of letting them know.

"I'll make 'em let you in," he said to Ratso. "I'll tell 'em they can't have me unless they take you."

"Big fuckin' deal!"

"So don't worry about it," Joe said.

"I ain't worried!"

"You're as good as in. Besides, they's nothing wrong with you."

"Who said there was?"

"If you had a haircut and some meat on your bones, you be all right."

"Thanks a million!"

"So I'll say, uh, 'Look, I don't go nowhere without my buddy here.' Okay?"

They walked a block in silence. At the corner of University Place, a cold wind blew at them until they got across the street where the buildings protected them again.

Ratso said, "You don't want me to go. Right?"

"Did I say that? I didn't say that."

"No, but I'll tell you something, Joe. I'm sorry, but I'm in the mood to let you have it. So listen: You are a very dumb person. You don't know how to get in out of the rain. You need me! You can't wipe your butt without me handing you the paper. So now you get invited to a party all by yourself and it's like you're the great man. Okay, are you ready for some news already? I don't *want* to go no cutesy-ass party with no Hansel and Gretel MacAlbertson." Ratso said their names in baby talk and then made a gagging sound in his throat. "Oooh, how kitchy-kitchy-*koo!* I'm nauseated already. The only reason I wanted to go in the first place was I thought, agh, they'll prob'ly have a ring of baloney and a couple of soggy Ritz crackers. What the hell, can't pass up a spread like that! Well, I lost my friggin' appetite, so goodbye already. Okay?"

He stopped walking.

Joe said, "Gimme that *add*ress!" He snatched the orange note from Ratso's hand and walked on. But he had gone no more than a block when his anger petered out. He stopped at Broadway and looked back.

Ratso was still there, standing in the middle of the sidewalk, huddling into his coat, watching Joe.

Joe gave him a signal with his hand, and Ratso started rolling toward him, hurrying to catch up, beating the air like a damaged bird. Joe wanted to shout at him, *Don't run!* but instead he turned away, purposely not looking. And then he heard the step-*drag* step-*drag* step-*drag* coming closer and closer. By the time Ratso caught up with him, both of them seemed to have forgotten their altercation.

They walked down Broadway to the corner of Harmony. Among several small signs in the outer lobby of a big loft building was one that said:

The MacAlbertsons. Two flights up.

Before proceeding up the stairs, Ratso leaned for a moment on the banister. His face and hair were wringing wet, and his breathing made a peculiar noise that was like a certain thin note on an organ. Joe had become so accustomed to hearing Ratso's sneezes and coughs, and his voice like rocks being dragged across an unpaved road, and he had become so used to seeing discomfort and pain in Ratso's face, that he had not for some weeks taken a really close look at the runt. Now he found that his coloring under all that perspiration was way off: His skin was more yellow than anything else, but it had some gray in it and a greenish cast as well; the whites of his eyes were a kind of pale peach in color, and lusterless; and his lips were lavender blue, edged with white.

Joe said, "What'sa matter with you?"

"Matter? What d'you mean, matter?"

Joe didn't know what to say. He kept looking at Ratso for a long moment.

Ratso became agitated. "What? What is it? Am I *bleedin'?*"

"No. No, you're not bleedin'. You're sweatin', though. Haven't you got a hanky?"

Ratso wiped his forehead on the lining of his coat.

Joe said, "You better dry your hair some."

Ratso made a swipe at it with his bare hands.

Joe took out his own shirt tails. "Come here. Gimme y' fuckin' head."

Ratso growled, "No." But Joe was louder. *"Come here!"* Ratso bent forward and offered his head to be dried. Joe rubbed at it with his shirt tails. "Can't go to a party with a wet head," he said. "Okay now, you got a comb?"

"I don't need a comb." Ratso started working at it with his hands.

Joe gave him his comb. "Few dozen cooties won't kill me, don't guess."

But the comb could not be passed through such a thick tangle of unwashed curls, and several of the teeth broke. Ratso handed the comb back and patted his hair into some kind of form. "Howd' I look? Okay?"

Joe looked at him carefully and for a long time.

The bare fact was that Ratso did not look okay. Joe was willing enough to lie about it and let the matter pass, but something else happened as he continued to look into Ratso's face.

180

What was it?

Neither of them really knew.

Some vague, awful thing had come into evidence between them, hovering in the air between them like a skeleton dancing on threads, something grim and secret that filled Joe with terror, making him feel locked out and alone and in peril.

As for Ratso, the signs of it, whatever it was, were subtle, amost not there. He simply turned his head away, somewhat sheepishly. There was a kind of stillness in his eye, a fixed look to his shoulders and the set of his head.

Joe opened his mouth to speak, but Ratso made a quick gesture of impatience and started up the wide, dark stairway.

Joe watched him. When Ratso was halfway up the first flight, Joe said, "Hey, *wait* a minute! Hey, *whoah!*"

Ratso stopped climbing and looked down. His eyes begged Joe not to speak, but for good measure he threw in this challenge: "Are we goin' to a goddam party or what?"

Joe was too bewildered to move. Something awful had just taken place here at the foot of these stairs. Or had it? He couldn't really be certain.

"Nothin's wrong, is it?" he said.

"Come on!" Ratso was impatient, then pleading. "Will you come on, please?"

He waited until Joe had begun the climb, then he took hold of the banister once again and pulled himself up the stairs.

part three

part three

1

the banister on the third-floor land-
ing was being used for a coat rack. It was piled high with
sweaters and scarves and parkas and every kind of winter
wrap imaginable. Ratso left his sheepskin on the stack and
looked over the rows of boots and galoshes and rubbers on
the floor.

"I'll pick me out a nice pair of rubbers when we leave,"
he said.

The door was wide open. Ratso led the way in. Joe felt
painfully self-conscious, not knowing what behavior was
expected of him. He walked with a swagger, frowning, not
wanting to be caught without an attitude.

The room was enormous; it ran the entire length of the
building and it was as wide as a house. There was a good
deal of noise but not enough for so large a crowd. Laughter was aware of itself, and so was conversation, and there
was a certain timidity in the sounds produced by a bongo
drum, a recorder, and a jug, suggesting that the musicians
had not yet hit any kind of stride. One couple was making
an effort to dance, and an even greater effort to do so
without being seen. There were many small groups, some
standing, some sitting on the floor, all loosely formed, and
many persons standing alone or near the periphery of a

185

group that did not quite include them. One couple—boys of college age, one white, one brown—sat in the middle of the floor holding hands, but it wasn't so much an inter-racial romance as a marriage of two shades of despair; they were joined at the hands but not at the eyes; each of them frowned into some distance of his own. Many of the lone persons, male and female alike, seemed to be ashamed of their solitary condition. You could see them casting about for a place to lose it, a way to camouflage it or something to attach it to: a drink, a cigarette, a corner, a conversation, a smile, a stranger, an attitude.

Along one wall was a big table with a good selection of cheese and lunch meat and crackers and bread, and on the floor next to it were washtubs filled with ice, ice water and cans of beer.

At the far end of the room Joe spotted the MacAlbert-sons, sitting on the floor at the feet of a skinny painted lady with long white hair.

Behind this trio, covering a portion of wall from ceiling to floor, were several long strips of butcher paper on which had been painted in black the legend

IT'S LATER THAN YOU THINK

and next to the sign was a bucket of black paint with a broom sitting in it, the handle leaning against the wall.

Joe kept looking at the MacAlbertsons. They sat before the sign like figures on an altar, quietly, and with that same unholy tranquillity that had caught his interest earlier at Nedick's.

The lady behind them was even more disturbing to him. He didn't like looking at her, but his eyes kept re-turning to her on their own. There was something wrong with her. But what? She had a blob of dark paint on each eye and a little red mouth. She blinked often. The lids of her eyes seemed to be operated by strings in the control of someone whose attention had wandered. Her head sat upon her neck in a loose way, precariously balanced, bobbing about like a toymaker's trick. Seen from a distance, she might even have been inhuman, something pasted together by those two silent, sinister children at her feet, an effigy perhaps of a missing parent, made from sticks and straw, candy sacks and Crayolas.

The boy had some jars in front of him, and he was shaking something out of one of them (a spider? a worm?) and handing it to a beautiful Negro girl. Whatever it was, the girl popped it into her mouth, downed it with beer, and then, in a comic imitation of sensual pleasure, she stretched her arms, wiggled her lean, jersey-clad body and danced across the center of the room into the arms of a splendid black giant, gaining and holding the attention of nearly every other person in the place.

But Joe watched the MacAlbertson boy, who was still preoccupied with those little jars. He drew closer, hoping for a look at their contents, when the one called Gretel caught his eye and beckoned to him with her head. Joe turned to get some guidance from Ratso, but Ratso was busy at the refreshment table, looking about furtively and stuffing his pockets with salami.

Gretel MacAlbertson, meanwhile, had risen and come toward Joe. Her face and voice were completely without expression. From close on, she was less sinister, and her tranquillity might even have been simple boredom.

"You're here," she said. "Do you need anything? I mean there's beer and . . ." She opened a fist and showed him a big brown capsule. ". . . *This*, if you want it." Reading

187

the question in his face, she said, "It's a bomber—good for about four hours."

Joe looked at the capsule, and then at the girl, smiling to cover his ignorance and wondering what to do.

She frowned slightly. "Well, *take* it," she said, her tone somewhere between a command and a dare.

Joe took the capsule and popped it into his mouth, worked up some saliva and swallowed it. Proud of himself, he smiled and looked to the girl for some sign of appreciation or approval. But all his bravado seemed only to have deepened her boredom. She pointed a languid hand toward the refreshment table. "Beer's all right with it," she said. This time there was *some*thing in her voice: gentleness, perhaps.

Ratso was at that moment approaching with two opened beer cans. He handed one of them to Joe.

Joe tried to perform an introduction. "This here is, uh, Ratso Rizzo, and—"

Ratso corrected him. "*Rico!*" he said.

But this sort of routine was clearly too taxing for Gretel MacAlbertson, who had wandered away.

Joe took a good, deep swallow of the beer and wondered what to expect of the capsule.

"If you want the word on that brother and sister act," Ratso said, "*I'll* give you the word: Hansel's a fag, and Gretel's got the hots for herself. So who cares, right?" He thrust a thumb into the air in the direction of the refreshment table. "They got salami up to here. So put some in your pocket already."

Joe felt himself being stared at. He turned to look and there, standing in front of the bathroom door, was a girl in an orange dress, smiling at him in a dark, provocative way. She leaned on the door frame in a manner that made

188

the bathroom seem to be her very own tent on a techni-
color desert—or perhaps she shared it with other members of the harem. She met his eyes boldly, opening her
own even wider, and then bared her teeth and gave a mad
little trill of a laugh. Running her fingers through her rich,
black hair, she came toward him. Joe liked her body: It
was slim-legged but thickly sensual, built close to the
ground.

She said, "I can tell, can't you?"

"Yeah," Joe faked it, "Hell yeah, I can tell."

"Well then," she said, "what'll we do? Leave now, or
what? Have you got a place? Because I've got this
damned roommate. Well, that doesn't matter, I can fix it.
Because we have this arrangement. Oh *God!* the second I
looked at you, I knew. Did you know right away?"

"Did I know, uh . . ."

"That we were going to make it?"

Ratso spoke up. "You really want to do business, don't
you, lady?"

Obviously the woman hadn't noticed Ratso; she looked
at him with surprise. "Who are *you?* Oh, God! Don't tell
me you two are a *couple!*"

"I happen to be his manager," said Ratso. "And he happens to be Joe Buck, a very expensive stud."

"Ex*pensive! Expensive?*" Her mouth dropped open. She
looked away, blinked, looked at Ratso again, and then at
Joe. "Is this *true?*"

"Well, now . . ." Joe began to hedge.

"Oh *God!*" she cried. "It *is!* I can't believe it." She wandered away—not escaping, just stupefied. She opened a
beer for herself, then leaned against the refreshment
table, looking at the tall cowboy, shaking her head, blinking.

Ratso said, "She's hooked. I'd say she was good for ten bucks. But I'll ask for twenty."

Joe said, "Listen, money or no money, I could *use* some of that."

"Oh hell yeah, you're *rich!* Go talk to her. I'll move in later." Ratso walked away.

Joe was beginning to feel weightless. He rolled his shoulders in slow circles, as if to test his ability to move, and found that he had some new possession of his body: It had become remarkable to him again, a thing of grace and power. And he even experienced that old longing for a mirror.

The black-haired woman was at his side looking up at him as if there were a vast difference in height between them.

"I'm *ter*ribly excited," she said. "This is the first time in my life I've ever been confronted by, well, that I've ever even heard of the mere existence of this sort of a situation. And I'm frankly terribly excited. I can't wait to tell my man but I don't have an appointment till Monday, isn't that rotten? Listen, I'm just speculating, you know, but what would happen if I said, 'Okay I'm buying'? *Oooh!*"

The woman suddenly shuddered. She had a fine, handsome nose. The nostrils dilated. She was breathing in short gasps. "I am em*bar*rassed," she said, "and this is *not Dexedrine!* I've had my *weight* in Dexedrine, and it never did *this* to me. I should *def*initely take notes: the breathing, the heart, the stomach, and *look! Goose pimples!*"

She showed him her arm; Joe smiled modestly.

"What *is* this? Buying a man, is that it? Well, I guess it's the most thrilling thing I've ever heard of. It's like, well, you take virginity, that's *one* end of something. And on the other, absolute opposite, farthest, most utterly dis-

190

tant pole is *buying a lover,* I suppose. Isn't it? Of course, leave us face this, I am a long way from virginity. *That* was never my problem. It's just that way way way back, *years* ago, I used to think I had to marry everybody I had an affair with. Primitive?"

She laughed, but her laughter did not interfere with the flow of her speech. "But after three husbands, count 'em, three, my man finally got it through my thick skull that I had become a perfect, living, walking example of Bronx morality in its most *stif*ling form, are you with me? *Then! Breakthrough!* And what do I do, I begin to act as if I have to have an *affair* with everybody I go to bed with! Don't you see? Just a *very* transparent extension of the same old morality bit. You have to agree, because what's an affair but marriage *sans* mumbo jumbo? I mean, *emo*tionally, you're taking just as much *pun*ishment! Aren't you? From a lover as from a husband? No argument there? Good! So!

"Suddenly it dawned on me: *What,* if you please, is wrong with just plain old s-e-x? I was *sure* this is what my man had been getting at. Of course they don't say it straight out, it has to come from you. Which if you're as dumb as I am, and I can be awfully dumb in certain departments, can be *terribly expensive.* Let's just not *think* about what this thing has cost me in terms of *good hard cash!* Okay? Anyway, I began to, well, walk through a few things, *you* know, just trying my legs, and baby, it was *no*where: I couldn't even reach a climax!

"*Then!* Tonight, when I came out of that bathroom and saw you, pure symbol—that's what you are, you know, symbol, oh yes, pure symbol, nothing more, nothing less. You didn't know that? I can't believe it. Anyway, I *knew* I was going to make a *real* breakthrough. No thinking,

191

either, my dear, huh-*uh;* feeling, just *feel*ing. You *see* the state I'm in, don't you? And didn't I walk right up to you? Well, I can tell you I've never done *that* before! What do you think I *am?* I simply had this feeling and there was nothing I could do about it, and furthermore I didn't *want* to do anything about it. Oh, when the time comes, naturally, I'll have to ask myself *why* do I choose a cowboy, and second, why a cowboy *whore.*

"But not tonight! No, sir. Being analytical *during* is the kiss of death. Your orgasm goes *right* out the window. Kiss me right now, will you? Before we talk the whole thing away? *Hey listen!* Would it embarrass you if I turned on this great big glaring ceiling light over my bed and looked at you *all over?* Because I've never really studied a man completely, I mean every square inch of him, and I'm *dying* to. May I? I mean aren't peculiar requests a part of your profession?

"And incidentally, how much is this going to cost me, anyway?"

2

joe watched the woman speak. But his hearing wasn't working in the usual way. All her talk might have been rain and there was glass between them. He heard her words and he saw them but they never got to him.

What he did hear was something that had to do with the capsule he'd swallowed, a high, thin, private sound, not really a sound at all. You could just as easily *picture* it: say it was a high wire he had flown to, at some altitude that caused a blending of all the senses, sight, sound, touch, making them one.

At one such moment, he chose to see the party from this altitude: saw a cowboy, himself, looking past a jumble of faceless party figures toward the end of the room where two young people in black sat on the floor at the feet of a woman.

But from his point of view these three people were not three at all: They were four: and one of them was himself. He belonged there with them. He was Joe Buck, the cowboy, and there was his blonde, sitting with the two beautiful children.

Now of course it was clear to him why he had been invited to the party: He was the missing member of something, always had been, but now everything would be straightened out.

There was a commotion at the other end of the room. Heads turned to watch what appeared to be the introduction of some sort of entertainment. The bongo player produced a drum roll and the girl on the recorder did her best to imitate a fanfare.

The MacAlbertsons, meanwhile, helped their lady to her feet. She seemed to be either drunk or drugged. But once on her feet she was able to walk under her own power, giving the effect of an imperfectly operated marionette. There was the clank and tinkle and jangle of costume jewelry as she pushed dozens of bracelets from her wrists up toward her elbows and made her way to the center of the room.

Joe believed that this was the moment at which the

purpose of the evening would be made clear to others as it was to him. A kind of wedding was taking place, a wedding of a somewhat unusual sort, more a reunion in which the principals had a deeper, more mysterious than usual kinship with one another. The fact that he had never actually seen these three people before tonight did not seem at all contradictory: His chimerical vision was such that any rupture in the usual logic of things achieved at once a new and higher order of fitness all its own.

For instance, what happened next was in a certain sense impossible, but nevertheless he saw it take place. The white-haired woman took one sweeping gaze at the people gathered there, and as she did so her eye touched upon Joe's for a moment and then moved on. He trembled and his entire body went cold with shock. For in that moment he had been looked upon by Sally Buck. She was much older now and more outlandish than he had remembered her. But still she was Sally Buck, and he had had this brief, coldly vivid view of her. And he knew now that it was his grandmother, returned from the grave, who had sent those two sad-as-death, poisonously pretty children into the streets of New York to search for him. And for what purpose? To tell him something urgent, of course. And here it was, the message was about to be spoken:

The MacAlbertsons, looking for all the world like dream children, slender and neuter in their tight black clothing, clearly the sort of young you'd send as messengers from the grave, had drawn close to the old lady, perhaps to catch her if she fell or to lend some other form of support. Now she raised her hands in a bid for attention, and when everyone was quiet, her hands flew to her face and she began to giggle and cough. She seemed to

194

have forgotten what she was supposed to say. There followed a quick huddle with the MacAlbertsons.

Joe's harem woman, the one in the orange dress, asked him why he was perspiring, but Joe didn't seem to hear the question. Then she said, "I think you ought to eat something, because the trick is to keep eating, don't you know that? Shall I get you a sandwich?"

He said something to her and she went away.

Now both the old lady and the girl were pointing at the boy called Hansel. Every eye in the room followed his movements as he painted a great black X on the sign, canceling out the words IT'S LATER THAN YOU THINK. He replaced the broom in the bucket and joined his sister. The two of them nodded at the old woman, restoring to her the attention of the room. She made more noises with her bracelets and coughed up some phlegm, which she spat into a handkerchief tucked into her waist. Then she held up one hand for silence, waited for it, got it, and spoke in a loud, flat, shaky, Midwestern drawl.

"It's not later than y'think, not n'more it idden."

She paused, sucking in her cheeks and pursing her lips as if they were too dry for more speech: The effect was of a series of quick desperate kisses being sent into the air of the party. Gretel MacAlbertson gave her a sip of beer. The woman licked her lips and gasped, then suddenly shouted: "Time!"—holding both hands motionless in the air and seeming to suspend the very commodity under discussion. There was another series of coughing spasms.

The party waited in silence for a moment, but slowly a murmuring started and grew, and Joe heard a man say, "She'd rather be here than in some doorway. Besides, she's too far gone to know what they're doing to her." And a woman answered: "Oh, don't tell me she doesn't know. I think it's cruel. These people still have minds, no matter how far gone they are!"

The old woman huddled again with the MacAlbertsons, obviously being coached by them. Then she faced the gathering once more and suddenly shouted: "Time is run out on us. They ain't no more of it!" Her lips rolled back, showing small yellow teeth and a mechanical smile that appeared to have no other purpose than to display the very last trick of the marionette master.

She looked at the MacAlbertsons for approval. They both nodded vigorously. Then, as if she had broken in the middle, the old woman's top half fell forward in a jangle of metal. She was taking a bow. The MacAlbertsons applauded. Everyone joined in. The noise grew to absurd, thunderous proportions, was further increased by whistles, shouting, foot stomping and even two or three screams.

Ratso was at Joe's side, nudging him with his elbow. "How come you're clapping? What the hell was 'at supposed to be, a song an' a dance? I thought they were gonna make her bite the head off a chicken at least."

Joe moved away from Ratso, threading his way through the noise, stepping over spread-out legs and around crossed knees and cocktail tables and benches and musicians, closer and closer to the old woman, who had returned by now to her chair behind the MacAlbertsons.

The dark lady in orange suddenly appeared in his path holding in both hands a big, thick sandwich. "I thought you *wanted* this!" she said.

Joe said, "Thanks," but he didn't take the sandwich. He touched her shoulder, she stepped aside, he continued to move toward the old woman.

He felt that the party had suddenly gone wrong. A moment ago he had known something. Something impor-

196

tant about his life had come clear to him, and then he had forgotten it. Or perhaps he had only been on the brink of knowing and it had been withheld from him. By this old lady. Who was she?

He studied her from this close range and found her to be even older than she had appeared during the entertainment. She was apparently in pain, too—seemed to have been knocked silly by it. Her forehead was creased with a network of tensions and lines. The face powder she wore covered some kind of skin eruption. Her eyes, blinking constantly, seemed never to have known rest. They were the quivering blooms of some endless suffering whose beginnings had long ago been forgotten. At odd moments, an inner contraction caused her to wince as if she had been kicked, her eyes would remain closed for a moment, and her face would buckle into a mess of painted creases like an exploded candy sack.

Joe tried to remember just what it was he had come to ask of the old lady—or of the MacAlbertsons, for that matter. He stood right in front of them, but they paid no attention to him whatever: They seemed to have no power to look upon anything or anyone, except one another. And Joe himself was no longer able to see them from high up. His special sense had somehow gone dead on him. He no longer felt any kinship with these people. They were just a pretty boy and a pretty girl and a sick old lady trying to have a party. He had always wondered about parties, and now he was attending one and he didn't much like it: If this was any sample, parties were even sadder than the streets were.

A big man with a shiny round face grabbed Joe's arm and said, "Didn't you hear what Mother Ceres said? She said you'd ticked your last tick-tock. So lay down, baby,

197

you're dead." The man laughed and moved on to someone else, saying, "Did you hear what I said to that guy? I said, didn't you hear what Mother Ceres said? She said . . ."

Joe went at once into action. He moved quickly to the man's side, took hold of him with both arms, and said: "Hey, how come you pick me?"

"Pick you," said the man with the round face. "What do you mean, pick you?"

"I mean, how come you said that to me? You think they's somethin' wrong with me, or what?"

"You're *crazy*," the man said. "Let go my arm."

"I ain't hurtin' your arm. I want a answer," Joe said.

Gretel MacAlbertson was standing there. "Thanks for coming," she said to Joe, "but we want you to go now."

Ratso was there, too. He said, "What're you, bombed?" Then to the MacAlbertsons he said, "He's just bombed, that's all."

As Ratso led him from the room and into the hallway, Joe said, "I'm not bombed. I was, but I'm not."

Ratso's coat had got buried; he began to rummage around for it.

Joe said, "I'm in a mess, is what I'm in. I'm in a big mess, and I got to fuck m'way out of it."

Ratso said, "I feel crummy. I got to lie down."

The woman with the orange dress appeared in the doorway. "Hey."

Joe looked at her and she said, "I asked you how much, didn't I?"

Joe kept his eye on the woman as he said, "Tell 'er, Ratso."

Ratso said, "Twenty dollars."

The woman said, "Sold. Mine's the dyed mouton. Under the gray herringbone. Let's go."

Ratso said, "And taxi fare for me. Twenty for him, and taxi fare for me. Okay?"

The woman said, "You know what I think? I think you ought to get lost, *bad* lost. Y'know? Like *dead!*"

"I agree," Ratso said. "And for that service, I charge one dollar for taxi fare."

The woman took a dollar from a small roll in her bosom and handed it to him. "When I count ten, begone. One, two, three . . ."

Ratso started down the stairs.

Joe helped the woman into her coat. "Hey," he said. "Uh, what's your name—honey?"

"Oh!" she said. "You don't *know*, do you? I *love* that. But I know yours is Joe. Which is fabulous. Joe could be just anybody. Kiss me Joe, hold me Joe, move over Joe, go away Joe. *Mar*vie! A perfect name for a male, um—person! Sort of like Rose for a girl."

Below them was the sound of someone falling downstairs. Joe ran down the two flights two steps at a time and found Ratso on the first floor struggling with the banister trying to pull himself to his feet. Then he took a second fall. Joe picked him up and Ratso gave instructions on how he was to be lowered to the floor. Joe lowered him onto his stronger leg. Ratso clung to the newel post, his teeth clenched and his face dead white.

The woman had arrived by now on the second landing. As she descended the final flight of steps, she said, "What's the matter?"

"He fell," Joe said.

"Is he all right?"

"What're you, smart?" Ratso said, then mimicked: "*'Is he all right?'* "

"Well, if you're all right," she said, "why are you hanging onto the banister? Can you walk or not?"

"Can I walk! *Natch*'ly I can walk." He took three steps, catching himself at the door. "What d'ya call that?"

"Yeah," Joe said, "but to the subway?"

"No no, I'm infirm, I'll never make it," Ratso imitated a damsel. "Carry me!"

The woman said, "He's got taxi fare." She turned to Ratso. "You're all right. Right?"

Ratso shouted, "*I said yeah already!*"

"He's all right," the woman told Joe. "Let's go."

3

an hour later, the woman, lying with her head supported on her elbow, touched at Joe with her free hand.

"That *hap*pens," she said. "Don't worry about it. I mean, are you worried about it? Well, don't be. Why don't we just sort of lie here and—see what happens. Maybe even nap a little, huh?"

Joe reached across the bed and took a cigarette from the nightstand. "That's something never happen to *me* before, you can bet your bottom dollar on *that*. Um, where's the matches, ma'am?"

"In the top drawer." While Joe lit his cigarette, she said,

"Maybe if you didn't call me ma'am, things'd work out better."

Joe lay on his back and blew smoke up toward the ceiling. "First goddam time 'at thing ever quit on me."

A short laugh came from the woman.

Joe looked at her quickly. "What? You think I'm lying?"

She made an effort to straighten her face out. "No! Of course not. Something struck me funny, that's all."

"Yeah?" Joe said. "Well, what was that?"

"But it's nothing."

"Nothing, huh?"

"Oh please now! Honestly."

Joe nodded his head and looked at the ceiling again.

"All right, I'll *tell* you," she said. "Suddenly I just put myself in your *shoes,* and I realized that being a pro-*fess*ional, well, that must be what really bothers you about a thing like this. Not that you *should* be bothered, because its merely human, but I had this sudden awful picture of a bugler without a horn or a policeman without a stick, et cetera et cetera, and I just . . . I think I better shut up, I'm making it *worse!*"

Joe's mind was working hard. He was turning over all the possible reasons for his failure, thinking of all the ways in which he had been weakened and wearied since his arrival in New York. And thinking of it, he felt the weakness, the weariness, like something running through him in place of blood. Little by little, the city had been drawing all that good juice from him, a little here, a little there, everything going out, nearly every second of the day, the sidewalks at every step drawing something out of him through his feet, the traffic noises sucking at his ears, the neon signs pulling something vital from his eyes, and nothing much coming in, coffee here, soup there, now and then a plate of wet spaghetti, a hamburger made of spiced sawdust, a bottle of beer. And none of it nourishing to anything in him except this weariness. . . .

When he awakened there were streaks of daylight at the edges of the window shades. The same thoughts, thoughts of himself being weakened, rushed through his head now with a kind of dream continuity. He saw himself being drained and robbed and swindled in a thousand impossible ways: Every smile cost him some ungodly sum, and every time he nodded in assent to a stranger, a vital substance was exacted from him. If a clock ticked or a breeze blew or a wheel turned in his presence, within range of his senses, it seemed somehow to have stolen his energy to fuel itself.

Nearly overwhelmed by these thoughts, he was surprised to discover that his power had returned to him while he slept. He put his hand on himself, touched deeply, almost to the point of hysteria, by a sense of relief and good fortune. But this passed quickly, giving way to a desire for some sort of vengeance. He wanted to say something with this power, wanted to make it count for something, use it for a protest, wanted to write his initials across the sky with it and a warning too in black letters that would make them tremble.

The woman next to him was asleep on her back. He reached out and placed his hand over her, curving his palm and his fingers in the shape of a cup and pressing them against her great warmth.

In a moment they were together and she was crying out with every breath. He drove at her in a measured, systematic way that seemed calculated not for his pleasure but for her punishment. But the woman liked this game. She bit his shoulder to earn more of this splendid wrath, and he had to cup his hand over her mouth and press on it hard to muzzle those teeth, and he continued to work and to work and to work and to work and the woman's eyes were wild and she moaned through his hand and slobbered in the palm of it and worked her mouth against it, and with her body she said, Oh yeah? Oh yeah? Oh yeah? and met everything he had to say with his, and they had established a kind of dogged and laborious and insistent fight between them, but she wanted more anger and so she clawed at his back with her fingernails and Joe knew she'd brought blood out of him, that he was being drained again. Now they were taking his blood. But this time he'd caught them in the act; well, he'd show them; and so he drove at her harder, and deeper, and deeper, and deeper, and now there were tears coming from the woman's eyes and all her breath came and went from her accompanied by some animal noise that was more vicious than a growl, and he took his hand away from her mouth and looked at her and saw that her face was something terrible, and so he called her something terrible and that helped her, something broke inside of her and she began to laugh and cry, alternating rapidly between the two like a madwoman, and it was clear to Joe Buck that the woman knew she was going to have her freedom, and he labored with greater and greater insistence to deliver it to her, not because he wanted her free but because he wanted to feel himself the deliverer, wanted to know that power again in himself, and then there was a long low cry like a deliberate scream coming from her, and he kept on for a moment as if he wanted to sign his name in blood and with a flourish to what he had done; and in doing this, something unexpected happened: He himself was set free. And then he allowed all of his weight to rest upon the woman. She kept her arms around him, smeared with her hand the blood she had drawn from his back. And she kept telling him over and over again the most common name for the act they had performed, as if the experience might be improved or prolonged or even somehow immortalized in the dirty-naming of it. And as Joe lay upon her, his eyes deep in the pillow, two young people in black walked into his mind, slender and blond and plain as day: the MacAlbertsons. And for a moment, briefly, while the woman recited her obscene litany of small words, he looked at these children in his mind and entered into their mystery. Saw them come into being full-grown before his eyes, saw them walking hand in hand against a backdrop of nothingness, together but unjoined, motherless and fatherless and without real gender, unconnected to the world or to who they themselves were, or where, or what, saw them wandering in search of others passing through the same empty regions, others born loose and alien and unconnected as they themselves were, and in this brief clarity Joe Buck had a sense of knowing just who the children were: his own. His own offspring, born full-grown from this very night's union.

4

When Joe left the woman's apartment that afternoon, he had his stomach full of food and hot coffee, he was freshly bathed and shaved, he had poured a lot of expensive-smelling cologne into his boots to counteract the odor, and he had twenty dollars riding on his hip.

At Times Square he bought a pair of socks and some clean underwear and changed into them in the men's room at the Automat. The old underwear and socks were in sorry shape, and, feeling extravagant, he flushed them down the toilet. Then he decided to spend fifty cents to have his boots shined, and while they were being worked on he counted his money and thought about what he might do with it. It occurred to him he should have bought some underwear and socks for the runt. And perhaps some food as well. And medicine.

At the drugstore on Eighth Avenue he bought aspirin, cough syrup and vitamin pills and then proceeded to the army-navy store, where he bought a pair of long underwear and two pairs of red woolen socks, one large and one small, to accommodate the difference in Ratso's feet.

Hurrying down Eighth Avenue with these purchases, Joe sang *The Last Roundup* in double time, oblivious to the stares of other pedestrians. The afternoon sun was melting the piles of filthy snow along the gutters, and he had to step deftly over the soft slush to keep from spoiling the new shine on his boots. Certain store windows and two or three mirrors along the way gave him a reflection of a cowboy passing by in splendid style, and at some of them he paused to smile at himself and tense his buttocks a time or two to savor all the power he had in there. His final purchase, a carton of hot chicken soup, was made at a good Jewish delicatessen in the block near 30th Street.

Arriving at the X-flat, he stopped on the stairs to check his parcels: socks, underwear, medicine, soup, cigarettes. Something about the socks stopped his mind. He placed the other packages on one of the steps and removed the socks from the paper sack, holding one pair in each hand.

He looked at them for a long time, straining after some thought or other. He pondered for a moment the peculiarity of Ratso's foot sizes, but that wasn't what he was after. He wanted something that would clarify a feeling he had in himself about all of these purchases, not just the socks. But whatever it was, it wouldn't stand still for him.

He gathered up the packages and climbed the stairs to the flat.

Ratso had a number of blankets wrapped around him and his teeth were clamped together to keep them from chattering. He swallowed two aspirins with a little water, but he couldn't get any of the soup down until the chills subsided. By then, Joe had to warm it again in a little pan over the canned heat, and now Ratso was sweating so that he wanted to remove all of his blankets entirely. They quarreled over the wisdom of this, and also over the question of a name for Ratso's complaint. Joe wanted to call it cat fever, a name Sally had liked to apply to a number of disorders he'd suffered in childhood on the theory that all sicknesses came from cats, but Ratso said he hadn't been *near* a cat, and besides, what he had was the flu.

While he drank the soup, Joe showed him the socks and long underwear. Ratso looked at them and shook his head.

"They wrong?" Joe asked.

"No. But while you was buying the underwear I could've *hooked* the socks. That's okay, though." As an afterthought, he added, "Thanks." Then he said, "Hey, Joe, don't get sore about this or anything, you promise?"

"Yeah."

"Promise?"

"*Yeah.*"

"Well, I don't think I can walk." Ratso looked at the

wall. He was obviously embarrassed. "I mean, I been fallin' down a lot and—uh."

"And what?"

"I'm scared." He put the soup on the floor next to the pile of blankets and began to shiver again. He clamped his jaws together and held his arms tight against his body.

"What *of?*" Joe said.

"I *tole* you already!"

"I know, but . . ."

"Of what'll *hap*pen," Ratso said. "I mean what do they uh, you know—*do* with you—if you can't, uh . . . Agh, *shit!*"

"Who? What does *who* do with you?"

"I don't know. The *cops*. Or the—how should *I* know?"

"You mean," Joe said, "like if you can't walk?"

Ratso nodded.

"Then what do they *do* with you?"

Ratso nodded some more. Then Joe got to his feet and began to shout. "Well, what's the cops got to do with that? That's none of their fucking business who walks and who don't! Man, I swear, you talk like a person with a paper asshole! Don't you know what you and me's going to do? You and me's going to Florida."

"Florida! What the—"

"Just a matter of bus fare is all."

"Come on with *Florida* already. Cut the crap." Ratso frowned and searched Joe's face for some sign of sense.

Joe said, "I been figuring main thing we break our ass for here is keep warm. Right? What you're doing now, you're shivering, see? Second main thing is food. Right again, right? Well, in Florida it's a matter of coconuts and sunshine and all that, and you don't break your ass at all.

Use y'head, Ratso, you know them things, we talked about all this shee-it plenty times, did you forget?"

He took out his money and displayed it, spreading the bills out like a poker hand. "This here's the start, what I made last night. Tonight I'm making the rest. It's all set, I was just waiting to let you know is all. Now tell me this, we figure the bus to take thirty-eight a piece, okay? So times two is how much?"

"What, you gonna take *me?*" Ratso said.

Joe nodded. "So times two is how much?"

"Seventy-six. Listen, Joe, I got nineteen. It's in that shoe."

"Where'd you get nineteen?"

Joe went after the shoe and pulled out the money.

Ratso said, "I went through them coats last night."

"What coats?"

"At the party, at the party, for chrissake! 'Member in the stairway? All them coats? Well, I got nineteen dollars."

"All right. And with this nine it makes what? How much more I got to get then?"

Ratso closed his eyes for a few seconds, then said, "Fifty. Let's say fifty. That's too much, huh?"

"Too much *fooey,*" Joe said. "Mood I'm in, it ain't *nothing.* I'll see you later."

At the door, he looked back. "You get into them long johns," he said. "And the *socks!* We ain't hauling ass onto no bus and you stinking it up with feet!"

Ratso was staring at Joe and past him. "I can't believe it, I can't believe it. I just cannot goddam be*lieve* it." Then he sat forward, "Hey, wait a minute!" He shook his head back and forth as he said, "You're not gonna do something real *dumb,* are you, and end up with your ass in a sling?"

Joe said, "Can't you shut up? Can't you? Can't you just once shut up and let me do something? I mean is they a law says Joe Buck can't have a one lousy i-dea 'thout getting his ass in a sling, just one puny little *i*-goddam-fuckin'-*dea*?" He came back into the room and flopped into a chair, making his feet land heavy on the floor. "Now you gone and shot m'whole mood right in the ass!"

But he rose again at once and returned to the door. "No you didn't neither," he said. "I'm *damned* if you did! You and me's leavin' town tonight."

He slammed the door and went down the stairs two at a time.

5

Joe scanned the doorways and theater lobbies and penny arcades of Times Square in search of a moneymaking opportunity, and for the first two hours nothing much happened. It was too cold to stand still for long periods. He wasted some fifteen minutes in Duffy Square on a prospect too frightened to speak up, and another even larger piece of an hour was squandered in following a pretty woman all the way over to Grand Central Station only to watch her board the train for New Haven. He walked back to Times Square and all the way up Broadway to 50th Street, over to and down Eighth Avenue and across 42nd again, then covered the same ground a second and a third time, warming up between trips in a dirty-books shop and at a gameroom called Fascination where he lost a dollar and twenty cents.

And then along about eight o'clock, having forgotten for the moment the object of his hunt, he was looking idly in the window of a Seventh Avenue magic shop when he realized that the liveliest possibility of the evening had shown itself less than three feet from him and was looking in the same store window.

This was a red, white and blue person of about fifty. He was stocky, almost fat, with very black eyebrows. He had a pleasant, round face that seemed always to be smiling, even in repose, and his eyes were anxious and uncertain of every single thing in the world. But the most vivid aspect of the man were those colors of a musical comedy American: the red of his complexion, the pure white of his hair and his silk muffler, and the lively blue of his eyes and his overcoat.

Joe had been taught that you weren't supposed to be the first to speak. You had to let them do that. There were a number of theories in support of this policy: For one thing, speaking first showed a certain eagerness that was apt to lower your price, and for another, if your prospect turned out to be a policeman in disguise, he would arrest you for soliciting.

But Joe felt the necessity of making a strike before the cold really got through to him. At a certain point on these winter nights in the doorways of Times Square his face became numb and pale and he was unable to think clearly or behave with any ease at all; from then on he would begin to look and act like a loser and no one would want anything to do with him at all.

And so he threw caution to the winds and screwed up a

210

good big smile and swung his eyes onto that red, white and blue face, and was about to speak when the man himself spoke up.

"How are *you*?" The big face broke open in the middle, showing still more red and white in the gums and perfect teeth, and he clasped Joe's hand in both of his own.

From his first words the man succeeded in establishing an atmosphere of extraordinary intimacy. A stranger observing the scene might have said that two friends of long standing had come together in a surprise reunion after years of agonizing separation.

His voice—he started talking at once in a way that suggested he might never stop—was deep and rich and vigorous and at the same time oddly prissy, giving him the aspect of a hysterical, somewhat sissified bull. Introducing himself as Townsend P. (for Pederson) Locke of Chicago ("Call me Towny"), he said he was "in paper" and had come to New York to attend a manufacturers' convention. "And frankly, to have a little fun, dammit," he added, like a person who has decided to put his foot down.

"This is my first night and I'll consider it a ghastly omen, clouding my entire ten days, if you don't consent to have dinner with me. Please! It's *aw*fully important to me. You will? You'll say yes?"

Joe found that his assent wasn't really needed. For he had hardly begun to nod when he found himself being almost forcibly conducted up 42nd Street. Towny did not once stop talking. What's more, he wasn't the kind of talker who required any sign of listening. He flitted from topic to topic in butterfly fashion: Chicago, food, his mother, the convention, New York, people in general, cowboys, the need for "fun," his mother again, the Midwest, restaurants, religion, Michigan Avenue, the art of conversation. ("That's what I like about you, you're such a wonderful conversationalist," he said at one point, causing Joe to open his eyes wide and nod in amazement.)

"Now where would you like to eat? I give you your choice of all the restaurants on the island of Manhattan. No, no, on the entire East Coast. If there's some place in New Jersey or Long Island or even Philadelphia that you absolutely hanker for, we'll hire a car. Now you say! Chambord? 21? The Luau? Never mind how you're dressed. They know me. I'll tell them you're with the rodeo, there's always a rodeo in New York. Besides, you look very elegant, and these places, the really good ones, never fret over neckties or any of that *nouveau* chichi crap. Oh!" —a snap of the fingers— "But dammitall, I'll tell you what we'll have to do, we'll have to eat in my room because I have this phone call coming at nine-thirty. My mother always calls me at her bedtime and I've got to be there. She's ninety-four and at that age it seems to me you can just damn well be there when they call up to say good night, don't you agree to that? So won't that be nice? To have dinner sent up? I've got a very modest, perfectly pleasant suite at the Europa near Ninth Avenue. All my fancy friends stay at the Pierre or the Plaza and they can have it! 'Why do you stay down there, Townsend, please?' Well, of course, I know and you know that fifty years ago the Europa was the only hotel in Manhattan: those high ceilings, all that marble in the bathrooms. *We* have an eye for real quality." He squeezed Joe's arm. "As opposed to mere fashion. Here! Look!"

As they turned into the lobby, a young man with a thin, cold, dedicated face pressed a piece of paper into Joe's hand. It said, *You are in a burning building and Jesus is the only possible fireman.* He crumpled it and put it in his pocket.

"*Look* at this magnificent lobby!" said Townsend P. Locke.

The lobby of the Europa had become a kind of arcade for small enterprises. One corner had been partitioned off for a passport photographer, another piece had been given over to a health club, and so on; and there were a number of vending machines for candy bars, soft drinks and cigarettes. The floor was of cracked tile and had been recently scrubbed in a slapdash way, leaving streaks of dried dirt and a faint smell of ammonia in the air. The room clerk, a gray, small, not-really-there-at-all person, seemed to have been selected for his ability to project to the guests a profound lack of interest in their comings and goings.

They stepped onto a creaking, slow, self-operated elevator, and Townsend P. Locke talked all the way up to the fifth floor and kept on talking all the way down the hall ". . . Macy's, the Park, the Village, the lights, the millions of strangers from every possible part of the world . . ." He was listing the aspects of New York that delighted him most. ". . . the utter and total privacy, the sort of, I don't know, madly forward thrust of everything; do you understand that? I mean, how shall I put it? My sense of *time* here is completely altered. And Chicago, mind you, is no mere cow town. But here, you see, there's this grinding forward of every second. Listen! Listen! Hear it for yourself! Time is a Colossus, and he's marching up Broadway! Can't you hear him coming?"

They were in Locke's sitting room, standing at the window, looking out over 42nd Street. The sound he tried to name could be heard. It was an all-pervasive, throbbing roar, as if all the millions of machines and people on the island were united by a central rhythm and spoke with one voice and could be felt and heard as a single being of tremendous force. "You and I," Locke said, "contribute to it. Yes! Isn't that exciting? Think of it, your heart goes tum-te-tum-te-tum, and the projector in that theater goes clickety-clickety-click, and each one of those cars goes *ggggrrrrrhhhhhoooooommmmmmmmmm,* and *oh!* Just thinking about it is more than I can stand. Would you like a drink? I've got some nice gin. But if you prefer something else, they'll send it up. Maybe you drink only *añejo,* or Irish, or saki. Do speak up."

"Gin's fine."

"And I really do find it unbearably exciting," Locke continued, "this time thing in New York. But on the other hand, the identical awareness can hurl me straight into the abyss. I'm manic, you see, and I have these *hairy* depressions, and they all have to do with time. For instance, in Chicago, I often have this feeling that time really stopped about *twenty years ago!* And that everything that happened since is some hideous mistake. Isn't that morbid? *Par exemple,* in that mood it seems to me absolutely grotesque that there should be in the world *any*where this white-haired gentleman you see before you. He doesn't ex*ist!* There was a war, there was a young man in uniform, handsome as handsome can be, with quite black hair—and he was *supposed to die in the war!* But he didn't. There was some idiot mistake in heaven, and he's still here! Isn't that amusing?

"All right, that's enough about me. I am through talking for the evening. Here's your drink. Now I want to hear all about you and conditions out West. I mean, what's happening in cattle, for heaven sake? But first let me confess something to you: The West holds a tremendous power over me, the vastnesses there and the romance, that whole society of tumbleweed and leather. So you see, even if you weren't an exceptionally fine person—which I know you are, I knew that at once, gifted and sensitive and unusual in many ways—but even if you weren't all that, I would still undoubtedly have felt this, this, this . . ." he waved the palm of his hand back and forth over his heart as if it were a magnet that would draw out the word he wanted ". . . *rapport!*" He thrust the hand forward now as if rapport were displayed upon it. "Simply because you come from the great West. My mother shares this with me, indeed she does, she would absolutely adore you, and when she telephones—" he looked at his watch "—at about nine-thirty, I want you to get on the wire and say, 'Hello, Estelle, I'm—' What *is* your name?"

"Joe."

" 'Hello, Estelle, I'm Joe. And Townsend's being a very good boy.' —Or something, anything. I'll introduce you, I'll say you're a cowboy and she'll be *so* thrilled. Ninety-four years old! And a mind? Like a steel trap! May I tell you what I did for her on her birthday? Oh, listen to me! You can't possibly care what I did for a very dear old lady you've never even laid eyes on on her birthday, can you?"

"Oh hell yeah," Joe said. "I want to hear all about that."

Joe sensed there was some advantage to himself in keeping the man talking. He needed to think. There was some sort of money connected with the man, not millions perhaps, but plenty. Joe guessed he had chosen this hotel over the better ones because it afforded him the freedom to indulge his special appetites. They were seated now, Joe on the couch, Locke in an overstuffed chair. Joe wondered how long the talking would continue, how long be-

fore the man made the inevitable trip to the couch, lowered his hand to the knee, etc., and what would be the
best strategy to follow at that point. Make a straightfor-
ward business proposition? Launch into a do-me-a-favor
speech? There was something likable about the man, but
he tried not to notice it. Straight business was easier to
manage.

". . . and there stood this string quartet. Picture it, an
old lady propped up in her bed, pale-blue lace coverlet,
hair all in tiny curls—I do her hair myself twice a week—
and the Vienna String Quartet standing at her feet playing *Happy Birthday to You!*"

Locke sang a chorus, ending in *Happy birthday dear Es-
te-ulll, Happy birthday to you.* "Oh God!" There were
tears in his very blue eyes. "And the night before, they'd
played Beethoven to twenty-five-*hund*red people! That's
the kind of thing I do for her. I mean how else can you
amuse a woman who's *twenty years older than time?* And
of course it makes *my* life so rich. People say, oh, you're so
good to Estelle. Nonsense, I tell them, I'm good to myself!" This was spoken with a kind of savage force. Proceeding more quietly, he leaned forward and said, "Let
me explain: My mother happens to be an exceedingly rare
human being of the most extraordinary sensibilities. The
privilege of enjoying her company is worth any sacrifice. I
don't wish to overstate the case, but if I were to describe
my mother in such a way as to do her the most meager
justice, I would seem to be guilty of the grossest excesses.
Therefore I am usually silent on the subject, silent as a
stone, for the simple reason that the average person, having a very limited concept of the real possibilities of the
human spirit, is unable to grasp . . . For instance, let me
interrupt myself, I am often told, and even by very close

216

friends—oh, this is so sad, and such a comment on the poverty of—you won't believe it, but this relationship that I describe, these persons call it 'sick.' And do you know why? Because I haven't married! Well, I haven't chosen to and why in heaven's name should I?"

This thought silenced the man. He seemed to have forgotten Joe's presence, and he sat staring at an arm of the couch, frowning, teeth clenched. Then, suddenly aware of the drink in his hand, he raised it, so suddenly that he spilled part of it on his trousers, smiled, wiped it off, proposed "a toast to the Wild West!" and began to speak again.

"You see, I happen to be passionate on the subject, and of course we live in an age in which all passion is suspect. All the old values have these ugly little clinical names now: Loyalty is fixation, duty is guilt, and all love is some sort of a complex! You should hear Estelle, she's *so* amusing on the subject! And you see, it's rarely the psychiatrist himself who talks such nonsense, it's your best friends! But don't you think it takes a *tiny* mind to hand down such judgments on the secret heart of another? Would you be so impertinent? Of course not. Let me tell you what a real analyst says, may I? And this man is fifty dollars per hour, need I say more about his qualifications? Well, he says it's an extremely successful relationship. And why? Because it works!

"It's all very simple: The ideal of the infant is to maintain its mother's love—forever. I have done this. I have lived this ideal existence. The problems are relatively minor: First of all, she will predecease me. *Perhaps!* Oh, you see, that's one of the marvels of my mother's character: *She won't die!*" He pounded the chair arm with his fist. "It's true. These women of my mother's breed, they refuse to die, they are on the side of life. They will not say yes to death. They have far too much love of life in them simply to let go of it all. That's courage. That's how this country was traversed in the covered-wagon days. The men were supported, cajoled, driven on by these women, and that's how the primitive was conquered, annihilated. Do you realize—and this is not at all off the track, this is the very heart of the matter—my mother went to Minnesota in a wagon? In other words—let me interpret, let me tell you what this means—in her lifetime, this country has gone from the pioneer stage to this complete *flowering* that all of us enjoy today. You and I, Joe, every day we reap the harvest in this garden spot of the world. And it's these women who planted the seeds, yes, we owe it all to them, this entire wonderful civilization of ours, every scrap of it is their making.

"And not only did they do their job, but think of the *speed!* My boy, there is no country in the entire history of the world that has progressed from the brute to the utterly civilized with such dispatch, such efficiency. And *there's* your reason." He pointed rather coyly to Estelle's picture and winked at it. The old lady in the photograph appeared to be modestly accepting the compliment. "Isn't she cute? The dead image of Queen Victoria. Our entire home is done in Victorian, pierced rosewood and red velvet, and we live in a glorious tower overlooking the lake, and with such grace and style. I take her to the theater and all the concerts in her wheelchair—when she's up to it. Don't I?" he said to the picture. And then he blew it a kiss and declared it was time to eat.

There followed a long telephone conversation in which the room clerk told Locke there was no restaurant in the hotel, and Locke tried assiduously to convince the room clerk that he was mistaken in this peculiar notion, there had to be a restaurant because he was hungry.

At one point he cupped his hand over the mouthpiece and described the impasse to his guest. "Joe, can you believe it, this poor man's got it into his head that there's no restaurant in this entire hotel. And of course there's no reasoning with these people any more. The railroads are the same way. You see why I'm forced to fly?"

At length the recalcitrant clerk "admitted" that there was a Chinese restaurant in the next block and promised to send someone for chop suey and egg rolls.

Before, during, and after this meal, and even while his large white teeth were being picked and sucked, Locke continued to spew out words. He seemed to be building something with them, one of those nightmare constructions that is constantly being undermined at a slightly greater rate of speed than one is able to achieve in the building. This one seemed to have to do with the identity of Joe Buck, for even though the conversation had little to do with him, it proceeded on the assumption that Locke's guest was a kind of ideal and perfect being, composed of all the manliness and heroism of an early Gary Cooper with the culture and sensibility and compassion of a Ronald Colman. Locke seemed to be afraid that if his visitor were allowed to speak so much as one full sentence, the construction would topple.

Meanwhile Joe Buck found it unnecessary to listen to what was said. He merely cocked an eyebrow, set his face at a certain tilt, and whenever the speaker smiled he followed suit and nodded agreeably. Occasionally he would tune in on a phrase or two: "My mother can't bear anything depressing!" "Of course you cattle people understand these matters far better than I, a mere paper merchant." "Back to my thesis then: The brutes tamed the country and the women tamed the brutes, the latter of course having by *far* the more difficult job, and succeeding, I'd say, *al*most entirely, wouldn't you agree?"

And Joe's thoughts would return to the problem of getting the evening onto a paying basis. But he made little progress. The words of his host acted upon him with a soporific, almost paralyzing effect. He had constantly to fight against falling into an actual trance of boredom by shifting his position, rubbing his neck, cracking his knuckles, squinting.

It was after eleven when the telephone rang. Joe seized this opportunity to go into the bathroom, where he could consult himself in the mirror. As he left the room, Locke was speaking loudly and distinctly into the mouthpiece.

"Do you want to hear about a coincidence? . . . Mama, a co-*in*-cidence. Guess who we were talking about at this very mo-ment? . . . I said, when the phone rang, guess who was being dis-cussed. . . . Dis-cussed. . . . No, not disgusted! Dis-*c-c-c-c*-cussed. Talked about! . . . Oh, Mama! Haven't you got it turned up? Which one are you wearing? . . . *That* one's no good, why aren't you wearing the Acousticon? . . . *A-cou-sti-con*! . . . Mama, dammit, this is im-pah-see-bull!"

In the bathroom, Joe splashed his face and neck with cold water until he felt that some blood had returned to his head. Then he leaned in very close to his own image and whispered: "Minute that sombitch gets off the telly-goddam-phone, you move into action. That's an order!"

6

•

Joe looked around for something to steal. There was an electric razor on the top of the toilet, but it was too bulky for his pocket. Besides, under a palm tree, where would you plug the thing in? There was nothing worth bothering about in the medicine chest either. But he did help himself to some cologne water again: took off his boots and opened his clothing and sloshed himself good with the stuff.

Then he listened at the door. Locke's telephone conversation showed no signs of terminating. Joe turned again to the mirror and began a rehearsal:

"Listen, mister, uh—I mean, Towny. Listen, Towny, did I mention to you my kid is sicker'n shee-it? Well, he is, and I got to get him South quick as I can. Yeah. Well, I, uh, I don't know *what* all he's got wrong. Had polio when he was teensy, and now he's snottin' at the nose, shivers and sweats all the time, busted leg, ever' damn thing. So what I thought, Towny, I thought I better get him on down South quick. Now listen. Now *listen*. *Listen to me, goddam ya!*—Sssssh," he cautioned himself and then continued the rehearsal in a whisper.

"Now if you'll just listen to me, Towny. Oh, I've had a hell of a good time here tonight listenin' to you for about forty-eight hours straight. Oh my yes, I've sure enjoyed it,

221

ever' goddam pissy-ass second of it. But now *you* listen awhile. I want some money. I got to have it quick, too, so if you want to swing on this thing, you better shut up and start in swingin'!"

In the sitting room, Townsend P. Locke sat on the edge of the couch, one hand resting on the telephone receiver, which had been placed in its cradle, and the other hand covering his mouth. His eyes were big with worry.

"Oh, Joe," he said as his guest returned to the room. "I behaved so childishly. I shouted. I was nasty. I was impudent. Should I call her back and apologize? She despises extravagance. Luxury she adores, extravagance no. She makes these *mar*velous distinctions. Well, I can't worry, can I? Shall we have a tiny?" He pointed to the gin bottle on the cocktail table.

Joe said, "Yeah, lemme pour you one, Towny."

"Thank you, that's very nice."

Joe poured until the glass was half full of straight gin, then he placed it in the outstretched red hand.

Joe remained standing directly in front of Locke, his pelvis on a level with Locke's face. There was a long silence. Gradually Locke's attention returned from Chicago to New York and still the silence continued. The man was aware of Joe's body standing in front of him and his face showed plainly the agitation he felt.

Joe fixed his face into a smile and looked at Locke. Locke looked up and met Joe's eyes and gave a small laugh. Joe nodded. Then he said, "What d'you want, Towny?"

Locke raised his black eyebrows and said, "What?"

Joe made a loose shallow cup of his hand and let it fall near his crotch. "What you got me up here for?"

222

"Oh!" Locke cried out, pressing his hand against his heart. His face showed genuine pain. "It's so difficult. So difficult. Impossible. You young people, you don't know what you do. You, you have this, this agonizing beauty. I know you're a splendid, truly lovely person, Joe. I knew that at once. I told you so in the street. And now you make this, this obscene gesture, and the combination, the innocence, the obscenity—there's something so agonizing in it, so beautiful. I'm not sure I can bear it.

"I should never have asked you up. I wanted so to be decent this trip, I was going to try so hard not to disgust myself. I suppose I hoped that we could have some communion in conversation, that I, as an older person, might convey to you some of my impressions of the world. What I mean is that I hoped we could find some higher level of exchange, isn't that ridiculous?" He took a long swallow of gin, and when he was used to having it in him, he spoke again, his voice dark and vehement: "I loathe life, I loathe every moment of it." He started to erase these words with a laugh, but gave it up at once. "Please go now, please. Don't make it more difficult for me. Just go, while I've got this scrap of strength left, the strength to ask you to."

"You mean, go?" Joe said. "You want me to leave?"

"Please understand, I just want, I don't want, well yes, yes I do. I want, I want you to, please, I want you to leave!"

Locke reached out and took Joe's hand, squeezing it between his own. "Please help me be good," he pleaded. "I don't want to be like I was in July."

Joe nodded. His own disappointment was great, but still he understood the man's plea. He started to walk away, but Locke held onto his hand. "Joe, listen, will you come back tomorrow and see me? Will you promise?"

"W-what's going on tomorrow," Joe said, "that ain't going on tonight?"

"I won't be the same tomorrow. I'll be different. I won't be so nervous. I can't tell you how awful I feel suddenly, like the bomb is going to fall. Which I want, you understand, I want it to fall, want it terribly! I'm just nervous about when!" He tried to laugh again and gave it up. "Look, sheer panic! Feel, feel my heart!" He placed Joe's hand inside his jacket. "A combination of things, I suppose, that awful traffic noise out there, room service sending up that inedible slush when I wanted everything so nice, then this disastrous telephone call from Estelle. But please say you'll come back tomorrow!"

Joe removed his hand and walked toward the door. "I'm going to Florida," he said. "I got to go to Florida."

"Oh, this is terrible!" Locke rose and followed Joe to the door. "I meet someone who understands me as no one *ever* has, and off they go to— Listen! Wait! I want to make you a present! For your trip! You'll let me, won't you?" He hurried into the bedroom.

Joe was astonished at this unexpected turn of events. He relaxed at once into a keen state of pleasure and anticipation, wondering how large a present was about to be made by the man whose tower overlooked the lake and who hired musicians for his mother's birthday.

He could hear the sound of a drawer opening and closing in the next room.

Locke returned. He was smiling. He walked toward Joe with one fist outstretched.

"I'd count it an honor if you'd take this."

Joe tried to find some words for his gratitude even before he saw the gift itself.

224

Locke's fingers uncurled near Joe's face, revealing a St. Christopher medal. "Please take it."

Joe looked at it.

"Go ahead! You don't have to be Catholic or anything. He's the patron of *all* travelers."

Joe shook his head.

"But I *want* you to have it," Locke said. "For helping me be good."

Joe allowed the medal to be placed in his pocket. And he went on shaking his head even after the man from Chicago asked him what was the matter.

7

the evening had taken a heavy toll of his spirits. He wondered as he climbed the stairs to the X-flat whether or not he'd have enough energy left to think up a story for Ratso.

"Ratso," he said softly, looking at the winter moon from the window of the third-floor landing. "No. Rico. I'll call him Rico. Rico," he continued, "I'm afraid this thing didn't work out none too good. I kind of pissed away the night on a bum lead. But I got a thing or two lined up for tomorrow, and I'd say we was going to be on that bus in two days at the latest. How's 'at sound to you?" He shook his head: It didn't sound good at all. Perhaps it would be better to say he'd raised part of the money, and the balance could be managed tomorrow. Well, Ratso, he would say, another twenty and we'll be on that bus.

He walked in with the intention of telling this lie, and found Ratso lying there awake looking up at the ceiling. Joe expected him to sit up and begin to question him about the evening's proceeds, but Ratso made no motion at all and said nothing.

Joe walked over and looked down at him. For some reason—maybe he knew the truth—Ratso did not meet his eyes. He continued looking at something on the ceiling, and he said, "I had shitty dreams." His voice was small and soft. All the gravelly harshness had gone from it.

"Ain't you gonna as' me," Joe said, "about how I done tonight?"

Ratso looked at him, but only with his eyes. His real attention was elsewhere. His face was empty of expression, and his eyes seemed to have lost some vital power. Not the power of sight, that was still there, but whatever power it was that made sight itself valuable, *that* seemed to be missing.

"I don't care about going nowheres," he said.

"You don't care about goin' to *Florida?*"

"Nah. So why don't you get some sleep already?"

Joe looked at the warm place next to Ratso and he thought about lying down. Then he looked at Ratso's damp, wasted, bone-colored face, and the eyes sitting too deep in their sockets, and in his mind he heard the sound of the opening and closing of that drawer in the bedroom of Townsend P. Locke's suite.

And then he knew he was going to have to get into that drawer. That was all there was to it. It had become a fairly simple matter.

226

"Well! If that don't beat the devil!" he said. "Here I got ever'thing arranged, and you don't care about going."

"You got what arranged?"

"The whole shebang. All I got to do is make one stop, take me two minutes. Then I figure we get on the next bus. But hell, you ain't interested, so I guess I'll have to go alone." He looked around the room. "I don't suppose they's nothing here I want. I got m'ass and I got m'elbows and I expect that's about all I need."

He walked over to the door. "Look, Ratso, I'll—uh—see you sometime, huh?"

Now Ratso was sitting upright with his mouth and eyes wide open. There was a moment in which he and Joe Buck simply looked at one another, and then Ratso said, "So long."

But he didn't move. Neither did Joe.

After a moment, Joe said, "You don' care nothing atall about going down there to Florida, is that it?"

Ratso licked his lips and frowned slightly. And then he said, "Nah."

Suddenly and swiftly Joe moved back into the room. "Get your shoes on, piss-ant! Time's a-wastin'!"

In a matter of seconds, Ratso had flung the blankets aside and was scrambling across the floor toward his shoes.

They took a taxi to the bus terminal. There was no luggage. Each had filled his pockets with odds and ends from the X-flat, and Ratso carried an Indian blanket. On the way, Ratso was breathing heavily and he complained often of the heat in his eyes. "What makes my eyes so hot? You know anything about hot eyes?"

Joe helped him onto a bench in the waiting room. It

227

would have been easier to carry him, but Ratso wouldn't allow it.

"Now wait here," he said. "I won't be but ten minutes."

"What if they get me for loitering?"

"You crazy? You getting the twelve-fifty to Miami Florida. That ain't loitering!"

"Okay, but what if that guy don't give you no loot?"

"You don't trust me, huh? Is that it? You don't trust me? Just say it! Go on, *say it!*"

"I *do*," Ratso said. "Only—"

"Only shee-it!"

At the door, Joe looked back and saw Ratso wrapping himself in the blanket. He waited until Ratso looked at him, and then he waved. Ratso waved back. Joe hurried toward the street, and once he was on Eighth Avenue he broke into a run.

8

He ran all the way to the Europa Hotel and up the stairs to the fifth floor without once stopping to think; he felt that any thinking he might do would be the ruin of his plan.

He knocked on Locke's door and then leaned against the doorframe, catching his breath. In a moment he heard a small *yes* from within the room.

"Towny?"

"Who is that out there?"

"It's me, Joe."

"Joe?"

"You know. That was here before?"

Joe heard the rattling of the safety latch, then the door opened. Townsend P. Locke was in a dressing gown, apparently naked underneath; he was barefooted.

"Good heavens!" he said.

"I got to talk to you."

Locke looked at Joe for a moment, his eyes twitching uncomfortably, and then he glanced quickly at the safety latch as if he regretted having opened the door.

"Joe, honestly, it's so late."

"Yeah, but this is important."

"Well, what in the world can it be about?"

"I, I can't talk out here."

"But I can't ask you in, not at this hour."

"Didn't you say we was friends?"

"Well of *course!* But—"

"But you didn't mean it, did you." Joe stated this as he walked past Locke and into the sitting room of the suite.

Locke remained at the door. He looked at Joe with a frown. "Please. Just say what it is. What is it?"

"Shut the door."

"Shut the door?"

"Yeah. You know. Shut it."

Locke drew a deep, careful breath. Then he closed the door.

Joe said, "I got to have some money."

"Oh." Locke smiled. "Oh, of course. Of course you do. I should've, should've thought. Oh, I'm so sorry to make you ask for it, that's not nice of me. I do understand these things. You boys always, uh, yes, and it's perfectly reasonable. After all, it's your—well, ha!—*income!* I'm afraid I was very selfish not to have thought of that myself. Just one second. You wait here.

Locke went to the bedroom. Joe followed. Locke opened the drawer of the table between the twin beds and removed a wallet. Then he took a bill from the wallet and replaced it in the drawer.

Then he saw Joe in the doorway. "Oh!" His hand flew like an overweight pigeon to his throat. He took a step backward in fright, bumping the table and knocking the lamp off balance. But he caught it in time.

"You frightened me," he said. "I thought you were waiting in *there!*" There was an edge of annoyance in his voice.

"Nah," Joe said. "I thought I'd just save you a step."

He looked at the ten-dollar bill in Locke's hand. "Is that for me?"

"Yes," Locke said. "And I consider that you've more than earned it, just for putting up with an objectionable old gentleman all evening. So don't even thank me."

"Towny," Joe said, "I'm afraid I'm gonna have to have more'n that *ten.*"

"Oh? Oh really?" Locke's voice was suddenly very thin, scarcely audible. His face was frozen in an expression that had little connection with the activity behind it. "Isn't that a pity! Because I'm afraid I don't have any more cash. I mean money."

"I got to have fifty dollars."

"Fifty!"

"This was a pretty long evening here, Towny, wouldn't y'say? Even if you did decide to be a good boy?"

"But Joe, I—I simply don't have it."

"Yeah, well I don't have no time neither, no time to set

here all night while you tickle yourself to death looking. I got family, goddammit, an' I got to get 'em down to Florida quick. Now you reach in there and peel me off fifty dollars."

Locke backed against the drawer.

"I understand, Joe, honestly I do. And I agree with everything you—" Joe came toward him. Locke gasped. "What're you going to do?"

"Get out o' my way."

"You're wasting your time. There's nothing—"

Joe hit the man across the face with the back of his hand. Locke fell against the bed, not from the force of the blow, but from his overreaction to it. He quickly pushed himself upright and fell to his knees, throwing his arms around the night table, blocking the drawer with his body. He lowered his head, watching Joe out of the corner of his eye, and began to whimper like a woman or a child. Joe grabbed a handful of the white hair and turned the man's face toward him. "Let go, let go that table."

"No, no! I won't! There's no money here! There's just private things!"

Joe hit the man across the face again, this time with his open palm.

The man continued to whimper and moan, but he didn't move. Joe struck him again, this time harder and with a closed fist.

Locke cried out, and then he said, "I deserved that! Oh yes, I did, I deserved it!" His moaning continued again, but in a much higher key than before. Still he clung to the night table with both arms.

"I brought this upon myself!" he said. "You should hit me again! My thoughts, all evening my thoughts have been disgusting, hideous. Is this blood on my face?" He

231

tasted the blood that was coming from his nose. "I'm bleeding! Oh, thank God, I'm bleeding! I deserve to bleed!"

"Turn loose that fucking table." Joe had begun to sense that he was coping with something more than a man protecting his money. There was in Locke's refusal to let go a kind of glee, almost fervor. His eyes were shining, his mouth and teeth were clenched in a stupid, smiling position, giving him the look of a fat, crazy fish. His face had deepened in color, and blood was running from his nose, into his mouth, over his teeth, down his chin.

Joe picked up the table lamp and held it high in the air. "You want to give me fifty dollars? Or you want your head broke open?"

The expression on Locke's face made his preference perfectly clear: He looked with longing at the lamp, and his body remained pressed against the table.

Realizing what was being required of him, Joe began to feel sick. It began to seem that the positions were reversed, as if Locke held the weapon and Joe was being threatened by it; that if further violence were to take place, it would clearly be against himself, but upon the body of Locke.

"Please let go that table, mister," he said.

Locke shook his head.

Joe swung the lamp down toward Locke's face, bringing it to a halt several inches short of contact. Locke cried out, but this time with pleasure. His body went limp and he loosened his grip on the table. Joe did not at first understand what had taken place. He hadn't struck the man, and yet Locke had given up the battle.

Then Joe looked down and saw the evidence of the gratification Locke had received. Locke was still in the

232

throes of some emotion, but Joe couldn't tell whether he was laughing or crying. But he did know in just what way he had been used by the red-faced, white-haired, blue-eyed man from Chicago, so that when he removed the wallet from the little drawer in the night table and found in it one hundred and twenty-one dollars, he put the entire amount in his pocket.

Joe left the room. Locke said, "Thank you, thank you."

Passing through the sitting room, Joe suddenly realized what he had seen as he left the bedroom: Locke, sitting on the floor, his head against the bed, his mouth wide open in a weird, blood-covered smile, and next to him, on the night table, a telephone.

Joe hurried back into the bedroom and found Locke scrambling to his knees, reaching for the receiver.

Joe called to him: "Hey!"

Locke cried out in surprise. He spun around and faced Joe. They looked at each other as if each of them realized that the worst part of the evening still lay ahead of them.

Locke said, "I wasn't going to call anybody! Honestly I wasn't."

"Keep still."

"Honestly! I was just—"

"Shut up."

Joe tried to think. All he could see was Locke and the telephone, the telephone and Locke, and he knew that one or the other of them had to be placed out of commission long enough for him to leave the building. So he went over to the night table and pulled at the telephone until the metal box broke free of the wall. But still the connection had not been severed. He had to set the telephone down while he pulled the cord loose from the little metal box. Then he picked up the phone again and listened. It was silent.

Locke had taken this opportunity to run into the sitting room, and he had almost reached the hallway when Joe, still carrying the disengaged telephone, arrived in the room to stop him. He shouted, *"Hey!"* and threw the instrument at Locke's head. Locke turned around just in time for the instrument to connect with his mouth, dislodging his dentures. He began to gag and spit, and then a set of teeth emerged from his mouth and he fell to his knees in pursuit of it.

Joe still held in his mind the image of the man and the telephone, the telephone and the man, and in his confusion he still felt it necessary to subdue the two of them. He therefore pushed Locke to the floor, sat astride his chest, and shoved the telephone's receiver into the toothless mouth.

There was blood on Joe's hands and, foolishly, instinctively, he wiped them on his jacket. Then he got to his feet and looked around the room. Locke's blood seemed to have spread in impossible ways. It was all over the man himself, it was on the carpet and on the woodwork. It was as if something terrible—call it evil and picture it a dragon—had raced about the room leaving its imprint everywhere.

As Joe left the room at a run, headed for the stairway, the last thing he saw was the man from Chicago, rolling onto his side, half naked, clinging to the object in his mouth like an enormous child struggling with its pacifier.

9

hey rented pillows for the trip and then the driver got on the bus. He climbed into his seat and pulled the switch that causes the door to close, and he spoke to the passengers through a microphone, told them there would be regular rest stops, and they were going to enjoy the trip and would arrive in Miami Florida in thirty-one hours.

Joe listened to this announcement carefully but not for its content: What he got from it was the comfort of the driver's voice, the strength and kindness in it.

"These guys are good drivers," he said to Ratso.

"They *got* to be," Ratso said. Then his teeth started chattering again.

The bus began to move.

"It's moving," Ratso said.

"Yeah."

"Thirty-one hours."

"Is what?" Joe said.

"What d'you mean, is what? Is *what* what?"

"Thirty-one hours."

"The trip is. Eight-thirty in the morning we get there. Not *this* morning. But the next one at eight-thirty."

The bus made a number of turns on its way out of town,

and pretty soon it entered a tunnel, and then a few minutes later they were on a speedway.

Joe said, "Do you believe it?"

"That we're on our way?"

"Yeah."

"No. I can't hardly believe it. I just can't hardly be*lieve* it."

"Me either," Joe said. "I just can't believe it."

They rode a few miles in silence. Joe turned around to see what the other passengers looked like. He thought they looked all right, the ones he could see. There were quite a few empty seats, which meant there'd be some places to stretch out for sleep.

"What'll be our first thing?" he said.

"That we do?"

"Yeah, when we get there."

"Well, I guess hook a bathing suit, huh?"

"And just go right on over to the beach," Joe said, "and start in? I mean just start right in *bein'* there, is that it?"

"W-what the hell else?" Ratso said.

"Shee-it, *I* don't know, *I* ain't the expert on going to Florida. I mean, *I* don't know what the hell you, uh, *do* and all. So I just *ast*. But Christ, I'm sorry I open m'mouth. Why don't you quit shivering?"

"I can't help it, that's why," Ratso said. When some more miles had gone by, he said, "You get your first palm tree in South Carolina."

"How do you know that?"

"I was told that."

"By who?" Joe wanted to know.

"This *guy*, that's who!"

"Well, to hell with South Carolina," Joe said. "We going

236

to Florida. And if you have to shiver, why don't you pull the blanket up more?"

"Hey, what's the matter with you already?"

Joe said there was nothing the matter with him, and for the next mile or so he was aware of Ratso's eye on him.

Then Ratso leaned in close and beckoned Joe with his hand. They put their heads together and Ratso whispered: "You didn't kill him, did you?"

Joe backed away at once, but just far enough to show Ratso the urgency in his eye as he whispered, "*Shut up, shut up, shut up!*" He took a quick glance at the woman across the aisle. She was asleep, her head against the window.

Ratso said, "You can tell me."

Joe leaned in again and whispered, "All I done was stick the phone in his mouth. I told you that. And it went *dut!*" He made a noise with his tongue against the roof of his mouth. "Like that."

"I know, but listen," Ratso said. "You got *blood* on your *jacket!*"

"From his nose, from his nose, I told you he had a bloody nose! You trying to get me all nervous or what?"

"No! I just wanted to know. I mean can't I ask?"

"Yeah, but why, why? You think blood has to mean somebody's dead?" They were silent for a moment, then Joe said, "You think a guy could get a telephone *stuck* in his mouth?"

"No. No."

"And then that person choke to death?"

"I said no, it's an impossibility! Now see how your mind is?" Ratso said. "You're gonna think about that. You shouldn't think about that. I mean it. Think about Flor-

237

ida." Ratso pulled the blanket up around his neck and
settled into his pillow.

When they had ridden a few miles more, Joe said,
"Ratso, you realize day after tomorrow, I mean the day
after to-goddam-*mor*row, you and me is going to have a
miserable pair of sunburned asses on us? Don't that grab
you like it does me?"

Ratso was silent.

"Don't it?" Joe said.

Ratso was looking at him, frowning, and he was touching his teeth with his fingers.

Joe said, "What's the matter?"

"I just wondered is all."

"What?"

"How'd you get it past his teeth?"

Joe was furious. "His teeth was *out!*"

"You *knocked* 'em out?"

Joe had to take a deep breath before he could answer.
"They was *false*, jackass, they was *false!*"

There was no more talking for a while.

An hour later, Ratso was perspiring and pushed the
blanket away. Joe put it back on, thinking Ratso was
asleep. But he wasn't. He opened his eyes and said, "Hey,
listen, I been thinking."

"You got to keep that blanket on you," Joe said.

"I been thinking, I hope we're not gonna have a lot o'
trouble 'bout my name down there. Because what's the
whole point of this trip, anyway? I mean New York is one
thing, but can you see this guy, imagine it, he's running
around on a goddam *beach*, and he's all suntanned and
he's going in swimming and all, and then somebody hol-
lers *Hey Ratso* at him? Does that sound good to you?
Admit it, it sounds like shit. And I'm not gonna have it.

238

I'm Rico altogether, do you blame me? Hey, look, this blanket is making me too hot. I'm sweating like a pig already."

"Oh. Oh, I see," Joe said. "Well, then take it off. Take your shirt off, too, and open the window while you're at it. Maybe you could get you a good case of pneu*mo*nia, how would that be?"

"I didn't *say* I was gonna take it off. I just said I'm sweating. But it's agreed, okay? We're gonna tell all these new people my name is Rico?"

Joe nodded.

He closed his eyes and tried for some sleep, but all he got was some foul dreams. He couldn't quite tell if he was asleep or not, but there were these dreams all the same, wild and ugly and vivid. In many of them he experienced a reenactment of the violence of the evening just past, opening his eyes in horror at the moment the lamp stopped short of crushing the skull of Townsend P. Locke. In these many awakenings it was always a relief to find himself on the bus at Ratso's side.

And then he began to have a number of these half-awake dreams in which Sally Buck's old boy friend, Woodsy Niles, was a dead man. The Woodsy dreams took place right there on the bus and they seemed real in every particular. The cowboy's corpse went through every kind of caper imaginable: In one of them it was propped up in the driver's seat operating the bus on hairpin roads and the passengers were screaming, *Help help the driver is dead the driver is dead!* In another of these terrible dreams, the bus arrived in Miami and all the passengers took their suitcases off the rack and left. All but one. The driver saw him there, apparently asleep in a seat near the back, and went down the aisle to awaken him. And then,

239

"Shee-it," he said, "I believe I got a corpse on m'hands here." At this point, Joe recognized himself as the driver and the corpse as his old friend Woodsy. He picked up Woodsy's body and began to sing to it *The Last Roundup,* softly and slowly, half lullaby, half requiem.

After these death dreams, Joe would awaken and study Ratso for signs of life, placing his hand under his nose to feel the breath coming out. At one such moment Ratso woke up. He looked at Joe and said, "What the fuck are you doing?" Joe just laughed.

It was about three-thirty in the morning, and they were having their first rest stop, somewhere in Maryland. Many of the passengers were asleep. Ratso said he wanted to stay on the bus. Joe got off and brought back some coffee in cartons. They sat there smoking cigarettes and sipping their coffee.

"Listen, Joe, we got to talk about something," Ratso said. "When you was gone, I tried to get up, but . . ." He shrugged, and then he shook his head and frowned. His face was grave. "I couldn't."

Joe listened.

"It's serious," Ratso said. "I mean, I *couldn't.* I couldn't get up. I mean I tried and all, and I just couldn't get up."

Joe nodded.

Ratso said, "What am I gonna do?"

"Well now," Joe said, "when we get to Miami, we'll carry you right on over to the doctor's."

Ratso shook his head quickly and grimaced. "Huh-uh. They can't do nothing with legs. They just go *tch tch tch* and they shrug their shoulders and grab your ten bucks and that's it."

"The thing you tend to forget," Joe said, "is all this sunshine we're coming into tomorrow."

"Course I know a dozen ways to screw a doctor out of his fee. But what's that got to do with sunshine? Oh, you mean like *healing* benefits and all?"

"Hell yeah."

After a moment, Ratso said, "All right, but look, what *if*, that's what I want to know, what if?"

"I–I guess we could get you a . . . *I* don't know what."

"A crutch?" Ratso said.

Joe looked at him quickly. "That's up to *you*, if you *want* one."

The other passengers were returning to the bus.

Ratso said, "And if I don't want one, what?"

Joe opened his mouth to speak, but he found he had nothing to say.

After one or two more false tries, he said, "Ratso. I mean *Rico*. Um, when we get to Miami, I'm fixing to go to work, did you know that?"

Joe hadn't known it himself. He hadn't known he was going to say that at all. His thoughts and his speech had become coordinated in some surprising way, so that what he said was as new to himself as it was to his listener. The bus started to move again and he kept on talking. "I got to do that, 'cause see, I'm no kind of a hustler. I ain't even a good bum. The way things is been, I ain't even nothing. So I'm gonna have to go to work, I don't know, sweeping, doing dishes, some damn thing or other. 'Cause we want it to be nice down there, don't we? Well, it not gonna be nice, it not gonna be all coconuts, it gonna be the usual crap, you can bet on that. Besides, I'm gonna be honest with you, I don't want to sleep on no beach. I

241

want a bathroom and some bay rum in the medicine cab'net, know what I mean? And some toothpaste? And a change o' shoes! 'Cause I am so sick o' lookin' at these goddam boots. I *am!* I'm gonna throw 'em in the ocean! Watch me. I want ever'thing new. And I don't care if I have to get a job picking flyshit out of a pepper box."

Ratso was looking at him with a very serious expression on his face, and he was doing a lot of nodding.

Joe laid a hand on Ratso's knee, and he looked past him and out the window at the dark landscape rushing by. "My whole point is, working, I'm gonna be able to look out for you, too. Not just me. Okay?"

A moment passed. They crossed a river and then there were more dark moonlit trees rushing by. Finally Ratso said, "Okay." Each of them was careful not to look at the other. They settled into their pillows and closed their eyes, each of them thinking his own thoughts.

Joe was astonished at the thing he had just said to Ratso, promising to take care of him, and even more astonished to realize that he meant it.

And so now here he was with this burden on his hands, responsible for the care of another person, a sickly, crippled person at that. But oddly enough, he liked the feeling it gave him. It was a curious kind of burden under which he felt lighter instead of heavier, and warm. The seat became exceptionally comfortable and his head fit the pillow better. He felt joined to everything that touched him, and pretty soon he fell asleep, dreaming his golden-people dream.

But there was a startling difference in it. They were marching to rodeo music, a wild march beat. And the rope of light that bound the people in their trip around the earth was on this night of a special brilliance and clarity so that Joe was able to see the actual features on the face of the marchers. The one that caught his interest was the face of a cowboy swinging a lariat, a lariat made of the same golden stuff that bound all the marchers. He looked hard, very hard at the face of the cowboy, longing to get his attention and disturbed more and more by an ever increasing sense of familiarity with what he saw, and lo and behold! There came a moment in which he knew the face of the cowboy to be none other than his own.

He was in the line with everyone else.

Finding himself in such a remarkable situation surprised him into wakefulness. A cool wintry dawn was coming in the window, washing everything with its own colors.

Ratso was wide awake, too, and he was in considerable distress. His face was wet with tears and misery was written all over it.

"Hey, hey, what's the matter?" Joe asked.

Ratso looked at him quickly and then he looked away again, and softly, almost inaudibly, he said, "I peed."

"You what?"

"Peed! Peed! Peed my pants!"

"So what? Is that so bad?"

"I'm all *wet!* And my seat's all wet."

"Hell, man, don't cry."

"Here I am going to Florida, and my leg hurts, my butt hurts, my chest hurts, my face hurts, and like that's not enough, so I piss all over myself."

Joe began to laugh. He realized that laughter was inappropriate, but he felt good and the whole thing seemed very funny.

"I'm falling apart," Ratso said. "That's funny?"

Joe nodded. And in a moment Ratso was laughing, too.

Then Joe said, "You just had you a little rest stop wasn't on the schedule." They both laughed as if this was the funniest remark they'd ever heard. They laughed for several miles. Ratso's face turned blue and his eyes were wild and bloodshot, and he complained that it hurt him to laugh so, but when he showed signs of letting up, Joe would speak out some new comment on the scatalogical aspects of Ratso's misery, and they would laugh some more. The last three or four remarks were clearly not very funny, but they enjoyed the laughing just the same. Then Ratso started to cough and choke, and he had to lean forward while Joe patted him on the back.

After this seizure, Ratso was weak and drowsy. His spirit had been quieted, but the interval of laughter had been exhausting. Joe told him there were plenty of empty seats and they would find a dry one at the next stop, and he promised that in one of these towns they would be able to buy some new trousers. He convinced Ratso that everything would be all right eventually, and by the time the bus stopped for breakfast near Richmond, Ratso was fast asleep. Joe drew the window shade to keep the sun from his eyes.

10

a few seconds later, when Joe stepped off the bus, he was surprised to find that the special quality of the dawn was spreading itself into the entire morning. He remembered having had some splendid dream but he couldn't recall the details of it. There was this almost painful prettiness about the day, even the air was pungent with it, and he supposed it all had to do with being out of New York City.

In the restaurant he ordered blueberry pancakes and a cup of coffee, and while he was waiting he was caught by some swift and profound emotion which he mistook for sadness. The feeling became so intense in him he thought he was going to have to vomit. He hurried back to the men's room, locked himself into one of the booths and bent over the toilet. He put his finger into his throat, but nothing came out but air. Then he started to cry. This surprised him. He wondered what these tears were all about on a day when he had been feeling so good. Soon they stopped. He blew his nose. Then he went back into the restaurant and ate his breakfast. The pancakes were good, but after the first bite he forgot to savor them. For some of the special quality of the morning had seeped right into the restaurant, so that all the while he ate he thought about the day he was having instead of the food, even ended up leaving half of his coffee to go out there and get right into the thick of it.

It was an awesome thing, this Saturday morning. It had simply taken over everything. Joe felt he could've reached out and closed his fingers around it.

But what made it this way? He walked over to the edge of the parking lot and looked at the ground. It was hard brown mud covered by some stubborn colorless weed that winter couldn't kill, and in the distance was a row of ordinary naked trees with nothing special about them. The sky had a very soft blue color you could look at without the least squinting, and the air was cool, very cool but not cold, so that breathing it was like breathing the soft blue of the sky and you knew you were getting the good of it in you. Joe stood there on the edge of the parking lot and cried some more, shaking his head in puzzlement at the tears streaming down his face, full of the wonder of this perfectly ordinary weather and pondering the freakish sadness that had come upon him.

The fact was that it was not sadness at all, but he had no way of knowing that.

He wiped his face on the arm of his jacket and then he got back onto the bus.

Ratso was still sleeping.

They rode on through the Southern morning, and the odd intensity of the day continued. Each little town they passed through seemed to have such Saturday things going on in it, people hauling Saturday-sized grocery loads, children running and bicycling and skating, gorging themselves on their Saturday freedom, young women already in curlers and lipstick headed for Woolworth's to buy still more beauty things to wear for their Saturday young men who filed in and out of every barber shop or stood about on the sidewalks of all these main streets jingling the change in their pockets, waiting for a shine or for new cleats to be put on, impatient for the Saturday night that was coming at them slow as a clock, slow but they believed in it, they knew it was coming at them, they could sniff it in the air, and Saturday's old women could be seen, too, in twos and in bunches they convened on every corner to cluck their teeth and speak of death while an occasional old man strutted by to confound them with his survival.

Joe saw all this, and at Raleigh in North Carolina he was happy to step right into it all.

He bought new corduroy trousers for Ratso at a dry-goods store near the depot, and for himself a cheap make-do jacket, a dark-blue one with white buttons. He told himself it was make-do but he liked it all right, and he placed the stained one in a trash receptacle.

Joe tried to move Ratso off the bus, so that he could take him into the men's room and help him change his trousers. But Ratso wouldn't wake up. Joe tried to rouse him by telling him they would soon reach South Carolina and it would be time to keep an eye peeled for the first palm tree, but Ratso was unresponsive. He did open his eyes for a moment, but he didn't seem to be seeing anything with them.

Two hours later, at Bennettsville, while most of the other passengers were off the bus stretching and having coffee and using the facilities, Joe carried Ratso to the back seat of the bus. The long underwear was wet, too, and removing it was a chore. Ratso was helpless as an infant. Joe had never seen him naked before. His pathetic little sex looked useless, just a token affair, something to pee through. His right leg was skinny and twisted as an old man's cane, and he was marked from hip to knee with large black and green and purple bruises from the various falls he had sustained in the past few days. He was like a plucked chicken, one who'd spent his life getting the worst of barnyard scraps and had finally cocked up his heels and quit. This history was written all over his body, and Joe read it well and with a feeling for the sacredness of it. For a moment he saw in his mind a motion picture of himself wrapping this naked, badly damaged human child in the blanket, taking him up gently and holding him rock-a-bye and git-along-little-dogie in his lap for the rest of the trip. But he snapped off that picture fast.

They settled into that dry seat on the back of the bus,

247

and then they rode on some more, rode on through more and more miles of this Saturday day that was as rich and mysterious as a memory. Ratso slept the deepest sleep in the world. Joe told himself that this was a healing sleep, and by the time they reached Savannah the sun had set and it was time for dinner, and still Ratso slept.

Joe didn't leave the bus. He wasn't especially hungry. He stayed at Ratso's side, and he went on feeling and savoring the special qualities of the day, even though night had come.

Among the many things he thought about were the astonishing remarks he had made to Ratso about getting a job and new shoes and having a regular life with its own bathroom. And he knew it was true that he would one day have those things, and real Saturdays like the one he had been watching out the window all day. Probably he would be a dishwasher or a short-order clerk. There would be other people working in the same place with him and at first they wouldn't look at him, they wouldn't realize he was just like them, one of them in fact, but gradually they would get the idea. They would begin to notice he was wearing regular shoes and somehow would come to know that he was no mere hotel person but had a place of his own with a private bathroom. And there would begin to be some dropping in and visiting back and forth, and no doubt one of these new people in due course would be a woman, not necessarily a blonde either or any one particular kind of woman, but she would have lipstick and curlers, they all have that, and she would be glad to have a man to take care of her, one who was good at lovemaking; and Ratso would be like a child to them and they would make him wash his hair at least once a week, or do it for him if he was too sickly. And the whole trick to having these things come out right was that you had to work hard and wait for them to come out right, you couldn't just say *oh it will never be it will never be;* you just had to keep on until it was, even if in the meantime your feet hurt and you grew a long white beard that reached to the ground. He had taken on a plan once before in his life, back in Houston when he decided to become a hustling cowboy and seek his fortune in the East. Well, he had carried that out, he had become a hustling cowboy and he had sought his fortune. There just wasn't any there, but he had sought it and that was the whole point. And now, this time, maybe there wouldn't be any ordinary life for him but he would goddam well do some seeking, and go on stubborn and hard-assed about it till the day he died.

It occurred to him that he was doing some thinking without the aid of a mirror, and he wondered if that wasn't some kind of an improvement.

He slept through the rest of the stops that night. He heard one driver say Jacksonville, and then he heard an altogether new driver announce Daytona, but he was only half awake. He was having a pretty deep sleep, considering it was a bus. The only thing he could remember from the night were those two calls for towns, and yet it was not surprising in the morning to awaken and find what he found.

Ratso's body had an abandoned look, rear end half off the seat, back bent at an awful angle, head slumped to the side in a breakneck position, arms splayed out like useless sticks, eyes wide open and not seeing a single thing. Obviously the thing in charge had gone out of it.

Ratso was dead.

11

and wouldn't you know it would be a beautiful blue-sky day with palm trees swaying everywhere just exactly as pictured in Ratso's folders and in *Florida and the Caribbean?*

But to hell with all that.

The thing to do was to see about getting him buried, no doubt a costly procedure. He took out his money and counted forty-eight dollars and some change. The thing would probably cost some fantastic sum, but if you were going to be the kind of person who went around offering to take care of people, you damn well had to look out for their corpses when they died.

His thoughts didn't seem right to him. He thought he ought to get upset, perhaps even hysterical and say *oh help help my friend is dead and I am all alone.* But he didn't feel that way. He just didn't, and that was all there was to it.

It was as if he'd known it was going to happen. Someone (who? Ratso?) had been whispering it to him for a couple of days now, whispering it to him in a kind of death language that you weren't supposed to understand until later. You get the idea somehow, but you don't *know* you know until it happens.

And now it had happened.

And so there would have to be a funeral, and he'd have to make some deal with an undertaker who would do the job right, but cheap and on credit.

No. First of all, he'd have to get the body off the bus, and then . . . and then they would . . .

Who?

The bus people.

The bus people would simply have to steer him to an undertaker, and then he would make this deal to get Ratso buried on the installment plan. (Ratso? Buried? Is he really dead? Yeah, Ratso's dead, he's really dead now. See, there he is, dead.) And then he'd get a job. And keep it. The thing was to *keep* it. And gradually pull together enough nickels to put a stone on the grave, nothing wild, just a stone with the name and all: Rico. Not Ratso. And he couldn't spell Rizzo, but he would find somebody who could. You had to have the spelling right on the marker so that when people passed by later they'd say, *Oh, look who's buried here, Rico Rizzo.*

Who was going to pass by and say that?

Never mind.

There'd be somebody around who could spell it.

That wasn't the important thing. The important thing was what to do first: tell somebody.

The driver seemed to be the person in charge.

Joe got up and walked down the aisle and stood next to the driver, leaning down and looking out at the Sunshine Parkway, having the same view the driver was having. After a moment, the driver acknowledged him. "*Yes* sir."

Joe said, "My friend is dead in the back seat but I don't know how to spell his name."

The driver said, "Your friend is *what* in the back seat?"

Joe said, "Dead. He's dead as a doornail."

251

"Is this some kind of a . . . ?" The driver looked at Joe quickly and then he turned his eyes back onto the Parkway. He looked into the rear-view mirror and then he slowed down and pulled over to the far-right lane and stopped the bus altogether. He climbed out of his seat, and as he followed Joe to the back of the bus, he said in his official bus-driver voice: "All right, folks, everything's fine. You be in Miami less'n an hour now."

The other passengers knew everything wasn't *fine.* Many of them craned their necks to get a look at the trouble, but they couldn't see anything. Those persons in the immediate area could have seen something, but they didn't want to be caught trying.

The driver took a look at Ratso and then he nodded at Joe. He began to take his hat off, but he didn't follow through.

"Is he kin to you?" he asked Joe.

Joe nodded.

Then the driver said, "Don't you want to close his eyes?"

"Close 'em?"

"You just reach over and you close 'em. That's all."

Joe closed Ratso's eyes.

"Well," said the driver uncomfortably, "I guess we'll just drive on, right? There isn't anything else to do."

Joe said, "Yes sir."

The driver made another announcement. "Just a little sickness, folks, nothing serious. We'll be in Miami in—" he consulted his watch—"forty minutes."

Joe went through his plans in his mind, and then once again, and still a third time until he was certain he had done everything there was to do up to this moment. And then he did something he'd always wanted to do from the very beginning, from the very first night he'd met Ratso at Everett's Bar on Broadway: He put his arm around him to hold him for a while, for these last few miles anyway. He knew this comforting wasn't doing Ratso any good. It was for himself. Because of course he was scared now, scared to death.